# BREATHLESS

## A Fish Monster Romance

Cat Wynn

To that untouchable sadness inside

# CONTENT WARNING

Breathless deals with topics some readers may find difficult including mental illness, child abuse and exploitation (past and off page), sexual assault (referenced, past, and off page), difficult parental relationships, parental death (off page), therapy, suicidal ideation and attempts, violence including blood and guns, and usage of chemical-alt substances. Please take care when reading.

# CHAPTER 1

I wake with a gasp, hand to neck, back to headboard, body bent to the darkness.

*I can't breathe, I can't breathe, I can't breathe.*

Except I can. I'm breathing right now. Oxygen pushes through me like a bike pump, labored and hard.

It's happening again. The suffocating. The drowning in my sleep.

*Use your grounding techniques.*

That's what my therapist would say. Well, before I fired her. Before I realized stepping out of my apartment was a nearly impossible task. She would say, "You won't suffocate in your sleep, Jules. Your body breathes for you. Trust your body."

"But what if it doesn't? And what if I don't?" I'd reply.

Bodies died all the time, morphed and changed and surprised their dwellers. There was nothing inherently trustworthy about them.

*Grounding techniques. Focus!*

Right. I turn my gaze to the sparkling rectangular glass across from my bed. My aquarium. An anchor of space and time in my bedroom. But there aren't any aquatic creatures inside. I could never be trusted to keep something alive. Not even myself.

Bubbles flitter from the pump at the corner. My heart rate slows while I watch the fleeting spherical dance. The aeration of oxygen throughout the water mimics the aeration of oxygen throughout my blood.

My breath settles.

My stare glazes over.

*Exhale.*

Sometimes, I wonder what it'd be like to be in that aquarium. I wonder what it'd be like to look through the glass from the other side.

I wonder who I'd see.

Chills run up my spine, and I shake them off, blindly grasping for my phone buried in the sheets next to me, its screen a comforting luminous glow.

Four thirty-five in the fucking morning.

Too early to rise; too late to go back to sleep.

I roll out of bed, naked save for the cotton granny panties, and sweep up last night's robe from the floor, shoving my arms through the green floral sleeves. My friend, Kate, gifted me this robe last year for Christmas, its slinky silk sticking like seaweed around my limbs. I tighten the sash in preparation. An inside girl's armor.

After I've scuttled to the kitchen and collected an enormous bowl of Froot Loops—"You shouldn't eat that junk." My mother's voice swims into my head. "Models don't eat sugar."—I wander back to my bedroom, plop down at my desk across the wall from my bed, and shove sweet, wet spoonfuls in my mouth.

I squint with a frown as the light blares from my computer screen.

I'm a copywriter, so I don't have to commute to an office. I don't have to mingle with coworkers. I couldn't even pick my boss out of a lineup if you put a gun to my head.

If it weren't for my friend, Kate, no one would even know I was alive. Like, what if I really did stop breathing one day? If my lungs just quit their job? No one would know I was here, shriveled up on the floor, like a dried-out sardine.

With that thought, my fingers type in the search browser. A familiar website, but it's not work. It's more of an interest. A hobby.

The Freemont Aquariumaniacs Forum

I visit this forum every once in a while. At least, it used to be every once in a while. Now, it's more like every single day or whenever the idea strikes me that I should put a fish in my tank. Or maybe a snail. A crab.

The people are nice, the community active.

And I don't *have* to participate; I can *lurk*. Scroll and read about the lives of others to my heart's content. I don't even have to leave my apartment . . . which is something I avoid at all costs anyway. I never go farther than the coffee shop next to my building.

For the most part, the forum members don't ask me about what I did this weekend. They don't poke and prod for details about my life, or lack thereof.

Instead it's just *betta fish this* and *scorpion fish that*. I like that.

Especially one person in particular. We've been messaging a bit.

But it's not *like that*, I swear. We just chat sometimes.

*About aquariums in the local area.* Mostly. And, fine, other stuff too.

Besides, I don't even know what he looks like. He's a total stranger on the internet, and I wasn't born yesterday. He could be a hideous, disgusting monster. Right? Or a total fucking catfish.

I glance around my bedroom behind me, the unmade seafoam bed, and a pillow surrendered to the floor, casing half off, cotton-white underbelly exposed.

An empty frame rests on the nightstand, which I've meant to fill with a picture of my mother, my only remaining family.

But somehow, I can't ever seem to find the time.

I check the updated posts on the forum and breathe in deep.

*Betta has fin rot . . . AGAIN. Think I'm going to kill myself.*

*Magic crab keeps disappearing and reappearing. Where's he going? A time loop? A portal?*

*Can a guppy suffer from depression?*

*Is my neon tetra pregnant? Because I am.*

Hmmm . . . I *scroll, scroll, scroll, click, click, click.* No new messages from my friend. A sensation in my belly droops.

May as well start this miserable day.

I change into sweatpants and an old T-shirt that says *Just Breathe* because it's good to live aspirationally, and pad my way to the front door, forcing the thong of my blue flip-flops between my sock-covered toes and sneaking down the concrete stairwell of my building.

Better the creepy stairwell than the risk of running into the creepy neighbor, Jason. Still, when I glance over the railing, the hole in the middle of the spiral curve gives me the feeling that I'm circling a drain.

I make my way to the hole-in-the-wall coffee shop next to my building, where I get the same thing every time with my scrunched-up wad of dollars. "Black coffee, please."

"How you doing, Jules?" the owner asks me as he takes my money in exchange for his goods.

I don't know how he knows my name since I've never introduced myself, but his face is crinkled from old age, little gray hairs sprouting from his ears and nostrils. He wears a black and white keffiyeh around his neck. A small sign hangs off the ninety-degree cliff of his counter that reads something in Arabic. I don't have the guts to ask him what it says.

His voice is soft. "You hangin' in there?"

I just nod, don't look up. Even though this small coffee shop is one of my safe areas, I'm still on high alert, muscles tensed. He's a nice man, but I can tell by the pitying look in his eyes that he feels sorry for me. As if he worries each time I turn up at his shop. That kindness lands flat, though. Sympathy makes me itchy to the gills. I'd rather he just not look at all.

I'd rather no one look ever.

He hands me my coffee, so strong it could strip the grease off an airplane engine, but I like it that way. I grip it hard in my fist as I scurry back into my building and up the stairs, the harsh LED overhead lights accentuating my eerie blue veins, almost luminescent beneath my pale skin. I shudder at the sight of my own flesh. Did it always look this way?

My reflection flashes next to me, distorted and dingy in a wire glass window but still unmistakable. The pale blonde hair, the light blue eyes, the tall, thin figure. I've been called beautiful many times before.

My mother used to enter me in baby pageants. That's how it all started. "And you hugged every judge! Never fussed!" She'd brag to her friends. As I grew older, the parading didn't stop.

Next came the clothing catalog shoots and the teen magazine covers. Then the runways and editorial spreads.

Until, one day, when I was around twenty-three, a woman approached me with a business card. "You look like someone who's searching for something new. Here, take this."

I flipped the card over. *Galaxia Business Conglomerates.* It looked like a scam, but I went to the website listed on the card and applied for a position as a copywriter. That's how I finally got out of modeling.

"You let your looks go to waste," my mother chastised. "Do you know how many girls would kill to have your figure? Your hair, your eyes, your nose? The opportunities I've gotten for you?"

"If they want to kill me for it, I wouldn't stop them," I mumbled back. That used to really piss her off.

"Ever since you quit modeling all you do is mope, mope, mope around the house all day. Don't go out like normal girls. Never even had a boyfriend! Really, Jules?"

But how could I have a boyfriend if my looks made me worthy of murder?

Not to mention, that's when the dreams began.

Well, not really dreams. Nightmares. And I don't even know if I can call them that because I never remember them. All I know is that for years now, I've had the same problem. I fall asleep, the world goes dark, and then I wake up . . .

Breathless.

The heavy emergency-exit door swings open loudly. I'm relieved to make it back to my apartment without running into Creepy Neighbor Jason. Once returned, I plop down in my chair, close out the Freemont Aquariumaniacs forum—still no messages—roll my head to each shoulder, then click on my assignment for work.

*The Infinite Web of the Multiverse*

I type.

*Scientists hypothesize that millions of other universes, collectively known as the multiverse, each with its own laws of physics, lie beyond our visual horizon.*

*Furthermore, some scientists conclude that any number of physical universes exist and that we each likely inhabit the one with the most appropriate characteristics for our best chance of survival.*

I let out a scoff. The idea of a multiverse, to me, a person who lives in this three hundred square foot studio apartment, is hilarious. My world is small, airtight, and compressed.

*The multiverse may function as an ever-expanding web-like system that connects each universe to the next. Scientist Theodore Lake recently shook the scientific community with his theory that portals might also exist in key elemental areas of each universe that may allow entry into other or parallel universe systems. This theory has been widely criticized as, at worst, "scientific mumbo-jumbo" and, at best, "optimistic science fiction."*

Whoever owns the company I work for is into some seriously weird shit, but as long as the assignments and paychecks keep coming, I couldn't give a shit. I glug down the coffee, shaking my head because it's so hot it burns my tongue. *Fuck.*

But a notification lights up at the corner of my screen.

*One new message from Mackthefishguy*

My pulse quickens, and I welcome the immediate distraction, clicking the notification. His avatar is a profile of a fish. A mackerel, I think, sleek, pale, and opalescent.

*Mack: It's Friday morning. Is your tank still empty?*

Mack knows about my greatest aquarium shame. About the total lack of aquatic creatures in my care. It's an inside joke of ours.

*Jules: As empty as my soul. Happy Friday.*

Small talk, I know, but I actually kind of like it with Mack. We're just two normal people having a totally normal conversation.

*Mack: Friday, Friday, Friday. You know where the fish crew goes on Friday nights, right?*

*Jules: Where?*

*Mack: Anywhere that'll drop the bass.*

*Jules: Booooo!!!*

*Mack: Okay, okay, okay, tough crowd. I'm a fish guy, not a jokes guy. But for real, what're you up to?*

I run my fingers through my hair, noticing all its knots. When was the last time I showered? I shake away the thought. More importantly, what would it be like to hang out with Mackthefishguy on a Friday night?

*Jules: The usual. The girls come over for drinks, we hit the town in miniskirts and heels, and then stumble home at closing time.*

A lie.

*Mack: Really? You strike me as more of an introvert, but hey, what do I know?*

*Jules: That's because I'm actually going to sit in my apartment and eat instant ramen. But the good ramen that comes with the oil packets, not just the powder. Although I like that kind too.*

The truth.

I send the message and chew on my lip as I wait for him to respond. I wonder what he's fishing around for—if anything.

Finally, typing bubbles appear.

*Mack: Don't you want to know what I'm up to?*

*Jules: Nah.*

I snort to myself.

*Jules: Kidding. What're you up to?*

*Mack: I'm expanding my tank again.*

*Jules: Again? But don't you only have one fish?*

*Mack: Yes, but he's growing. Even if I don't want him to.*

*Jules: Don't you think he could use another fish in the tank with him? Isn't he lonely?*

*Mack: Other fish don't like him.*

*Jules: What? Why not?*

*Mack: He started out cute, but now he's turned into kind of a freak. Too ugly.*

*Jules: I don't believe it!* Then I pause before typing the next words. *Send me a picture.*

It sounds like nothing, right? Asking for a picture of a fish. But this is an escalation of our conversations. We've never exchanged pictures before. And even if I don't want to admit it, I'm testing the waters. What else can we exchange . . . ?

*Mack: Sorry, he's camera shy.*

My heart sinks a bit at the rejection, even though it's silly. We're talking about fish. Fish *tanks*, at that.

Typing bubbles appear again.

*Mack: But I'll send you a picture of the new tank, how about that? I haven't switched him over yet.*

I raise my brows.

*Jules: Deal.*

*Mack: Incoming.*

As I wait for the picture in my inbox, I click through my open tabs. *Multiverse. Aquariumaniacs. Fanfic.*

I click back, and the message from Mack has arrived with an attachment.

Why am I so nervous to see a picture of an empty tank? Something about it feels so personal.

I open the attachment and gasp, hand to mouth.

The tank is *huge*. Bigger than anyone could possibly need for one fish, unless he's keeping a shark or dolphin in there, which the Freemont Aquarium forum people would find highly unethical. But the enclosure takes up half the wall. Next to the tank, tacked up, is a framed picture. It's too blurry to make out what's inside, but it kind of looks like the face of a man.

*Hmmm.* Could it be? Could that be Mack? Why would he have a picture of himself on his own wall? Then again, he *is* a man . . . they do weird shit like that.

And what could he possibly need with a tank this enormous? But also, we *did* meet on a fish forum filled with fish fanatics on a local forum called the Aquariumaniacs.

What was I expecting?

I click my mouse to zoom in on the picture, narrowing my eyes to inspect closely. There's a reflection in the tank of the room in front of it, but it appears mostly empty other than a long white couch.

Then something in the corner of the reflection startles me. I blink hard to determine the image, and then my adrenaline spikes.

What the fuck is that?

There's a *creature* in the picture. Or at least part of a creature. Surely that can't be a fish? Can it?

But it looks like a fish.

I lean in, mind racing.

At least, it looks fish-*like*. But also . . .

Also, it looks like a man.

# CHAPTER 2

I zoom in on my screen and put my face right up to it, but that does nothing but blur my vision even more. I lean back again and squint, and the image clarifies.

In the very corner of the picture is a face. Almost one that looks like a fish but also oddly like a man. It's white and translucent in color, I can only see about the top quarter, or at least what I think is the top quarter. A large opalescent light blue eye, a high forehead, or at least what might be called a forehead. But also . . . an ear?

The fish has ears? Like human ears? Something like that. Ears but with pointed little fins circling the outer shell.

I sit back in my chair. *Relax.* It's an illusion what you're seeing. A reflection of a reflection. It's just his fish. He only has the one, so it must be really, really big. Also, there's gotta be fish in the world that resemble people.

My fingers type quickly, and I search the internet for "fish that look like humans."

Results pop up, videos with creepy, human-like aquatic creatures swimming in murky, gray waters. Despite the off-putting images, I sigh in relief. It's totally possible that this fish has a human-like face. A weird mixture of genetics that got us to where we are today.

Maybe that's why Mack doesn't want to share any pictures on the forum. A rare fish like he has could potentially put him in danger. Someone might want to steal it. Do experiments on it. Fry it up for dinner. You know how dangerous aquarium forums are.

I laugh a little to myself and shove another soggy spoonful of Froot Loops in my mouth, chewing thoughtfully on the soft grains.

All this isolation has done a number on me apparently. I wasn't always a shut-in. But it happens easier than you'd think.

I pick up my phone to text Kate. She'll set me straight, although Kate is a weirdo in her own right. She has four boyfriends, none of whom I've ever met, and one of them, I'm pretty sure, is a ghost.

She didn't always have a ghost boyfriend. She used to be super normal, and we went to college together.

I guess I used to be *super normal* too, according to a lot of people.

I save the image and tap Kate's contact from my phone.

"Good morning, my darling," she says, answering on the first ring.

"Damn, why are you up so early?" I look at the clock and realize it's now six fifteen in the morning.

I probably should've checked before calling, but I've always kept weird hours, and Kate never seems to mind. At least, ever since she's been with her four boyfriends, she seems infinitely happy.

I hear a big yawn and stretch on the other end of the phone. "Gabriel just brought me breakfast in bed. He's an early riser, so I like to get up with him. The other three . . . they're more night owls if you know what I mean."

I don't want to get into a conversation about Kate's sex life at six in the morning, although I know she's always waiting for the chance to indulge me, so I get right to the point. "Hey, I saw something weird today from Mack. You know the guy I'm talking to online?"

"Fish forum Mack?" Kate asks.

"It's an aquarium forum, but yes, essentially."

"Okay, aquarium forum Mack. Tell me all the dirty details. Unsolicited fish pic?"

I zoom in and out of the picture. "That's the thing, I'm not really sure. Can I send it to you?"

"Sure, you know I love weird shit."

"This is true." I attach the image and send it over. "Check your messages."

I wait a second and speak again. "Do you see it?"

"Hang on. Hang on . . ." Then there's another pause. "So, what am I looking at? This just looks like an empty tank. Why's he need a tank the size of his wall?"

"Look in the corner, do you see a fa—"

"Holy shit, what the hell is that?" Kate cuts me off.

"You see it too!"

"Yeah, of course I see it. Is that some kind of monster head?"

"I don't know!"

"It's so creepy!"

"I know!" I'm practically shouting into the phone. "Do you think that's his fish? He says he only has one."

"This dude has an enormous tank with only one fish in it? That's really fucking weird, Jules."

I close the image on my screen. It's freaking me out. "Well, he did say his fish was too ugly for the other fish."

"Hmmm. Maybe there's something else going on here. May I say something crazy?"

"Have you ever said something not crazy, Kate?"

"Touché. So . . . here's the thing. You know I'm a believer in the supernatural, right?"

"I'm aware." *Ghost boyfriend.*

"Well, maybe this is some kind of . . . paranormal creature we're looking at. Have you considered that?"

I scrunch my face. I'm a skeptic, not a believer. "I think of all the available possibilities, that's probably one of the least likely."

Kate sighs. "You're never any fun."

"I'm very aware."

There's a pregnant pause between us before Kate speaks again. "When's the last time you left your apartment? You've never even met the guys."

The guys she's referring to are her four boyfriends. "I go to the coffee shop every day. Besides, I've been super busy with work."

She doesn't need to know *all* the details about my agoraphobia. *Yes, I know it's agoraphobia. Yes, I've googled my symptoms before.*

"A likely story."

I don't like where this topic is heading, so I veer it back. "Do you think I should ask Mack for another picture? Maybe he'll accidentally send more clues about the fish creature."

"I think you should just ask him outright what the hell that is."

"I can't do that!"

"Why not?"

"Because he clearly didn't mean to send it. It was an accident."

She *tsk, tsk, tsks.* "No such things as accidents in this universe."

I scoff, picking at my nails. "Pretty sure my existence disproves that statement."

"Jules!"

"Look, I gotta go, Kate. I'll call you later."

"Wait, hang on!"

I hang up, cutting her off, and lean back in my chair in frustration. I go to drink my coffee and realize the cup is empty. Damn, I've been distracted.

I rub my face, cheeks gritty against my fingertips. I can't remember the last time I showered.

I scuttle to my front door again, this time flipping my hood over my face and hugging my chest tightly. I have to risk another trip to the coffee shop. The sun is peeking through my window now, so I know more people will be out. But I'm addicted to this coffee. I think I like to punish myself with how strong it is.

I walk out of my apartment and close my door inch by inch so it doesn't make a noise. I wince when the latch catches. *Don't let Jason hear, don't let Jason hear, don't let Jason hear.*

But when I tiptoe past my door, the familiar jingle of Jason's front lock sounds in the hallway.

*Fuck.* My flip-flops don't allow me to run—I've tried before and ended up wiping out on the cold white industrial tile in the hallways.

"Hey, Jules!"

I stop dead in my tracks. He's up. He's out.

Then, fuck it, I keep walking. But he calls my name again.

"Jules! Hey!" He barks at me like I'm on a football team with him. "Did you hear me?"

Ugh.

I turn around slowly, sure to have the worst scowl on my face I can muster. How ugly can I make myself? How much more unappealing? I haven't showered, so while still thick, my blonde hair is getting a little on the swamp-witchy side. I also haven't washed my face, so my skin is gritty. And my clothes? The sweatpants with the spicy ramen noodle stain on the thigh. The sweatshirt that has a hole in the shoulder and surely sweat stains in the armpits by now. Haven't done laundry in weeks.

Not to mention the flip-flops forced over the mismatched socks.

The message I'm clearly sending to the world: *Back off. Don't get close. No looking.*

But, of course, that doesn't deter Jason. He's always looking.

Still, when he approaches, a weird smile on his face, my fingers tighten around my keys, and my mind introduces a million scenarios in which I have to stab him in the side of his neck.

"Almost missed you. Like you were trying to run away from me or something," says Jason as he leans against my doorframe, chewing gum.

He doesn't have a shirt on, and his chest is smooth, rippling abs down his front side. His hair is cropped close. Usually, he's got a gun clipped to his hip, which trips my pulse every time I see him. He's a cop, so that's why.

He's probably in his late twenties, about the same age as me, give or take. But we couldn't be more different.

"I'm heading downstairs to get coffee."

He smiles and points to his door. "Coffee? I've got coffee. Come in. I'll make you a cup."

I stare at him blankly, hoping to make him uncomfortable. Most people can't stand to be under my stare for too long, but it doesn't seem to be working.

"I'm good," I deadpan, but when I pivot around, I freeze in place when his hand grips my shoulder, spinning me back around.

"You should smile more. You'd be really hot if you smiled, has anyone ever told you that? It's not that hard, just lift the corners of your lips. C'mon, if you smile, I'll get you that cup of coffee you want."

His fingertips tighten ever so slightly when I move away, and my body recoils involuntarily. Although he's smiling, I don't like the glimmer in his eye. I don't like it one bit.

I jerk my shoulder from his grasp. "No thanks!" I shout awkwardly, then before he can say any more, I turn and jog away.

I must look crazy, but I don't care. When I hit the stairwell, I think I may have made a tactical error. He could chase after me here, and I'd have no place to go.

He could push me, and I'd fall to my death right down the center hole. Flushed like a goldfish down the toilet.

I'm rushing now, panting because I'm pushing my legs to trot down each step so quickly. My hand slides along the railing. *Don't fucking trip.*

By the time I reach the bottom, my legs jiggle like jelly and my lungs heave.

But I welcome the air outside. He didn't follow me.

*Of course he didn't follow you. As always, you're scared of nothing.*

I'm annoyed with myself for acting like such a victim.

I step into the shop and nod at the owner.

One simple interaction with Jason has my parasympathetic nervous system on fire . . . or that's what my old therapist would've said. *Flight or fight.*

And I fled.

It's a good lesson. I don't need to be curious about things.

My apartment is safe, and that's where I'll stay.

When I step outside the confines of my safe spaces, bad things happen.

Forget about Jason.

Men are dangerous. And I don't want any in my life.

The only thing I want is to hide. And to breathe.

# CHAPTER 3

There's drama on the Freemont Aquariumaniacs Forum today. Big drama

I slouch in front of my computer screen, crunching on Froot Loops, empty coffee cups crowding the surface of my desk.

I installed a padlock to the inside of my front door this morning. Ordered it online, watched a tutorial, and did it myself. I haven't seen Jason because I've stopped going out for coffee every morning. Instead, I ordered coffee grounds from the grocery store online and then had someone deliver them directly to my house. The coffee's not the same, but at least I don't have to go outside to get it, shrinking my world down by approximately half.

I'm wrapped in a blanket, dark green and warm, and the blinds are drawn, but the sun's not up yet anyway. I don't think, at least. I've lost track of time. Is it morning, is it night? I'm not sure. My hours are off. I've been avoiding sleeping.

Every time I doze, I wake up the same way. Dying for breath.

I scroll on my computer and pass the pop-up ads for natural gonorrhea medications and foot fungal treatments to read the never-ending list of messages on the Aquariumaniacs forum.

*Where are the mods? Why are you allowing this psycho to ruin our forums?* AquaFriend2023 writes. Her post has three hundred likes.

*Free speech is a human right! Let them talk!* Clownwithafish writes. His post has nearly the same number of likes.

There's a debate going on about a new user. Specifically user *FishKiller1234*. Definitely an interesting choice for an aquarium forum, but I suppose it's no worse than *JulesLikesToSwim*, which is my own username and also a blatant lie since my own flippers haven't seen a body of water in years.

FishKiller1234 has been posting some very incendiary comments on forums the last few days, and they've got everyone in a tizzy.

It started out small, with just a few posts.

*Hello everyone. I'm FishKiller1234, and you all need to be very, very afraid on these forums.*

People took the bait and responded.

*What are you talking about?*

*Afraid for what?*

*The only thing I'm afraid of is using the wrong method to adjust my $CO_2$ levels.*

After a few days, FishKiller1234 went away, but then they returned.

*You fish people are extremely sick. You should shut down this forum right now. Do you know what's happening to regular, normal humans now?*

Another poster bit, responding again.

*We're keeping our aquariums appropriately clean?*

But FishKiller1234 wasn't having it.

*No, you're turning into monsters. FISH MONSTERS.*

I laughed out loud when I read the post, wiping away the dribbles of milk on my chin. *Fish Monsters* is honestly hilarious. Because what even is a fish monster? Kate might know, given her love of the supernatural.

But reflexively, my mind wanders to the picture from Mack.

Was that a fish monster? Does FishKiller1234 *know* something . . . ?

Their newest post is from this morning.

*Please remove yourself from these forums and repent. It's the only way you won't mutate into fish monsters. I have proof of these monsters. They live among us and they're dangerous. They want our children. They want our homes. They start out just like us, but then, slowly, they're tempted by their unclean desires to turn into fish. And then they transform into their final forms. FISH MONSTERS. They walk among us! Message me and I'll show you. Or join my Facebook group.*

A message pops up on my screen. It's from Mack. I nearly jump out of my seat.

Ever since that picture, I've been avoiding Mack. I've been avoiding everyone really. I have four missed calls from my mother and one from Kate. My mother . . . well, that's just par for the course. I haven't spoken to her in months. Kate, on the other hand, will call back.

Part of me doesn't want to talk to Mack, but another part of me is missing him just a little. Okay, fine, missing him a lot.

So sue me. Who knew there was a part of me that liked to flirt? That was still reaching out for human contact.

I hem and haw in my computer chair, the rusty hinges creaking loudly as I rock back and forth, and then, finally, I open the message.

The picture still freaks me out, yes. But surely, a reasonable explanation exists for what I saw. There are always reasonable explanations.

What harm could talking to someone do? Mack doesn't know where I live, and he doesn't know my full name. And vice versa.

And weirdly, I really do miss him.

*Mack: Are you okay? Haven't heard from you in a few days. Did the fish monsters get you?*

Instantly, relief rushes to the pit of my belly. Surely, he wouldn't be joking about something *if he was that something?*

And despite it all, when I talk to him, I experience a little bit of joy, like a tiny pinprick of adrenaline in a sleepy fugue. Joy that I don't really deserve. Joy that I almost never feel.

I chew on my lip but then set my fingers to type.

*Jules: Sorry I've been away. I've been fighting my evil desires to transform into a fish. I've been repenting on a shrine of pebbles and sand. Fishkiller1234 has opened my eyes to my unholy ways.*

He responds almost immediately.

*Mack: So we've both been up to the same thing! What're the odds?*

*Jules: Yes. What're the odds of two weirdos on an aquarium forum having the same weird interests?*

*Mack: FishKiller has really stirred up a storm in our community. Maybe we should start a protest. Are you pro or anti fish monsters?*

*Jules: I just told you, I'm fighting urges myself! If there was a pill to fight off this fish desire, I'd take it. But the dark call of the sea compels me . . . beckons me . . . whispers my name.*

Although I might be a copywriter, I still have some good creative chops. Nothing wrong with showing off.

*Mack: Wow, I didn't know it was that deep. Are you this serious about anything else in your life?*

*Mack: Or anyone, perhaps . . .*

My fingers pause on the keyboard. Is he asking what I think he might be asking? Even with my perennial fears, I can't seem to stop talking to him. I have this desire to just spill my guts. Maybe it's the anonymity. Maybe it's because he just seems kind. Maybe because he can't see me.

My eyes float to the padlock on my front door. *Danger.* And still, I want to know more about Mack.

*Jules: The only thing I'm serious about is filling up this aquarium. What about you? Will you stay a single fish forever? Just like the guy in your tank?*

I type only these words, but I have so many more questions.

*Mack: Nah, he and I are living the solo life.*

*Jules: Is it because you're a terrifying, scaly, horrible fish creature?*

There's a pause in the messages.

*Mack: Maybe. Would that scare you if I was?*

I laugh a little.

*Jules: Send me a picture and I'll decide. Maybe I like to be scared.*

The biggest lie I've ever typed in the history of my life. I hate fear, mostly because I spend so much time experiencing it. But you can't quell curiosity forever without it rearing its ugly little inquisitive head. Plus, I think we're flirting.

And I like when we flirt.

Even if fish monsters were real, and Mack was some kind of out-and-open fish monster, it's infinitely better to flirt with the monsters who are out in the open than the ones who lurk behind their doors. Like Jason. Like all the other men in my life.

*Mack: I have a rule about sending pictures to strangers on the internet.*

*Jules: So do I. Always use a ring light. How about I send one first?*

Where is this boldness coming from? I guess the more you isolate yourself physically, the more you emotionally rebel. Could that be true? What would my therapist say? Dammit, I wish I hadn't fired her.

But Mack has already messaged back.

*Mack: You're sure you want to do that?*

*Jules: It's just a picture. I'm just a person like everyone else.*

*Mack: Right. Aren't we all . . . ?*

*Mack: All right. If you feel safe, I would very much like to see a picture of you.*

*Jules: And you'll send one back.*

*Mack: I'll send one back.*

*Jules: Promise? You swear on the single, sole fish in your tank.*

*Mack: I swear on the single, sole fish in my tank.*

*Jules: Picture incoming.*

My heart races. I still haven't showered in days, brushed my teeth, changed my clothes. Shit. I can't just look like a slob. I can't look like my everyday, true self for this picture. Compulsions are so strange. The compulsion to send Mack a picture is so strong, though. Strong enough that I rise from my desk, unzip my hoodie, tear off my shirt and let it fall to the floor, and push down the waistband of my sweatpants and trip out of them.

I'm in the bathroom, fully naked, before I can even blink. I reach into the shower and turn the old crystal handle. Water bursts from the shower head, and for a second, the rushing noise falls over me like a soft summer blanket.

Then I lift my arm and get a whiff of my underarm, and *yikes*.

It really has been too long since I've bathed. Gross! Talk about fish monster. She is me.

The heat of the water hits me hard as I stand directly under the stream. For all my complaints about my shitty apartment, the water pressure is A-plus.

I grab a washcloth and some soap and begin scrubbing at the dirt and grime.

As I scrub, I notice my skin doesn't feel as soft as it used to. It's almost a little rough in nature. Man, I've been really negligent in the upkeep.

And my eerie blue veins . . . ugh, when did they get like this? Maybe a direct result of a vitamin D deficiency.

Still, I scrub until my skin has smoothed. Next I tackle my hair, squeezing on a glop of shampoo and massaging it deep into my scalp.

Despite myself, the entire thing calms me. As I'm rinsing off, I realize this is the best I've physically felt in days.

Showers. Maybe I should try them more? Why did I stop taking them anyway? But I know why. I know the deep depression that holds onto my insides and sucks me beneath the surface every night. But I can ignore that problem for now. Because now something exciting is about to happen.

I slather on lotion to counteract the weird roughness of my arms. Seems to work. The lotion soothes and absorbs, although my skin still feels a little damp. And then I open my closet door. I haven't visited anything inside this room in weeks, but I can't wear my sweatshirt.

This calls for totally normal clothes. For all Mack knows, I'm a normal woman who does totally normal woman things: walks the dog, shops for groceries, showers on the daily, visits her family, interacts with maybe more than one single friend.

I choose a green slip dress, shimmery but dark, and pull it over my body, flipping out the ends of my wet hair that get stuck into the back of the dress. The straps are thin, and the front is a V but not too deep. The dress is old. From college.

I catch a glimpse of myself in my full-length mirror.

*Have you sent your pictures to that agency I recommended?* The voice of my mother echoes in my head. *You could make a lot more money with modeling than you can with writing.*

I'm still beautiful. I almost do a double take since I so rarely look at myself in the mirror. I'm beautiful but a little gaunt, but that's to be expected given my hermit-like mentality. I almost thought it'd be worse really. In my head, I'm an old crone, a witch covered in jellyfish; *touch me and die.*

But on the outside, I don't look like that at all.

Except for the weird blue hue of my veins, of course.

Still, I'm physically beautiful. I know I'm beautiful. I've always been. It's the one thing I've always known to be true about myself.

I open the blinds, and bold morning sun blasts through the glass of my window.

Well, at least I know what time of day it is now. The light is convenient.

I turn on my forward-facing camera and snap a picture. I don't need another try. First one did the job. I have a small smile, but I can't bear to show my teeth. I don't smile big in pictures; this is the most anyone will get out of me. Even Mack.

He'll like what he sees. I know he will. In that sense, I'm a little giddy with glee.

But in a much bigger sense, I know I'm a liar. I'm the real catfish. The real person inside me is not the person reflected on the outside, aesthetically correct though she may be.

Luckily, the internet isn't real.

It's been fifteen minutes. He's been waiting.

I attach the picture to a message and send it to him.

A reply immediately appears.

*Mack: Oh. Okay.*

*Oh. Okay?* What the fuck? But another message pops up right after.

*Mack: You're . . . gorgeous. I had no idea.*

Hmmm.

*Jules: You sound disappointed.*

*Mack: No, of course not.*

*Mack: Maybe a little worried.*

*Jules: Worried? Why?*

*Mack: You might be disappointed with what I send back.*

*Jules: I've never been the kind of girl who cares about looks.*

I don't mean it in a *not like other girls* kind of way. I've just never held physical attraction in high regard. I never found the male models who had their hands on me on shoots sexy. Their touch didn't turn me on. I googled it once, and I think I'm something called *demisexual.* But to be honest, I've never really thought about it much. I'm no virgin, but I'm pretty inexperienced sexually. Agoraphobia will do that to a girl.

Mack is quiet for so long I'm convinced he's not going to respond. My heart sinks at the thought. After we've opened this little door to each other, I'm sparking with curiosity now. I want to know who I'm talking to. And the fact that he isn't responding makes me surprisingly and deeply sad.

Until I see typing again.

*Mack: Here goes nothing.*

I rub my hands together in anticipation. He must be ugly. Maybe fat. Maybe bald. Maybe he's missing some teeth. Whoever he is, whatever he might be hiding, I want to see it.

I click on the attachment to open the picture and tilt my head in confusion at what appears before me.

Mack is . . .

Attractive. Huh.

I don't know what I was expecting. The picture is of a man, maybe in his early twenties, which would mean I'm a little older than him, which also surprises me. His hair is a sandy blond verging on ginger, and his eyes are a deep-set gray-green. Striking, but there's also a surprising amount of darkness behind them. They're larger and a little far apart. His jaw is wide and square. And his body is that of a man who goes to the gym. Wide shoulders and thick biceps covered with a light gray-green shirt that's almost an exact match to his eyes.

For some reason, this surprises me as well. Maybe I just assumed he was like me. Maybe I'm a little let down at the thought that he's not a shut-in. A hermit. An Emily Dickinson type. But no . . . he looks really normal. Hot, actually. Like a guy who goes for a run out in the city, and when he stops at a traffic light, a woman might tap on his broad shoulder and ask for his number.

Why am I so disappointed? God, I'm such a fucking weirdo. As if I didn't need more reasons to feel like a freak. What was I expecting? A fucking fish monster?

*Mack: So, what do you think?*

*Jules: Hm. You're beautiful too.*

*Mack: Now you're the one who sounds disappointed.*

*Jules: You look like a movie star or something.*

*Mack: And you look like a model.*

*Jules: Don't worry, like I said, on the inside, I'm nothing but a black hole.*

*Mack: Well, I don't think you're a black hole. I think you're funny. And smart. And a great conversationalist.*

*Jules: You wouldn't feel that way about me if you met me.*

*Mack: I think I would.*

Warmth trickles into my belly at his words. The thing about Mack is that he's liked me even before seeing me. I don't think I've ever had a relationship like that.

But the more I stare at his picture, the more it looks off to me, a little distorted and glassy, actually. Like it's a reflection of something. A picture of a picture.

Until I realize it is.

I scroll through my old messages and open the picture of Mack's tank. The one with the weird creature in it. Next to the tank is a framed picture.

The general shape and color are familiar.

I toggle back to the picture of Mack and then back to the framed picture. The color scheme is the same until I'm positive that, for some reason, Mack took a picture of the picture.

Why wouldn't he just take a selfie and send it?

*Why* would he take a picture of a picture? It's so weird, and it doesn't add up.

And then in the very corner of the reflection on the glass in the alleged picture of Mack's face, almost completely camouflaged against Mack's sea-green T-shirt . . . I see another face. That same face from before.

This time I see the whole thing.

The creature in the reflection isn't Mack's fish.

The creature in the reflection is the one taking the picture.

# CHAPTER 4

"You should ask him to do a video call." Kate's face is shoved in the crack of the door between the chain and the lock.

It rattles as I pull the chain and release the door.

Kate walks in and toes her shoes off, handing off a cup of rocket fuel coffee from the shop downstairs. I haven't gone in over two weeks now.

"Thank you, thank you, thank you!" I say and sip the liquid, letting it scald my throat. It's painful. I love it. "You didn't see Jason out there, did you?"

I flip the lock on my door.

Kate narrows her eyes and plops down on the couch. She pulls out a small takeaway box that I recognize from the coffee shop from her purse and pops it open to reveal a trio of Makrouta cookies. "No, not today. You know last time I saw him he grabbed my ass? But that was years ago. I let it slide. But now . . . Now I'd punch him in his fucking face if he tried that again."

"Don't try it. He'll have you arrested. There's no winning with cops. And why didn't you tell me about that?"

"I didn't want to worry you. But look . . ." She gestures at me in the robe she gave me, hair in a messy top knot. "You're already worried about everything, so at this point, I don't really think I could make you worse."

I scurry to the couch and sit next to her, crisscross applesauce with the sacred sludge between my hands.

Kate reaches into the box and offers me a cookie. I accept and shove it in my mouth. I haven't even eaten breakfast today, and it's already one p.m. I know because that's the time Kate said she'd be over.

"So, what was such a big deal that I had to come over in person? You know you can come to me as well. When's the last time you left your neighborhood?"

"It's been a hundred years, at least," I mumble, pushing hair out of my eyes and then pulling up my phone. "I couldn't send you this picture because I didn't want you to freak out. This stays between the two of us."

Kate's delicate dark brows knit together. "Okay," she says slowly, taking the phone from me. "What am I looking at? This guy?" She turns the phone to face me. "This hot guy? I'm lost, fill me in. Are you back on the dating apps? Wait, you were never on the dating apps."

I shake my head. "Not the dating apps. The forums."

"The *fish forums?*"

"Aquarium forums."

Kate's eyes go wide. "Aquarium guy looks like *this?* Damn, girl."

I shake my head. "You aren't looking closely enough. Remember the last picture. With the reflection?"

She looks even more concerned now. "Yes. Of course. The fish with the human face."

"Here's the thing. I'm not so sure it's a fish with a human face anymore."

Kate fiddles with her dark hair, the strand winding and unwinding around her finger. Then she leans toward me. "This is some supernatural shit, isn't it?"

I wince but also roll my eyes. "Could we not bring the supernatural into everything? Isn't it horrifying and grotesque enough simply to be part of the natural?"

Kate shrugs, but then her eyes widen, and her hand flies to cover her mouth. "Jules, what the fuck . . . I mean, *who the fuck* is this in the corner of the screen?"

"I don't know, but I'm pretty sure it's not a fish with a human face anymore!"

"No . . . no . . . this is a human . . . with a fish face."

The reflection is small, and you wouldn't see it at first, not with the way it blends in with the color of the picture. It's almost like one of those magic eyes where once you know how to find the hidden picture, you can't shake your focus away. You can't see anything else.

I can understand how he missed it. I could understand how any average, normal, non-anxiety-ridden person could miss something in a picture like that. But my job is built in the details. Copywriting is an exacting practice. And I'm used to looking at not just the words but also the spaces between the words.

And that's, unfortunately, what I've done with Mack's picture as well.

"Jules, what are you going to do?" Her voice quiets. "Are you gonna confront him?"

I let my jaw drop. "Am I going to confront a fish monster?" *Oh my god, the fish monsters are real.* "I think not. This isn't a horror film. I'm not trying to get eaten alive or something."

"Oh my god, you know what you should do?"

"I'm afraid to ask."

"You should go to his house and take a picture of him and sell it to a tabloid!"

"Kate! Be serious. And that would be a horribly cruel thing to do, anyway."

"I know, I know. I'm just kidding about that, just trying to lighten the mood. But really, you should meet him in person."

A small flicker of adrenaline pings in my stomach at the thought. But I tilt my head down, brows angled upward. "For what reason would I ever do that?"

"To find out the truth! Maybe he's a human. Maybe he isn't. Because you never know. A fish monster guy might be super cool."

The picture of the reflection flashes in front of my eyes. The strange, smooth head. The aquatic features. The peculiarities of the image. My brain has questions. My body does too.

But I shake my head. "You're crazy. And this whole thing is insane. Of course I don't want to see him in person! I regret ever sharing a picture with him. I regret ever talking to him."

"So, you're just gonna block him or something?"

I lean back on the couch as Kate flips through the pictures on my phone. Normally, I wouldn't let someone flip through my pictures, but Kate's different. She won't judge me for the million random screenshots I've taken in the fish forum. Or the artistic shots I take down the center of the spiral staircase. Since I haven't been out for a while, I haven't had much to take pictures of anymore.

I let my head flop back. "Ugh! Why do I feel so guilty? I can't just block him. Even if he is a dangerous fish monster, he's still my friend, or was my friend, or something like a friend. I don't know. Plus, he called me beautiful."

Kate glances up from my phone. "Everyone calls you beautiful. I would hate you for it if you just didn't seem so completely uninterested in exploiting that beauty even a little bit. Hey! Whoa. This is so weird." Kate stops her fingers as she's flicking through an album.

"What is?"

She holds up the screen, showing me the first picture Mack sent me of his aquarium.

"This picture was taken in the same place as the other one, right?" she asks.

I nod, unsure what she's getting at. "Yes . . . I think so."

"Well, guess what, Jules? I know where your fish monster lives."

***

Twelve hours later, and Kate's gone. It turns out Kate probably does know where Mack, a.k.a. the Fish Monster, lives. The crown molding in the picture is what gave it away. A very specific and custom crown molding that only exists in one building in the entire United States of America. Apparently, Kate's asshole ex-boyfriend used to manage the property there, and as a result, she learned all about it.

"Joe specifically hand carved this custom molding. I remember because it's all he ever talked about. Vasser Estate this and Vasser Estate that. They said *spare no expense*."

"Vasser?" I asked.

"The building belongs to this huge real estate tycoon named John Vasser. He's nearly a billionaire."

She could even tell what floor Mack's unit was on.

The fifth floor.

The news hit me like an anchor, heavy and mooring.

Now that Kate's gone, I pace around my living room, arms clasped behind my back, forehead tilted, surveying the limited inside world around me. Unmade seafoam bed, desk against the wall, aquarium bubbling in the corner, empty silver picture frame resting on a nightstand.

*I should really put that picture of my mother up.*

I shake myself out of my thoughts, halting in the middle of my living room.

Because now I know two things.

One: I know Mack is a fish monster. Or at least, I believe it. I believe it with my whole entire brain even though rationality screams at the back of my neck.

And two: I know where Mack lives.

Oh, and three. For whatever inexplicable, morbid, weirdo reason my brain might have, I can't stop staring at his picture.

Not the fake picture of the blond guy with the green eyes.

The picture within the picture, of course. The real picture. The picture that exists in between the spaces. The aquatic one with the eerie blue gaze and the almost see-through white gauzy scales and the high forehead and smooth head and . . . also there's some kind of fin growing out of his chin. Like how a betta fish has fins floating beneath it. Like that, but it falls like a beard.

I genuinely can't stop looking. I'm a woman obsessed.

But I'm also a woman on a deadline, and I've never missed a deadline before.

I can't afford to lose my job, of course. What other job would allow me to hide away in my apartment, staring at the walls, navel-gazing about fish? If I had to venture out of my safety, I wouldn't survive.

Mental illness is the real monster, isn't it?

For a second, another thought crosses my mind.

Maybe there's no fish monster at all. Maybe there's no Mack. Maybe I've just totally cracked? Maybe I'm hallucinating. Maybe I've succumbed to the spiral of madness that I sometimes feel is just bubbling beneath the surface.

My gaze wanders to the four corners of my room. Seafoam bed, sparkling aquarium, empty picture frame . . .

Yes. Losing my shit entirely? Definitely a possibility that I can't count out. In fact, a possibility that I've never counted out.

But then another peculiar thought strikes me.

If I'm afraid of being crazy, but I'm already crazy, then isn't that its own kind of freedom? A freedom to do whatever it is I really want. Whatever that might be.

I roll out the creaky chair to my computer, and instead of opening my work assignment, I open the Freemont Aquariumaniacs Forum again.

My hands freeze, eyes unblinking at the screen. There's a message from Mack.

But I can't open it. Not yet.

I click back. First, I have a deadline to meet.

# CHAPTER 5

I finished the first portion of my assignment and turned it in to my boss minutes before the deadline. This project on the multiverse is extensive, and it's going to take me the better part of the year to finish it, even though my only role is to research and condense copy in an easy-to-consume format.

Sometimes I wonder who my boss is. I've never met her. She's just some woman who hired me off the internet. And in that sense, I love her and she's a hero. But also, she could be anyone. I never really considered who I might be working for. Maybe a mad scientist?

*Wow, I really might actually be going crazy.*

Being in this apartment for so long has warped my sense of reality.

Once I sent off my assignment, I paced around my apartment again, looking at it with renewed vision, a novel perspective. Like . . . what might Mack think about this place?

The furniture is secondhand for the most part. I'm a saver when it comes to money. If I ran out, what would I do? Face the world? I don't think so.

When I'm old enough to retire, I'll never have to talk to anyone ever again; I can have all my goods and services delivered. I can sit on my couch and stare at the wall, and no one will know the difference.

Well, except for maybe Kate.

And Mack . . .

Okay, fine. I let myself think about Mack again, and like magic, I wander my way back to my computer chair, and sitting in front of the screen where his message sits, I open the forum.

I chuckle at myself. *You are definitely crazy. Mack is not that weird fish creature. You've convinced yourself of nothing.*

He's a normal guy with blond hair and green eyes and a wide jaw and broad shoulders. He's a normal aquarium forum guy with whom I've developed a friendship over the past several months. Nothing more, nothing less.

I click on the message.

*Mack: I just wanted to let you know I'll be leaving the aquarium forum. I think this place is starting to have a negative effect on my personality . . . Too much of a good thing, you know? I have loved getting to know you. But you'll probably never hear from me again. I hope you have a great life. You brought a little bit of joy to my day every day, and I can't say that about anything or anyone else in this world. Even my ugly fish thinks so. I'll miss you, Jules. You have no idea.*

My mouth drops open.

*What?!*

He's . . . he's leaving me? He's just up and leaving?

Disappearing like a raindrop in the ocean? Like a pebble skipping past the surface?

*How fucking dare he.*

I thought we had something.

I thought we were copacetic.

I thought . . . *I thought he liked me.*

Suddenly, my world has shrunk even more; the walls push toward me like an inflating balloon house, threatening to brush against the skin of my arms.

If I don't have Mack, who do I have?

All my ambivalence evaporates, and my fingers frantically type out words. Maybe I can convince him to stay. Maybe it's not too late.

*Jules: Leaving? But I haven't even shared my deepest, darkest secrets with you yet. Who else am I going to confess to about my special instant ramen recipe or the time I accidentally made all my desktop icons invisible or the time I downloaded porn onto my work laptop and it was emailed to the entire company? You can't leave me, Mack. I thought I mattered to you. I thought you cared. I thought we were friends. Where are you even going?*

It's a frantic, confessional message. The tone is desperate, and for once, I don't care. The confession is the point. Don't go. Please forgive me. Redeem us. Return. But when I hit send, the message bounces back.

*User Mackthefishguy, account deleted 10:22 p.m.*

In the corner of the screen, the last digit of the clock increases by one. 10:27 p.m.

I missed him by five minutes.

***

After Mack's message, I dove deep beneath my comforter, head cloaked beneath the cover. I didn't come out for hours. Not when my stomach rumbled or my phone buzzed or my tongue scraped like sandpaper against the sticky pillow of my inner cheeks.

At least I know I fell asleep at night and not in the morning. Tiny wins.

Now, it must be past sunrise. I've woken up three times already, gulping for air, my hands at my throat. But my dreams amount to nothing more than a distant, wispy idea, not a picture or a memory. The only image I can conjure up is green and goopy, dark and floaty, like air or water or space. Sometimes, I swear I see spiderwebs. Glowing. Or maybe fiery webs. I'm stuck in one like a bug. Unable to move.

Someone or something is going to get me.

That's the most I can remember. Which, admittedly, is more than before. But less than the average bear.

I pull at my collar, which now feels tight at the neck. I'm in my sweats from days ago. They've dampened at folded junctures of my body with perspiration. I'm like a wrestler trying to make fighting weight. The desire to fall back into the abyss is strong, to succumb to the darkness of a dreamless sleep. But nonetheless, that desire is irrelevant. My body decides when it's time to rise, and there's no denying what my body wants.

Fuck it. *Get the fuck up.* There's no more hiding in the bed.

I force myself through my normal morning routine: Mouth to coffee, spoon to Froot Loops, robe to body, ass to creaky computer chair. Ass out of creaky chair. Hand to door locks.

Ear to door. I'm listening for Jason.

Anything to avoid Jason.

Fingertip to phone messages.

There are four from my mother. I delete them without reading them.

One from Kate.

*Kate: Um, hello? Where have you been? Do you need anything? Break-fast sandwiches? A new therapist? An edible?*

I don't respond to her either. What's the point? Kate can't change anything in my life. No one can, not even me.

*Especially not me.* I let out a grunt of agreement with myself.

It's not until I plop down again in my creaky chair and flip on my computer that I let the feelings rush back into my consciousness.

*Mack is gone.*

And I don't know anything about him. I never even got an email address. A real name.

The only thing I got was a picture of a fake person. And a terrifying creature.

Who is Mack?

Maybe he realized what happened. Maybe he knows what he sent me.

Or maybe he just never really gave a fuck about me the way I gave a fuck about him.

That part seems more likely.

Suddenly, I don't care so much about whether or not he's some kind of fish creature. My perspective has shifted again, crystal clear.

There are only a few things that matter in this world. Mack was a kind person. Someone who told corny jokes. A guy with a big tank, whatever he might be using it for. And he was nice to me. He liked me for more than my looks.

That's who Mack is.

And the feeling of missing him is deeper and darker than any feeling I've ever had in my whole entire life.

*Fuck!* I shove my hands in my hair and then pick up my phone again.

*Jules: Mack is gone. He left the forum.*

*Kate: What?! Not our fish guy? Fish guy left under suspicious circumstances after sending you suspicious pictures? No . . . shock of the century.*

*Jules: It's not funny. I think I was starting to really like him. I don't know what to do.*

*Kate: Go to his house. The fact that you know where he lives is actually huge information. Tell him he can't just abandon you like that. You're a person too! You have feelings.*

A knock on the door has me jumping almost an entire mile.

My heart races. Who the fuck is knocking at my door?

I sit completely still. I don't answer my door as a general rule unless I know it's my mother or Kate. Not even my mother, really.

No one else is allowed. I even include specific notes on my deliveries never to knock. I tell them I have a heart condition.

Seconds tick by, and then I relax again. The knocker must be gone by now.

I pick up my phone to text Kate back when the sound occurs again.

*Shit. Go the fuck away already! No one's welcome here.*

Another knock, again and again. Then a voice.

"Jules? Hey, Jules. It's George. From the coffee shop. Can you open up? Or just let me know you're here. I'm worried about you."

*George? Holy shit.*

I clamber to the door and open it just as wide as my chain lock will allow.

"What do you want?" I ask through the space in between the door.

"You haven't been by for coffee in days. I was worried something happened to you."

Something *has* happened to me. My whole life has happened to me! But how do you explain that to a kind, near stranger who is only trying to treat you like every other normal human in the world?

"Are you doing okay?" he asks.

I clear my throat. "I'm fine. It's fine. Everything's fine. Can you leave now?"

But he doesn't. "I don't mean to bother you. Do you have family or anything? Someone who checks in on you regularly?"

*Family.* What a question.

"I gotta go, George. Thanks though," I say and close the door in his face, each lock dully clacking as the lugs flip.

The more people in my life, the more likely they are to let me down. The padlock secures my door. I stare at it. Nothing on the outside is coming in. Nothing on the inside is going out. But George's voice, his very presence, the act of interrupting my life without me asking. It has me slightly shaken.

I flip around, and right away, the sparkling rectangular aquarium at the side of the room catches my eyes. Bubbles flitter up. Water pushes down. Up and down and up and down. I breathe in and out and in and out.

Mack's disappearance has me feeling powerless. And there's nothing scarier than the thought of losing your own power. Especially when you barely had any to begin with. What would my old therapist say?

A realization slams into me.

I've been doing this whole thing wrong. Mack might have cut me out, but Kate is right about one thing. *I know where he lives.* And that kind of knowledge is power. And then, I get an idea.

# CHAPTER 6

It's two p.m. I've been waiting by my front door for three hours. Sitting. Listening. Biding my time.

I heard Jason talking out in the hallway to some stranger yesterday. He's going out of town for a while, catching a flight around three thirty. I'm waiting for him to leave so there's no chance I'll run into him.

Nervously, I finger the hem of my shirt; odd for me to wear anything but my robe or sweats inside my apartment. But right now, I'm in a black sweater with little embroidered green flecks all over. My jeans are new. Well, they were new three years ago when I first bought them. I never even opened the package. They languished in a corner of my closet, but today is the day to wear them.

My mother's voice floats into the ether. *Why do you wear such dark and dreary colors, Jules? You're a bright spring! But you dress like the sludge at the bottom of the ocean.*

I give another cursory sniff under my arms to make sure I'm not about to offend the general public, and I breathe in a sigh when I realize I smell as fresh as the sea breeze. Usually, not so much the case.

I've showered, that's why. Got up first thing in the morning and shuffled myself inside the little glass stall in the corner of my bathroom. I've used all the best soaps and lotions too.

My skin is still feeling a little rough though. Scaling off a bit like I'm drying out or something. That, with the blue veins, has me wondering what's been going on with my body lately.

I slathered on extra lotion.

*Jesus fuck Jason, will you fucking leave already?*

Finally, my ears perk up at the sound of his door. Then heavy footsteps.

I clamber to my feet and peer out the peephole to see Jason and his tightly trimmed hair and workout pants trotting to the elevators.

*Thank fucking god.* He's gone.

I wait another ten minutes, just to be safe. And then, for the first time in weeks, I turn all the locks one by one, finally pull the chain from its little brass holder, and open my front door. The cool air from the hallway catches me first. I'm unused to the smell anymore. I breathe in deeply and struggle a little. Maybe I have allergies. Then, I scurry out to the hallway, circling the drain of the stairwell, and suddenly . . . I'm outside.

Sheepishly, I stroll up to George's shop, meeting him at the counter. His eyebrows go up when he sees me.

"Jules, so good to see you out and about. And looking so . . ." He puts out a hand.

I smile, looking at him for as long as I can stand, then look down at my hands again. "Black coffee, please," I interrupt before he can finish his observation.

Yeah, I know I'm not usually showered or dressed in outside clothes or wearing walking shoes. George might try to be kind to me, but it doesn't mean I want any comments on my appearance.

In fact, one of the reasons I stopped leaving my apartment at all is because of the comments. I just became so sick of everyone always having a fucking opinion on how I look.

"Enjoy . . ." George hands me the coffee. Same old look of concern on his face as always.

I almost turn back to my apartment out of habit. Just as I've done hundreds of times before. But this time, I close my fist in my pocket.

I'm not going back to my apartment today.

I'm not scurrying back to the darkness.

Instead, I'm finding Mack.

***

Kate gave me Mack's address. I don't know his specific unit, but I'm sure I can find out. The building is huge, but so is each individual apartment. He lives on the fifth floor, and there are only five other units on the floor.

Finding the right unit isn't the hurdle. The hurdle is . . .

I look down the sidewalk. The sky is gray and cold. I'm almost unused to the cold anymore, keeping my apartment at the same moderate and almost balmy temperature every day. Can I even adjust to cold weather anymore, or have I gone completely cold-blooded?

My veins glow especially blue and eerie beneath the natural light.

*Ugh, gross.*

*Come on, Jules. You can do this. You used to do this all the time before. You used to ride the subway in New York for your go-sees. You used to take the L in Chicago. Now, you can walk seven blocks to this apartment. You can do it.*

*What did your old therapist say?* A journey of a thousand miles begins with the first step.

She really did love a platitude, but hey, they come in handy every now and then.

With some effort, I push one foot in front of another. George is probably staring at me from behind his counter with that concerned look on his face. The weight of his judgment barrels down on me, even if I can't see it. The weight of everyone's judgment everywhere . . . And yet . . .

Another step, and another.

Step, step, step, step, step.

And before I know it, I'm past my building to the end of the block on the edge of the sidewalk and the street, a pedestrian sign about to turn green. It flickers, and I walk again.

I'm doing it! My blood is pumping, the world around me blurs green and white and gray and blue, and my hand is balled up in unmovable fist at my side, but nevertheless, I progress.

Forward and onward. I shutter my gaze. Avoid the wandering eyes of onlookers. Especially the men. I pull the hood from my coat over my head. Squeeze my cup of coffee. Swallow tight. Trot ahead. Push faster and faster.

By the time I reach the building, my nerves are shot, knees trembling, lungs heavy.

But also . . . *holy shit.*

I haven't gone this far in years!

But now that I'm here . . . That's a whole other story.

The building itself is old. It might be a part of the preserved historic buildings in the area from the look of it, with splattered ivy snaking up the side of the mottled red brick. The large gold art-deco-era sign above the entrance reads The Dome. Dizziness swirls through my head when I crane my neck to catch a view of the top floor. It's about ten stories high. *Whoosh.* Another wave of dizziness, and I almost crumble to my feet.

*What am I doing? No, but really, what the fuck am I doing?*

An almost magnetic pull has me shifting my weight from one foot to the other toward the direction of my apartment building.

It's crazy to come here. It's crazy to show up at someone's apartment unannounced in general, but to show up unannounced to the home of a near stranger you met on the internet? Someone who you suspect might be catfishing you? What am I, some kind of stalker? Or worse, someone with a death wish?

But a small voice inside me won't shut up. *You made it this far. He can't just abandon you. He can't just leave you. Who does he think he is? Your father?*

A laugh hits the center of my chest at the thought, but it breaks the panic. So, I tighten up my coat, toss my now-empty coffee cup into the wrought iron trash can in front of the building, and approach.

I push out a breath as I open the front door.

The lobby of the building is ornate, vaulted, shiny, but it has a haunted quality. Old paintings of men at sea are on display. Also, large, lacquered fish are hung high on the wall. Well, whoever decorated the lobby is certainly consistent. A small waterfall is situated on a coffee table next to a book. I tiptoe over as if I'm breaking the law and look.

*Moby Dick.*

I'm sensing a theme. Mackthefishguy lives in a fish building. Interesting.

The elevators are off the lobby in a narrow hallway. A doorman snores behind a desk, his brimless navy cap tilted just over his brow. Otherwise, not a soul in sight. Definitely for the best. I might die if I had to get in an elevator with another person.

I press the button and get inside. It's rickety, lurching a bit as it rises. I cross my arms, gripping onto my chest.

For the millionth time, I doubt this decision.

For the millionth and first time, my desires override my rationale.

The dull orange numbers light one by one as I ascend through the floors until finally, *five* illuminates. Another lurch of the elevator and then an off-tune ding. And before I know it, the metal doors slide open, revealing a new territory. My own road less traveled.

Now, all I need to do is figure out which unit belongs to Mack.

*Hmmm.* The last thing I want is to have to see or talk to anyone extra, so knocking on each door is out of the question. I've got to keep the interactions down to a minimum.

It's a good thing I'm an expert at that.

The hallway, at first, appears liminal. Never ending and otherworldly. The low-ply carpet is navy with a turquoise swirl traveling like a wave up and down the strip of rectangular flooring. The lighting is a warm, dull yellow.

But there are only a few doors.

My brain scrambles. How do I figure this out? Work smarter, not harder.

First thing. Doormats.

I don't think Mack would have a mat outside his door. Most men don't. And if he is the man with blond hair and green eyes in the picture, then he *definitely* doesn't have a doormat.

That eliminates two of the doors in the hallway. The first doormat reads *Come as You Are.*

The second has a million pictures of a man's face printed on it that reads *STEP ON ME.* A custom joke doormat. Definitely not Mack. At least, I hope not because there's a fetish I'm not trying to explore.

Okay, three left. I feel like I'm playing *Carmen Sandiego* or something. I was always good at that game as a kid.

The door closest to me has a winding green pothos. This could be Mack's. He likes aquariums, so the odds are good that he also wants to keep a plant alive. But upon closer inspection, a sheen of dust indicates that the plant is plastic. For some reason, I just know that's not his. He's not a plastic plant guy. No way. In fact, in the Aquariumaniacs forum, he specifically ranted about how he wasn't a fan of plastic plants. The fish can tell the difference. Some plastic plants can even irritate fish fins.

That leaves me with two more doors.

I put my ear against one of the doors and hear a TV blaring. It's loud. A blustering conservative news station.

There's no way in hell that's Mack.

I can't. No, I refuse to believe it. I won't even allow it into the realm of possibilities.

So, that leaves me with one other door.

There's no mat, no plant, no sound. Just a regular wooden door.

And behind it? Behind it is do or die.

The fact that I've made it this far is, quite frankly, astounding. Part of me wants to call Kate, but a larger part of me pulls away. Keep this a secret for now. A secret close to my heart.

And the thing I want to know most of all? Mack's secret. What's he hiding?

I bring my fist to the wood and knock, knowing there's a chance that absolutely nothing will happen. In fact, I'm kind of banking on it. If nothing happens, then I won't get an answer I don't want to know. Schrödinger's Mackthefishguy.

But when I get no response, I'm surprised to find that it actually kind of pisses me off. I don't feel relieved at all. If anything, I'm a little more wound up.

I knock again, but this time with more force.

*Boom, boom, boom, boom, boom.*

I wait for a beat, hands on my hips.

Still nothing.

I haven't traveled *this* far (a few blocks) to get nothing in return (the attention of the person who has not asked for me). It's cosmically wrong!

*Fuck it.*

I use both hands, fists pounding the wall, until suddenly, a noise. A rustling inside the apartment. A flicker of a yellow light beams through the crack at the bottom of the door.

Time both speeds up and slows down.

"Can I help you?" A man's voice comes through the door. The voice is deep and smooth but hushed and guarded.

Goose bumps ripple up my arms.

I swallow hard. "Mack?" In comparison, my voice comes out like a squawk. I clear my throat.

"What?"

"Mack. Open up. It's Jules."

There's a long pause. And then his voice comes again. "Jules." It's as if he's trying out a new word for the first time.

"Yes." This time, my voice gains strength.

"I don't know any Jules."

*How dare he!* But the insolence gives me even more strength. "Yes, you do. You know me pretty well, actually. From the forum."

Another pause. "I don't believe you."

"It's me. I know you're looking through your peephole. It's me. I sent you the picture. And then you sent me a picture, remember? And then suddenly, you just disappeared?"

"What do you want?" The coldness in his voice shocks me.

It shouldn't. I've shown up unannounced like a psycho knocking on his door. This is exactly what I should expect, nicer, in fact, than what I deserve, all things considered.

"I . . ." My voice trails off. "Can you just open the door?"

"No."

My jaw drops. "What! Why not?"

"Why would I open the door to a complete stranger I haven't even invited? How the hell did you even find this place? Do you live around here? Are you fucking serious right now?"

I scoff.

I should feel ashamed, but I don't. I should scuttle back to my little hole, but I can't. I'm actually kind of pissed. This is a new feeling. A feeling I haven't felt in a while. Indignation paired with a completely unjustified, righteous rage.

"Are *you* serious right now? I thought we were friends! Friends don't abandon their friends. Friends don't just disappear out of nowhere!"

"We're not friends. We were just on a forum together. Nothing on the internet is real."

I cross my arms over my chest, legs spread as if I'm squaring off with the door. "Okay, well, it's one thing to be an asshole, it's an entirely other thing to be intellectually dishonest." Again, my indignation is rocketing upward, unjustified as it might be. "I'm as real as they come, you son of a bitch."

Then I hear a little chuckle behind the door, the sound taking me off guard. His voice gentles. "You know what? You're right. I'm sorry for the way I left the forum. It wasn't a very kind thing to do."

While he's talking, my eyes are searching the door, the smooth frame, checking the knob. Why won't he open up?

"I won't accept your apology unless you let me in." I have to see. For myself. With my own eyes. I have to know who he is.

"That's not happening."

"Why not?"

"Because you're a total stranger and this is crazy. How'd you even get here?"

"I live down the street. It wasn't a big deal." *It was a huge deal.* "I just walked." Yes, I just walked. Like the way a pirate walks the plank.

Another pause. "You live down the street?"

"Yes, this whole time we've lived right next door basically. Can you believe it?"

"Jules, I truly cannot, not even in my wildest dreams, believe any of this."

While he's talking, I glide my fingertips along the door frame. As a woman, I would never keep a spare key where someone could find it. But men never seem to have those same concerns, do they?

"What are your dreams like anyway . . ." I murmur.

"Huh?"

"Because you have them, right? I don't. Not really . . . I've been having nightma—" My finger bumps something metallic on the very top of the frame, and I have to stand on my tippy-toes to reach. Then it clatters to the ground.

*It's a fucking key.*

"Hello? What are you talking about? Jules, I really think you need to leave."

I hold the key between my thumb and index finger.

"I'm gonna give you one last chance to open the door, Mack."

"Is that a threat? Are you threatening me?"

"Not a threat, just a heads-up."

"What are you talking about?"

Before he even finishes his sentence, I shove the key into the little lock on the gold knob, twist, and open it.

# CHAPTER 7

"Holy mackerel," I stand frozen in the doorway. My blood runs cold, my body stiff.

*Run! Move! Go!*

But I can't. I'm stuck.

There he is. Standing before me. Not the blond-haired green-eyed man from the picture frame. Of course not him.

It was never him.

But instead, it's the iridescent blue-eyed fish creature. With the large head and scales, the wispy fins flowing beneath his chin. The fan around his ears.

And now I see the rest of him. "Man who looks like a fish" is right. He looks halfway between evolution. Or maybe he looks beyond evolution. Maybe that's closer to the truth. Fish emerges from the primordial soup only to be sucked back in once again, but this time with more tools. Because he has legs. Hands and feet, although slightly webbed, are attached to arms and legs. Both of his sides have fins running down the length. And he's covered in pearly scales.

*I think I might throw up.*

"Close the fucking door!"

His voice shocks me back to life. In reality, only a mere second has passed. Startled, I push the door closed behind me.

I'm still just standing here, but he stalks over near me, and I almost flinch at his reach. But he's simply turning the locks on the door.

Then he puts out a webbed hand. "Give me the key."

My hands shake as I grasp the key in my palm. "No."

He puts his hands on his hips, standing before me. He knows I'm staring. He knows he's on display like a four-hundred-pound tuna at the Tsukiji Market. Or like one of those oversized fish men take pictures with on boats. This brings it into a totally different perspective somehow.

"Are you scared?" he asks, but not in a threatening way. Almost in an apologetic way, with his head tilted, watchful eyes trained on me.

"I—I . . ." I can't get the words out. The shaking in my body won't stop.

Behind him is a tank. The huge one. And from the water prints on the hardwood floor of his apartment, I suddenly realize who the tank was for.

It was for him.

I clear my throat. I might be an agoraphobic coward, but I'm not a little bitch. I cross my arms over my chest. "You shouldn't keep a key outside your door."

"What?"

"It's dangerous."

"How do you know I'm not dangerous?"

"Are you? Are you the same guy I've been talking to all these months?"

He shifts his weight from one leg to the other. *He's not even wearing clothes.* Except, wait, he is. He's got on swim trunks. They're nearly the same color as his scales though. An opalescent pale blue.

I can't help but notice he's tall too. Much taller than I am.

"You really aren't scared of me?"

I shrug. "Answer the question. Is Mack your name? Are you the guy from the forums?"

He nods. "Yes. That's me."

I squeeze myself for comfort. "Then no, I'm not scared of you."

I search deep within every nook and cranny of my body to evaluate whether or not what I'm saying is true. I think my body is still in shock. I can't feel my hands or my feet. I can't stop staring. My mind is quite literally blown at the creature in front of me. Creature?

Is he a creature though?

He seems like a human.

"Jules."

"Yes?"

"I need you to leave now."

"Are you serious?"

"Deadly serious. I need you to leave and never come back. I need you to leave and forget you ever saw me. Do you understand?"

I scrunch my face. "Excuse me. That's a very rude way to talk to your guest. The least you could do is offer me some coffee."

He gestures around his barren apartment. There's not much in it except for a white couch and his large tank. Next to the tank on the side that was out of the frame of the picture is a tall desk that comes all the way to the top of the tank.

On the surface of the desk is a laptop.

"Does this place look like it has coffee?"

"You don't drink coffee? Weirdo," I scoff. Then my eyes go big when I realize the implications of my words. "I didn't mean it like that."

"I'm going to ask you one more time, politely, to leave. And if you don't listen, then I'll have to physically remove you."

I glare. "I came *all the way to your apartment* just to be treated like a criminal?"

"You said you lived just down the street." *Because he has no idea the strength it took me to get here.* "And you quite literally are a criminal. You broke into my house."

"I used a key."

"That doesn't make it any better."

"And we're friends."

"Then I'm sorry, we aren't anymore."

Well, that just pisses me off. How could he treat me this way? First of all, he's a liar. He doesn't have a fish in his apartment. Second of all, he's denying our friendship, and I think that's the part that hurts most. And third of all, now that I'm here, I don't want to go.

I know it's weird. Normally, I'll do anything to return to the safety of my apartment. But now . . .

Tears nip at the corners of my eyes. I feel betrayed.

I wipe away the feeling. "I can't believe you'd say that to me," I say and swing around, my hand on the doorknob. "I thought I knew you. Guess I was wrong."

Then I turn around one more time, throwing the key as hard as I can. It splats against his scaly abdomen, where I notice the outline of abdominal muscles, like a six-pack. What a strange combination.

The key falls to the ground with a sad little clink in the middle of a wet spot.

"Fuck you, Mack! You're an asshole."

And I slam the door.

***

I don't remember coming home. I don't remember walking back into my apartment. I don't remember slinking into my robe and then fully submerging myself into the bathtub. I don't remember any of it.

Until I wake up. My eyes pop open, and I'm in the water.

I emerge, breath heaving.

*When did I fall asleep in here?*

*What the hell have I been doing?*

But then the memories of the day fall back into my consciousness, and a familiar sick feeling trickles over me. I step out of the tub, my wet feet slapping against the floor, and peel off my robe, hastily throwing it onto my drying rack and wrapping myself in a warm towel.

I scrub myself down. And then I notice a small little green dot on my forearm. I scratch at it with my fingernail.

A mole?

It doesn't look like a mole; it kind of flicks back and forth. I clasp it between two fingernails.

"Ouch! Fuck!"

Okay . . . don't do that again. Must be a skin tag or something.

Skin tags seem like something old people get. But maybe I'm aging exponentially because of my lifestyle. Shut-ins don't age like fine wine, I'm pretty sure. We age like old milk.

I check my phone, but I don't know why. There's never anything interesting or new on it. I slink over to my bed and fall down, scrolling through the internet.

I'm tempted to google fish monster. Is that what Mack is? Is that the technical term?

He said he could physically remove me. He said that maybe I should be afraid of him.

But I wasn't. I'm not.

In fact, upon reflection, without the shock of the moment, I realize that fear wasn't the motivating emotion at all. Instead, I was . . .

Intrigued. Very intrigued. I can barely shake the image of his slick pearlescent, white body out of my head.

And what's even weirder is that I think I was dreaming about him. I can never really be sure though . . . I so rarely remember anything about my dreams. A pearly exterior. A fiery, electric circle spinning in the open air. Blood.

His voice too. Now that I've heard his voice, I can recontextualize all his messages. Because I know his intonation. Who he is. What he sounds like.

Out of habit, I go back to the Aquariumaniacs forum. I know he won't be there, but I still have access to our old messages. I scroll through them and read them in his voice now.

There are thousands, so I have a lot to choose from.

*Jules: What's your favorite movie?*

*Mack: Would it be a cliché to say* Jaws?

*Jules: Would it be an even bigger cliché if I said* Splash?

Jeez. I guess all the clues were there all along. I mean, who spends all their time on a forum about fish and aquariums and also says their favorite movie is about an aquatic animal while making tons of fish puns?

Well . . . other than me.

Not to mention, the messages on the forum itself have really piled up since I've been away.

*FishKiller1234* has also seemingly made a return.

I click on his posts.

*FishKiller1234: There are those who walk among us that are not of god's light. They have warped and mutilated bodies. They mean to change us all into them. The Fish Monsters want to warp and mutilate you as well. Join my Facebook group to learn more.*

*Clownfishlover2: Dude, get the fuck off the forums. Nobody cares.*

I scratch my head. Is Mack a fish monster? Does he want to warp and mutilate other people and turn them into fish monsters too, like zombies or vampires?

But if that were true, why would he be trying to kick me out so quickly? I mean, other than the fact that I showed up unannounced.

Why wouldn't he have tried to attack me or something? He could've. He was standing right in front of me on dry land. And he must be strong. I peeped the rippling muscles down the lines of his body.

*Hmmm.*

I scroll through messages. I'm angry, I realize. Not afraid. And more than anything else, I have a million more questions than I did before.

Who are you Mack the Fish Guy? And where the hell do you come from?

I think I'm going to try to find out.

# CHAPTER 8

My phone buzzes in my pocket, but I ignore it for the fifth time. I do glance at it furtively, though, before shoving it back in.

*Kate: JULES WHERE THE FUCK ARE YOU I HAVEN'T HEARD FROM YOU IN DAYS*

The caps lock is overkill, in my opinion, even if I do appreciate her concern. But I can't respond now.

I'm sitting outside Mack's apartment. Back against the door, hands on my bent knees. Regrouping. The door's locked . . . I tried opening it, and of course, there's no key.

I regret giving it back to him now. I should've swallowed it or something and shit it out that night for later use. A giggle wells up at the disgusting thought.

Maybe I could call a locksmith and get them to open the door?

Jesus, I'm one hundred percent a stalker. Besides, what would happen if someone else saw Mack? I've seen enough sci-fi movies to know that nothing good can come of curious eyes seeking out mysterious monsters. But am I the one with the curious eyes?

And is he a monster?

Whatever, enough of this. I'm knocking on the door again. I jump to my feet and swallow the knot in my throat.

The knock is hollow against my knuckles, and I tighten my fists, digging my nails into the tender flesh of my hand, waiting for an answer.

Of course, there isn't one.

"Mack, open up!" I shout.

"I know you're in there!"

Nothing.

"You can't hide from me."

Menacing but untrue. Also. Still nothing.

"I have a picture of you. And I'll show it to others if you don't let me in."

*Yikes.* What a thing to say. But I can't help it. I have to see him again. I have to know what's going on. The questions I have about him haunt me unrelentingly.

"Wait!" A muffled sound comes from inside. The smooth, deep voice. Then a splashing nose and a *splat, splat, splat.* "Just wait."

*He must've been in the tank.* How *fucking* weird. Then again, who am I to judge? A woman who considered hiring a locksmith to break into his apartment.

My eyebrows lift in anticipation before the door opens an inch, and I see his eerie pale eyes and smooth, scaly face peeking through. A chill runs down my neck. His presence does something to me.

"How do I know you're alone?" But his voice remains deep and smooth as ever. Still guarded. Still cautious.

"Because I'm a loser without any friends?" I say, lifting a shoulder. Sometimes the truth is the most persuasive answer.

His large eyes move left and right as if he's considering the veracity of that answer, and then the door opens. He hides behind it as I shuffle inside.

Once I'm in, he immediately locks the door.

He holds out a hand. He's wet, slick with water, leaving a trail on the floor. "Show me the picture."

"You can't delete it, I've saved it to the cloud," I say.

"Yeah, I get how blackmail works. I just want to see it."

"You can't see my phone."

"Send it to me, then."

"I need your phone number. Do you even have one?"

He briefly shuts his eyes and brings his hand to his forehead. "I'm a fish, not a Luddite. Of course I have a phone."

The gesture is so human. So is his voice. His posture, the way he moves and speaks.

But his appearance is so . . . not human.

"555-7632."

I smother the surprise that I'm sure is on my face. I can't believe he gave up his number. I type it into my phone and send him the pictures.

He furrows his brow. "These are the pictures I sent you. I thought you secretly took one of me or something. You've tricked me."

I shake my head and reach out toward him. He backs away, as if afraid. "Sorry, I'm not trying to touch you . . . I was just trying to show you where to look in the photos."

"Oh," he says and scratches at his forehead.

I get a closer look, and he doesn't have fingernails, but this gesture, in particular, looks very human. I wonder where he learned it.

"May I?" I ask.

He thinks for a moment. "Fine."

I walk closer to him, filling in the space between us and stepping to his side so we're not in an intimidating face-to-face stance. I know firsthand just how intimidating that posture can be.

"Here . . ." I say, reaching toward the phone in his hand and making an open-pinch motion on the screen with my index finger and thumb. I zoom in on the area in the corner of the picture, the one he sent of the framed man. "Look closely, look here right in the corner."

He glances over at me, and now I'm sidled up next to him. I can really see every detail of his form. Each small iridescent scale, like they're drawn on with ink and oil paint. His ears too, like holes in his head, but they're tipped with little triangle-like fins. Almost as if to mimic a human.

"You noticed that?" He lowers the phone, again turning his gaze to me. "You saw me?"

I nod. "Yeah, I can be observant sometimes. Not all the time. Just sometimes."

He shakes his head. "Why did you still talk to me after this?"

I shrug. "How was I supposed to know what I was looking at? I knew you were a catfish, I just didn't know you were a cat . . . *fish*. You know what I mean?"

To my absolute surprise, he chuckles at that, lowering his focus to his feet. "And now that you see me for who I really am?"

"Now that I see you, I have more questions than answers."

He nods. "Me too."

A trickling sound comes from behind us. He turns his head and then makes a quick start toward his tank. "*Shit*. The tank is leaking. Overfilled."

"What?"

"Listen, Jules," he says as he leans toward the bottom of the tank and flings a towel down from a small white rack, wiping the floor and Plexiglas. "You're a better person than I imagined. If I were you, I don't know what I would've done if I saw . . . well, *me*. But you can't stay here. And you and I can't be friends."

"Why not?" I ask.

His jaw falls. "You can't be serious."

"I am serious. We were friends before. Why can't we be friends now? Do you need any help with that leak?"

"No, I got it. I promise you. I've done this before." He scrubs the ground aggressively, as if he's trying to rub the wood right off the floor.

"Are you sure?"

He pauses, eyes down. "I'm not used to people in my apartment. Not anymore. Can you just . . . can you just leave?"

I don't want to go. He hasn't answered any of my questions. I haven't asked them. But at the very least, I can understand this struggle. I don't like people in my apartment either. The only person who's ever been in there is Kate. The very thought deflates me like a pool float.

I rub my lips together, disappointed in the moment. I'll have to figure out another way to get through to him. "Fine. I'll leave. But I have one other question."

He rubs his webbed hands over his bald head. Again, another very human gesture. "Yeah?" he says in a mildly exasperated tone.

I back up to the door, my hand on the knob. I know once I leave, I may never be allowed to come back. "What's your real name?"

"I told you." He looks down at the floor, where he's squatting now, while tiny drips of water plummet from the tank. "It's just Mack."

"Just Mack. So you used your real name?"

"Did you?"

I nod. "Yes. My name is Jules. Short for Juliet. My mom had a whole thing where she thought I was going to be a famous actress."

"Juliet."

"But call me Jules."

He stands and flings the towel back over the short rack. "Jules. Will you leave now?"

***

I can't sleep, but what's new? I'm not only thinking about Mack, but I'm also thinking about his tank. It was nearly the size of the entire wall, but surely there are limits to how much weight those floors can bear. His apartment is otherwise barren. No TV on the wall. No chairs or blankets or throw pillows. Does he sleep in there? Does he live in there? Because clearly, he can also be *outside* the tank.

So, what does it mean?

I get out of bed, tossing the blankets to the floor, and I sit at my desk to do some work. I've been running behind on my deadlines, which I'm usually fastidious about. But I've been so distracted lately with this *Mack* business. It's like . . . how am I supposed to live life as a normal human now that I've seen what I've seen?

Nevertheless, I type away. A job's a job.

*The multiverse may include inhabitants of many different varieties. If one can conceive of an idea, it likely exists. Scientists, however, have no way to conduct an experiment to prove this hypothesis true or false, leaving much of the multiverse ideology to forever remain in the ether of the theoretical or the hypothetical.*

I lean back in my chair. Damn, if only I could call up a scientist and tell them what I've found.

Even at the thought, my body recoils. Telling anyone is off limits. Mack is vulnerable. He's literally a fish out of water. And I know what it means to be vulnerable. I know what it's like to live a life that's hidden.

Granted, I've already told Kate quite a bit, but Kate's kind of a loon. A loon who would never . . . ever fucking snitch. I'd trust her with my own life. And god knows I don't trust many.

I pick up my phone and scroll to the new contact I added.

*Mackthefishguy* is how I saved it. The only messages between us are the ones I sent earlier with the picture.

I just keep staring at it. Maybe it's not safe to keep on my phone. But I want to keep it, as if it's proof that we've had contact. As if it's proof that our relationship existed.

Because now it feels like nothing but a dream.

Mack's no longer on the forums. He doesn't want me at his apartment. He doesn't want to be friends.

And I'm not saying the guy doesn't have his reasons.

But the more he pushes me away, the more I want to swim against the current right back to him.

What an odd feeling.

As if I'm practicing, I type a few words in the message box to Mack on my phone. I won't actually send them; I just like knowing I *could* send them.

*Jules: So what's it like being a fish*

I delete the message. Then I type again.

*Jules: So what do you have underneath those shorts? Is it normal like a person?*

I laugh a little and hold down the delete button. How about that? I like the feeling of typing these never-to-be-sent messages. A little part of me is tickled with joy at the inappropriateness. It's freeing. Unserious. Fun.

I type some more.

*Jules: So how do you fuck though?*

But like, for real. How does he fuck? Is there a dick under the shorts? I know it's none of my business. But alas, I'm only human. We all wanna know what we don't know.

I go to delete the message when I'm interrupted by a phone call.

*My mother. A-fucking-gain.*

Hastily, I ignore the call. She's the last person I need to talk to. I know she's been trying to get a hold of me, but I don't fucking care.

A memory flashes from the past, but I push it away. Photo shoots. A man's hands. My mother's back turned conveniently away. I don't want to think about her. And I don't want to think about what she did to me . . . what she allowed to be done to me.

The screen clears, but when I look again, my stomach drops.

Because yes, I've ignored my mother's call, but I've also done something else.

I sent the fucking message to Mack!

There it is, in a little blue bubble on the screen, like a little whale peeping above the water.

*Jules: So how do you fuck though?*

I clap my hand over my mouth, and a series of maniacal, horrified laughs burst from me.

*Really, Jules?!*

*You meet a perhaps mythological creature, make friends with him, stalk him at his own house, get his phone number, get banished, and then the first message you send to him is* so how do you fuck though?

Really?

I'm beside myself now, fallen to my mattress and laughing like I'm on drugs.

If only I had drugs to blame instead of whatever mental illness this is.

Now, I stare at my screen.

What can I do? I can't unsend the message. Should I send another one and try to cover it up? Or does that only deepen the transgression?

The cover-up is always worse than the crime, isn't it?

But nothing's happening on the other end anyway. He's not responding.

Then it occurs to me.

*He's in the tank.*

He's in his tank! He probably never even looks at his phone. When I was at his apartment, he had his computer propped up eye level to the tank. I imagine him floating to the top, propping his hands out and typing on the computer. At the very least, he must've done that because he chatted with me almost every single day.

But his phone. Maybe he keeps that somewhere else? Maybe he doesn't use it as much.

I don't know anything about the social life of a fish monster.

I stare at the nothingness beneath my inappropriate question.

I shouldn't call him a fish monster. I'm a monster, after all. Look at my behavior.

I'll call him something else instead. How about a fish king?

Fish King. Sure, why not . . .

No, what about a fish daddy?

Oh my god, I laugh in that horrified way again.

What is wrong with me!

Then . . . typing bubbles appear beneath my message.

# CHAPTER 9

I'm biting my cheek so hard while I wait for the bubbles to turn into text that pain bursts through my skin right up to my eyelid. But then the bubbles stop.

*Excuse me?*

I exhale when they begin again.

It's one thing to be a fish daddy, but it's another thing to be a fish fuck boy.

Oh shit, fish daddy is going to become a thing, isn't it?

But then the text appears.

*Mack: I know . . . I KNOW you didn't just send me this after breaking into my house and interrupting my otherwise perfectly fine and peaceful life. I know you wouldn't do a thing like that, would you, Jules?*

I giggle. He sounds angry, but also . . . he asked a question, right? A question means: *continue on.*

I take this as a sign. I shouldn't because, as per usual, I'm acting as unhinged as a broken front door, but I can't help it.

This is the most exciting thing that's happened to me in years.

No, that's happened to me *ever*.

And I don't want it to stop. I can't remember the last time I felt so alive.

Before I respond, because I want to think about this, I pad my way over to the bathtub, strip off my clothes, and flip on the faucet.

The sound of the water soothes the deafening silence of my apartment. I toss in some bath salts and dip in a toe, letting the heat from the water spread from my leg to my heart, goose bumps rippling up my skin along the way.

Once I'm submerged, I settle in with my elbows on either side of the porcelain tub, my knees bent—one leg crossed over the other, swinging cheerily—my head resting against the wall, and the ends of my hair damp with moisture.

*Jules: If you know, then why are you asking?*

Typing bubbles appear on the screen. Excitement bubbles in my belly.

*Mack: Because I just want to verify exactly the kind of crazy you actually are.*

*Jules: Are you really one to judge?*

*Mack: I might look crazy, but I'm actually incredibly reasonable. More reasonable than you, at least.*

Now I'm extra excited. I kick my feet in the water. We're flirting again. Talking, like friends, like we used to on the forums. Or at least, we kind of are. We're on the path.

*Jules: So, does that mean you can't fuck?*

*Mack: We're really doing this, huh? We're really going to talk about . . . me.*

*Jules: You can't blame a girl. You can't act like you wouldn't have a million questions either if the tables were turned.*

*Mack: Sure, but I wouldn't break the ice with questions about how someone fucks!*

*Jules: Oh, the ice has been broken, my friend. The ice was broken when you sent me those pictures. Consider yourself the breaker of the ice. I'm *merely just testing the waters now. Dipping my toe in to feel out the temperature. But I didn't get here on my own.*

*Mack: I can't deny that you make a good argument.*

I shake my shoulders and smile smugly. Why am I enjoying this *so* much? Really, an unprecedented amount of satisfaction surges through me given the situation.

*Jules: Then answer the question.*

*Mack: If I answer the question, then we'll be done talking?*

*Jules: No, of course not. If you answer the question, that'll just be one question off the list of the many, many, many questions I have for you.*

*Mack: But what if I don't want to answer your questions?*

*Jules: You do.*

There's a pause in the typing bubbles. We've been rapid-fire texting back and forth. And maybe I've pushed him too far.

*Mack: The truth is. I don't know if I can fuck. It's embarrassing, honestly.*

*Jules: You're a virgin?!*

I'm shocked at the very idea. Even I'm not a virgin, and I'm practically a hermit crab.

*Mack: Why does it feel like the idea of me being a virgin is more shocking than . . . well, the other thing?*

*Jules: So you are a virgin!??!*

*Mack: No, I'm not a virgin.*

*Jules: Then how come you don't know what it's like to have sex . . . like as the way you are?*

*Mack: It's a long story, Jules.*

*Jules: What, you have other friends to talk about it with? Tell me.*

There's a pause. I nibble on my lip while I wait for the next message.

*Mack: I wasn't always this way.*

*Jules: What way were you?*

*Mack: That picture I sent you. The first one that's hung up on the wall. That wasn't a catfish. That was me, or maybe still is me, who really knows. But that was me a few years ago. Before I became what I am now.*

My heart sinks in my chest. What does he mean? Does he mean . . . he transformed into a fish?

Then my mind spins because if that's true, then that could mean other things are true. Like . . . FishKiller1234. *They walk among us.*

Although, Mack doesn't seem to do any walking. Instead, he has a tank. A tank he lives in.

*Jules: You used to be human.*

*Mack: I guess so. I don't know if I'd even take it that far. I think I always felt a little different. Like maybe I didn't fit in. I used to worry about things other people didn't. And then one day, those worries started to come true.*

*Jules: What do you mean by worries?*

But then there's another long pause.

*Mack: I don't think I can talk anymore tonight. I've had a long day.*

*Jules: But I worry too! Maybe we have the same worries? Worrying is a totally normal human thing though!*

I'm frantically tapping away at my screen for some reason. What is he talking about? What are these proverbial worries? Are they the same worries I have day in and day out? The nightmares. The dreams. Whatever you want to call them. The emptiness.

But it's too late. He's gone radio silent.

The conversation lasted as long as it took to fill up the tub. With my toes, I push the knob down and halt the stream of water.

Now, I'm just sitting here. Alone. In this bathtub.

Normally, I'd be thirsty from all the salt I dumped in with me. But instead, I feel filled up.

I flick the little skin tag on my arm back and forth and back and forth, thinking about Mack.

First, I think about the picture he sent me. Of the attractive man with green eyes and blond hair.

And then I think about his form now. Most people would describe it as creepy. As worthy of a horror film.

I search my brain and scan my body, what my old therapist taught me to do in challenging emotional situations. What do I feel when I think about Mack? What do I see? Where is it in my body?

The truth is, I'm not sure.

But despite all this, my hand begins to trail down my belly.

In my other hand, I'm holding my phone, our messages still sitting there. I want to will him to keep typing, but I know he won't. He's done. Maybe forever.

But that doesn't stop my hand from exploring farther. Lower and lower until I've reached the blonde pubic hair, the little triangle patch at the top of my pelvis, and my fingers search for that familiar little nub at the center of my body.

I haven't masturbated in . . . a long, long time. When I do, my mind is usually blank. Thinking of nothing at all. Not of a man or a woman. Like I said, looks don't really do it for me. It has to be something else, something I rarely find in anyone.

But my mind is floating toward visions of Mack. I can't even really see him in my mind, but I can feel him, his energy, his voice—*that voice*—his messages. I open my eyes and read them, and my fingers are circling my clit now. The little bursts of energy are electrical and spherical in nature. The feeling builds and builds and builds, and my hand is working faster than before.

Any thoughts about what I'm doing are quickly pushed out of my consciousness. I don't have time to question why I'm turned on right now, but I am. I'm leaning into it instead. Until the wave of pleasure begins to wash up from my clit toward my belly, growing and growing in strength. My hearing goes fuzzy . . . like a seashell against my ear. The ebb and flow and crash and receding of each wave of water.

And then, my eyes shut.

***

# CHAPTER 10

FishKiller1234 has taken over the forums.

It's been a few days since I've checked them, but the pump in my aquarium has broken, and I need advice on a new one. And yeah, I know that nothing lives in my tank. I know that! I do.

But maybe if I just create the perfect environment, something can or will survive—or already is surviving—in there. Maybe I just can't see it yet.

My aquarium is my own multiverse. I chuckle at the thought.

Also, I make my second ever post on the forums. This is new for me.

First, it starts out as my simple question. "Which is the best water pump for a freshwater tank?"

But then . . . then I scroll for a bit.

*FishKiller1234: You people are idiots! Poisoned by your own selfish, debaucherous desires. Repent now, or you will turn into the fish monsters. To learn more, follow me on Facebook.*

*TankNerd1979: Dude, relax. Maybe you need to take a trip to the pharmacy to refill your meds. I have an aquarium because my kids like it. Do you think my kids will turn into fish monsters too, you fucking nutter?*

*FishKiller1234: THE CHILDREN ARE IN DANGER. To learn more, follow me on Facebook.*

I shake my head. Fucking hell.

And even though I may have technically met my own fish daddy, these messages are starting to piss me off. FishKiller1234 doesn't know what the hell he's talking about. In fact, he's spouting nonsense all over the internet, and I, for one, won't stand for it.

I muster up the courage to hit reply. I know replying to people who are off their rockers is like shouting into a void and expecting it to answer back, but I just can't stand for it anymore. The disinformation is frustrating. We just want to talk about our fish and be done with it.

As I type, my hands shake lightly. I'm not used to this kind of public confrontation.

*JulesLikesToSwim: @fishmonster1234 And so what if there are these so-called fish monsters among us, huh? They aren't coming into the forums and harassing people. They aren't posting insane messages every single day to disrupt our usual conversation. I don't see any fish monsters acting as CEOs of any petrol companies or snatching up any children or working on the police force. So what if there are "fish monsters" among us? Let them be! They aren't hurting anyone. Live and let live, my man.*

*FishKiller1234: YOU'RE ONE OF THEM. WE'LL FIND YOU AND ELIMINATE YOU FOR THE SAFETY OF ALL. To learn more, follow me on Facebook.*

I sigh when I read the response and shake my head. He can't be fucking serious? But, of course, he is. And I didn't expect anything better.

But then, another message pops up on my screen. A new person on the forum.

*AverageJoeGuy: Hey, are you okay?*

I glance around my apartment. I haven't showered again. Although, at least I took a bath the other night. Still, as usual, my skin is grimy. I guess that's just a thing now. The clothes I wore to Mack's are still on the floor. I haven't bothered to pick them up. It reminds me that I'll probably never see him again.

My phone is also on the floor at three percent battery because I've been staring at it for so long, willing Mack to reply. Which, of course, he hasn't. I want to send him another message, but I can't yet.

Why am I so desperate?

And my desk is covered in coffee-smudged mugs and empty ramen bowls.

So . . . am I okay?

I don't know. *You tell me.*

A part of me is a little alarmed by this message. Usually, I would just ignore it. It's rare that I want to bring new people into the fold of my life, even through a forum conversation. Mack was an exception because his first message made me laugh.

*Mackthefishguy: Welcome to the forum. Are you originally from Freemont?*

*JulesLikesToSwim: Yep. You?*

*Mackthefishguy: Finland*

*JulesLikesToSwim: Really? Wow, you've come a long way.*

*Mackthefishguy: No, sorry, actually, I was just making a joke. I'm not really from Finland. I'm from Freemont too.*

So, I almost don't reply to AverageJoeGuy. But then, my eyes survey the scene again. One more time but through a different lens.

*You're brave, Jules.* Talk to a goddamn stranger.

I click the Reply button and type back.

*JulesLikesToSwim: Are you asking because only a person doing exceptionally poorly would try to have a real conversation with FishKiller1234?*

*AverageJoeGuy: Yeah. Pretty much. I get that FishKiller is an annoying guy. But I wouldn't say he's entirely crazy. You know?*

I narrow my eyes. What the fuck does this guy know?

I drum my nails against the only available surface on my desk before replying.

*JulesLikesToSwim: You can't tell me you believe in fish monsters?*

*AverageJoeGuy: I do. And I think you do also. But my only question is . . . why?*

*JulesLikesToSwim: I don't know what the hell you're talking about, buddy.*

*AverageJoeGuy: I'm not trying to be weird. If anything ever starts to feel off . . . though? Maybe you're experiencing something you can't explain. Just know that I have answers.*

My pulse races. I don't like what he's implying. Of course I'm experiencing things I can't explain. That's how anxiety works. Panic disorder. Agoraphobia. And I don't want to talk to this guy about it.

*JulesLikesToSwim: Whatever you say. Goodbye.*

I click off the screen, but that doesn't feel like enough. I completely shut down my computer.

My gut is screaming at me. Maybe it's all the spicy ramen. But I also think it's the messages.

What does AverageJoeGuy know? What does he know that I don't?

# CHAPTER II

Kate arrives, and she doesn't knock on the door, she kicks it loudly. So loudly that I can't ignore it.

"Where've you been, bitch? Open up!"

I grimace but pull myself from the couch, my dark green blanket wrapped tightly around me. When I get up, I nearly fall over. My feet are asleep, and I only have one sock on. How long have I been sitting here in front of my TV?

I don't watch TV very often because I prefer my phone's small screen close to my nose, dangling near my pillow at night. But I've decided I need a break from my phone.

I haven't heard from Mack.

And I need a break from my screen. I'm ahead on my assignments. And I can't bear to read the messages on the forum.

So, instead, I've been a lump on a log, a.k.a. my couch.

I let Kate in, although begrudgingly, and she immediately looks around with disgust, clutching a large paper bag filled with groceries.

"Ew, gross, this place is filthy. God, you're kind of a slob, but I didn't know you were a *slob* slob, you know what I mean?" She sets the paper bag on my table, which is small and round. Her dark hair is tied up in a bun, highlighting the beautiful cheekbones on her heart-shaped face.

Olive skin, luminous and clear. "Um, excuse me? Are you watching porn right now?"

Blankly, I stare at the TV screen and then nod my head. "Yeah, it's the only thing my TV plays. I've been sitting here watching it for . . ." I lift up my wrist as if I'm wearing a watch, but I'm not. "For a long time now. It's surprisingly boring."

Kate marches over to the coffee table, grabs the remote, and turns off the television. The image of a man fucking a woman from behind disappears. I've been watching silent porn for god knows how long now.

"I'm taking you out of this apartment," Kate declares.

"No! No, you can't! I refuse."

She puts her hands on her hips, looking at me in frustration. "You can't live your whole life this way, can you?"

I collapse back onto the couch, cocooned in my blanket, feet up at the end of the armrest. I turn the porn back on. "I don't see why not."

"Can I bribe you to go out with me again? Like we used to do in college?"

I shake my head. "No."

"Okay, but you know it's my birthday in a few weeks. What about a drag party? There's an amazing one on the east side. They're doing Drag *Little Mermaid*. Everyone dresses up. It's the best time you'll have in this whole godforsaken city. C'mon. Please? Please? *Please*?"

I narrow my eyes at her, shooting what I hope looks like a glare. But also, a part of me feels guilty. She doesn't expect anything from our friendship really. In fact, it's so one sided it's almost laughable. I don't even leave the house. I've never seen her apartment, but she's seen mine. I've never met her boyfriends.

And well, she's never met mine because I've never had any.

My mind involuntarily wanders. And all I can see are large fish eyes and opalescent scales.

I'm a bad friend. Normally, though, I'm numb to the feelings. But now, a pang of guilt stabs my chest. And I don't like it. I haven't felt this pang in a long time, something has awakened. "Fine. Maybe I'll come to Drag *Little Mermaid* with you. Maybe."

"Yay!" Kate claps her hands together excitedly.

"And also." I pull the blanket up around my mouth as if it will cushion what I'm about to admit to next. "I have to confess something to you."

Her smile drops. "What do you mean?"

***

I'm relieved to be alone in my apartment again. Sometimes, Kate overstays her welcome, which doesn't take much, really. My tolerance is low.

But now the place spotless. The clothes are washed and hung up, the dirty mugs gleaming and sparkling in the kitchen cabinets. The fridge is filled with things I'll never eat, like tomatoes and cucumbers and kale. Ugh, fucking kale.

But despite myself, I appreciate the effort. I'm grateful.

Plus, I appreciate her advice. The weirdo that she is.

Because I spilled my guts to Kate. I told her everything about Mack. That I saw him. Who he is. Fish daddy exists.

"I'm crazy, right?" I asked her.

And she only had one thing to say to me. "I believe you."

And then she said, "I think you should keep talking to him. I think there's a lesson for you to learn here."

"But he doesn't want to talk."

She sighed. "You know how our friendship is one sided?"

I looked off to the side guiltily.

"Don't act like you don't know what I'm saying. And I want you to know that it's fine. Because I know you're going through stuff. I've gone through shit before too, and I came out the other side of it, and now I'm happier than ever."

"Yeah, but I've been going through this for years now. And you still hang around."

She grabbed my hand. "That's right. I do. Because I understand. And there's no time limit on how much time you might need. There's no limit to that. So, I meet you where you're at."

"Okay, what does that have to do with anything?"

"Mack . . . he's clearly going through something too. And he says he doesn't want you around. And that might be true. But also, you were friends, you say so yourself, and you never say that about anyone. So, maybe you need to be there for him as well. A little push and a little shove to get someone out of their shell never hurt anybody."

I was surprised to hear her say that, but now it makes sense. She's always been there for me, it's true. And she's also given me space. I worry about breathing. About suffocating in my sleep. But maybe Kate would be the one to find me, shriveled up on the ground like a dried-out sardine, before it was too late.

Maybe I'd never considered it before.

Either way, it gives me the strength to pick up the phone after Kate leaves my apartment.

*Jules: I'm coming over.*

Suddenly, bubbles appear.

*Mack: Jules. You've got to give this up.*

*Jules: I think there are other people on the forum who know about you. Or your kind.*

*Mack: FishKiller1234? That nutjob?*

*Jules: No, others. There might be more of you out there. Aren't you curious?*

*Mack: That has nothing to do with you.*

*Jules: I know, but . . . I miss you.*

Silence.

I pull on my jeans as the silence persists, then a sweater over my head. A navy blue. According to my mother, the colors are too heavy for my delicate coloring, but the insides have never matched the outsides.

He's gone silent on me again. But then I put myself in his shoes. I know what it's like to feel overwhelmed by interactions with other people. Like all the times when Kate expresses something to me that is beyond my emotional skill set. Now I'm the Kate in the equation.

That makes me feel brave.

Brave enough to leave my house for the third time.

***

Okay, I've made it to the sidewalk again. I take a big breath, only choking briefly before regaining myself, coughing into my hand and approaching the coffee shop.

"The usual. Wait, no. Two coffees, actually," I correct myself.

George's eyebrows go up. "Two coffees?" he asks.

"That's right." I even offer a smile. Or something close to it. It still feels so weird to be looked at.

But this time George just nods and hands the coffee over. "Enjoy your day, Jules."

I nod back, take the coffees, and begin my epic journey seven blocks north to Mack's house.

I think it's easier this time around, and also, excitement propels me, spurs me forward and into action. I didn't realize excitement and anticipation could override so much of my anxiety, but it turns out that's a thing. Maybe my therapist could've mentioned it once or twice.

Even when I get to his building, I'm emboldened. Confidently, I march inside, swinging open the heavy entryway door and marching to the elevator. Luckily, no one ever seems to be in the building. Maybe it's filled with old people. Maybe it's filled with weirdos like me. Either way, I'm alone in the elevator all the way to the fifth floor, and I thank my lucky stars.

I only waver in my bravery when I make it to Mack's door.

But I force myself ahead and knock.

I almost drop my coffees when the door opens in less than three seconds.

And my heart flutters, or maybe it's my stomach, or maybe it's my adrenal system going haywire. Either way, something crazy pumps through me at the sight of him again.

"Come in," he says.

His deep, smooth voice fills me with anticipation.

# CHAPTER 12

The first thing I notice when I step inside is the changes he's made to his tank.

He's filled it with all kinds of things. Plants mostly, water plants, swaying on thin green stems with furry little fronds puffing out in different directions. The tips of their stems breach the surface with flowers and leaves. And now the tank is a beautiful blue filled with beautiful green. Also, there's a light inside. It glows a soft purple, like a mermaid shell.

"I like what you've done with the place . . ." I joke. But also, I do like it. It's beautiful by anyone's standards. "The Aquariumaniacs would go wild for this shit."

Mack sighs. His footprints aren't leaving wet marks. And there aren't wet marks all over the floor like last time. Instead, towels are hanging on a rack next to the tank, and there's a towel on the ground in front of the couch.

"Now that you're here, I suppose I should offer you a seat." He gestures toward the white couch.

I toe off my shoes and leave them by the doorway. I'm not sure how much propriety matters in these situations, but I'm not going to track dirt inside. However, now I'm walking around in my bare feet. That feels vulnerable too.

"Thanks for the offer," I say and sit on the couch. "Are you going to sit with me?"

Right now, he's standing in front of me, his hands behind his back, rocking back and forth a little bit. He looks nervous. He's got a shirt on as well as his swim trunks. He's all dressed up, I realize. I think he's done it for me.

"I guess that's what a normal person would do, right?" he says, then he settles in next to me, long, muscled legs spread wide, leaning forward, with his large hands clasped in the middle.

I prop myself on the edge of the couch cushion. I'm sitting primly. Back straight. Knees together. Both hands holding coffee cups. I never sit this way at home. Who am I trying to impress? I think I'm just nervous.

Nervous by his presence.

His body.

His energy.

"You shouldn't manspread."

"You shouldn't show up at people's homes uninvited."

I laugh a little. "Touché. I brought you coffee." I offer the cup to him, extending my arm.

I know he doesn't want me to get too close. I know he doesn't want me to touch him. I can tell by how he flinches almost imperceptibly when I make a move.

"I won't touch you. Just take it." I wiggle the cup at him.

To my surprise, he accepts the cup and brings it to his lips, sipping gingerly. "Shit. That's like rocket fuel."

"So, you can drink coffee." I take out my phone and sip my own coffee with the other hand.

I've written down a list of questions I want to ask him, and I don't want to forget.

"I can drink anything I want. I just don't . . . always want to."

"Why are you drinking it now, then?"

He takes another sip, his gaze briefly flitting to mine. "Because you gave it to me."

Unexpectedly, heat creeps up my cheeks. "Oh."

A small smile plays on his lips. His lips are the same opalescent as the rest of him. But they're also full and bowed at the top. In some ways, they are the most human-like thing about him.

"Go on, then," he says. He holds out his hand, palm upward, then beckons his fingers.

I shift my hips back and forth. "Go on, what?"

"I know you have questions to ask. So ask them."

I glance down at my phone screen. I'm dying to ask so many things. "You mean it?"

He shrugs, looking a little incredulous. "I think I do mean it. You're persistent. Undeterred. What can I say? I admire it a little."

I lick my lips. "Okay, then. I have been wondering about some things."

"Thought you might."

"First thing. Why do you have the tank if you can sit here next to me on the couch?"

"Why do you have a bed if you can sleep on the floor? Why do you have a chair if you can stand? I can spend quite a bit of time outside of the tank, I won't die instantly or anything. But the tank is where I'm comfortable, where I rejuvenate. I can sit here with you on the couch, but I'd much rather be floating in the water."

"You can breathe out here though?"

He nods. "I can. But it's easier in there." He gestures toward the tank. "And . . . well . . ."

"Well, what . . ." I prod, although I'm trying to be gentle. I don't want him to go radio silent on me like he did before.

He scratches at his ear with his fingernail-less finger. The web in the valley of his fingers stretches and moves as he does. "I used to spend a lot more time outside the tank. But slowly, day by day, I spent more time inside it. I'm not sure what it is really. I guess I'm just changing. Just like everyone else. I have my preferences."

"You mean, you didn't start out this way? It was a slow transformation?"

He looks a little pained as he bites his lower lip, looking downward. "It's been going on for years. And I just keep turning more and more and more."

"More and more . . . into a fish?"

He looks up at me, his face somber, and nods.

"You're still changing?"

At that, he shrugs. "There's no telling, although I think it's mostly slowed at this point. It's not like I can go to a doctor or something and get a test. Not that I've tried. I don't think anything good could come of involving a doctor. You understand that, right? You can't tell anyone that you know me. You can't tell anyone ever."

"Yeah, of course. I'm not an idiot. I wouldn't do that to you."

"I guess it doesn't matter at this point anyway. If you wanted to, you could ruin me."

I shake my head. "I would never do that."

He gives another little smile. "Sure, Jules."

A moment lingers between us, and I realize I've scooted a little closer to him. When did that happen? I'm not at the edge of the couch anymore. I'm leaning forward now, my knees pointing toward him, now inches away.

I set my coffee on the hardwood floor.

"When did the changes start?"

"When I was around twenty-one or so. You've seen the picture. That's me up there on the wall. Was me. Still is me? I don't even really know anymore. I keep it there as a reminder."

"A reminder of what?"

"Of who I no longer am."

I swallow hard and nod. I think of the old portfolios of my face and my body. Of a person who now only exists in print but nowhere else. "Were you happy before?"

"What do you mean?"

"In the picture, were you happy?" Because to me, I can't quite tell. In the picture, he's smiling, but his eyes . . . his eyes belie something else entirely.

"I have no idea how to answer that question. Is anyone happy?"

I scratch my head. "I think some people might be."

"Are you?"

I shrug. "I wouldn't know anything about it."

"Yeah." He nods. "Can I tell you something weird?"

I laugh at the absurdity of his question. "Weirder than this?" But also, I'm excited that he wants to confide in me. I want to know everything.

He chuckles quietly, his chin down. "Sometimes, I ask myself if I feel more like me now than I ever did before. Here I am, a freak of nature. I can't even leave the apartment. I haven't left in years. And I can't hide it anymore. What . . . I've become. But also, I'm still me."

I inch even closer. I want to put my hand on his hand. To comfort him because I understand. I understand the confusion between what's on the inside and what's on the outside and all the opinions and judgments others carry because of it. Part of me wants to withhold, and another part of me wants to confess in a way I've never done with another person before.

"You know before, when you said I look like a model . . ." It's an obvious leading question. I know even bringing it up seems like I'm fishing.

"I remember."

I lean forward like I'm sharing a secret, because I am. "Well, I am. Or, I was, I guess I should say. Ever since I was a little kid, and it's what I did growing up and even after college. But the truth about me is that my outside has nothing to do with how I feel on the inside. My mother always used to tell me that appearance is what everyone will judge me on the most. That it's my most valuable public asset. That so much of what we get in life is because of what we were born into. What we look like. And she's completely right. And that's why I don't leave my apartment anyway. Because my outsides are a lie. And I can't stand to be a liar."

He tilts his head a little, and my eyes zero in on his neck. It's shaped like the neck of a man, but there are three little slits alongside it. Of course there are. He has gills. But he must also have lungs.

"But you must go outside. You're here, aren't you?"

I lean back in the seat. Heat creeps into my cheeks a bit. "I had to make an exception."

"For me?"

"I wanted to see you." My voice comes out small but honest.

I sit on my hands. The urge to fidget is too great. He's looking at me a little seriously now, and I think anyone would squirm a little under that light blue gaze.

When his gaze doesn't falter, I lower my own. "What? What are you looking at?"

I sneak a peek, and he shakes his head as if coming out of a trance. "I'm not sure. You tell me."

"Huh?"

"Who are you, Jules?"

I scrunch my face. "I-I . . ." I don't even know how to begin to answer his question. Who am I? Am I the beauty? Or am I the beast? "I thought I was the one asking the questions."

But he rubs his face with his hand, and again, I watch his fingers closely. "I think I have energy for one more question. You better make it good."

I nod and ask the only thing I want to know. "When can I see you again?"

# CHAPTER 13

I made a deal with Mack. Well, maybe not a deal. Maybe I kind of begged him to agree to see me again.

I don't think he trusts me, and I get it, I really do. He's vulnerable in a way most men aren't. He's vulnerable to the outside world, to what strangers might say or do or think about him.

I feel like this too. Not just because I'm a woman, although all women are vulnerable in the outside world, but also because something else lurks inside me as well. A secretive part of me that I can't let others see. Hidden. Protected. Locked up.

I wasn't always this way. Don't get me wrong, I was never outgoing or the life of the party or anything. I always had really small friend groups. But I wasn't locked away. I lived something of a life.

Until my mother stepped in and took it over. Let's just say the modeling world wasn't for me.

Let's just say the limelight wasn't for me.

Let's just say older men's groping hands with cameras and booking agents with leering eyes asking me to put on skimpy underwear in front of them . . . wasn't for me.

My mother used to exploit my body. And so did so many other people. Yes, I was paid for it. But I wasn't ever asked if I wanted it.

And now I'm grown, and I've made a decree all to myself.

Nobody gets to see my body. Nobody gets to see me. And nobody gets to touch me.

Because now I protect myself. I protect myself for all the times when there was no one there to protect me.

Mack needs protection too. I get that. He's more than just a body.

His body though . . .

One would think I'd be disgusted. And at first, I thought I was because the sight of him made my whole body shake, sent goose bumps running up and down my flesh. But then, upon closer self-examination, I think I was more . . . intrigued than disgusted.

And it's true that if I saw him in the dead of night, I'd probably run.

But only if he were a stranger. I'd run from any stranger.

He's not a stranger. He's a friend.

He's the only friend I leave the house for, and that has to count for something.

Speaking of, I'm getting ready to leave my apartment right now. I've texted that I'm coming, and he didn't respond, but I know he'll let me in. My intuition tells me so.

I brainstormed some ideas about what to bring when I visit him. Thinking about ways I can distract him so that I can ask more and more questions.

We've been texting in the meantime.

*Jules: I have to show you something.*

*Mack: What?*

The first thought that popped into my head was what Kate always does when she comes to see me.

Cleaning.

I'm going to clean his tank. I've already got my bikini on underneath my clothes because, if nothing else, I'm going to assume the sale. It's better to ask for forgiveness than permission, or however the saying goes. My therapist might've said that. Or maybe it's just something I saw on TV.

And if you want to get to know somebody, you have to get on their level.

This is what Kate does for me. She gets on my level.

And I'm going to pay it forward by getting on Mack's level.

Which is probably below the sea.

Although I chuckle at my own pun, other thoughts occur to me. Like . . . could Mack live in the ocean? What would happen to him if he left the confines of the tank? He prefers the water, but does he *need* the water? Does he have to come up for air sometimes like a whale?

The questions are too daunting to even comprehend. Besides, why do I need all this to make so much sense? The only thing stranger than fiction . . .

I pinch my arm hard, dull pain shooting up from my elbow.

*Get yourself together. This isn't a fantasy, this is reality.*

Sometimes I forget that in real life, we don't always discover explanations for every little peeping phenomenon. Sometimes we're just left to wonder, wide eyed and slack-jawed. We're just left to live with whatever mysteries we've been dealt.

I want Mack to agree to see me again, so I have to be crafty.

*Jules: The thing I want to do for you is a surprise. You're going to have to invite me over again if you want to know.*

*Mack: God dammit.*

*Mack: I want to say no . . . but also, I hate not knowing what you might be talking about, even though I suspect you're up to something.*

*Jules: I guess you'll just have to find out then. See you at three?*

***

I reach Mack's apartment in record time. Because I've done something huge.

I've taken the bus.

Yes, me. Jules Lowe. Your unfriendly neighborhood shut-in has stepped onto public transportation, sat down on a public seat, and waited the two and half minutes and seven blocks.

I don't know what compelled me to do it.

Okay, if I'm honest, I do know what compelled me.

I want to see Mack, and I want to see him now. I'm literally jittering with anticipation.

When I reach his door, there's an envelope on the floor in front of it.

I pick it up, turning it over in my hand.

*Mackenzie* is scrawled in ink. Bubbly letters. A woman's writing.

*Knock, knock, knock.*

"Open up. I've brought a surprise! Don't worry! You're gonna like it," I say with a little too much singsong in my tone.

For all I know, he won't like what I'm planning to do at all. For all I know, cleaning a fish daddy's tank is akin to searching through somebody's bedside table.

But if I've learned anything at all from my model days, it's this one thing: everything in life is all about framing. And I'm framing this as a gift.

I knock again, but before my hand even makes contact with the door, it opens.

Mack's not there of course. He's hiding behind the door for obvious reasons.

Still, I smile. *Yes, I've made it here again.* The joyous excitement rockets in my chest.

I walk inside, and the door closes behind me, the locks clicking one at a time.

Then there he is.

"Hey . . ." he says.

I'm still smiling, and now he smiles back, if not a little hesitantly.

Is it possible he looks different than I remember? Probably not. I think I'm just noticing more and more now. For instance, his pale white shimmering scales are changing color now. There's more green in them, like an ocean-y reflection glowing from within.

Maybe it's the lighting. Maybe not.

But I won't forget it.

"This was outside your door." I shake myself back to reality and hand him the note.

He narrows his eyes and closes the gap between us by taking the envelope out of my hand. In that second, I'm so acutely aware of the fact that we can't touch.

It's not like with a regular person where you might bump into them or offer a hug or a handshake.

This is different. The space is purposeful.

He won't come near me. He wouldn't even try it.

The more he stays away, the more curious I am about what would happen if he inched closer.

Mack takes the envelope and places it on the high table next to his tank. He has to step up on the side of the desk to put it there, and he does so with complete ease, as if he's weightless.

"Who's that from?" I ask.

Of course, it's none of my business, but at this point in the game, all pretense of social etiquette has flown out the window. Or up the aquarium pump.

"It's from no one."

"Okay, be secretive, I see how it is . . . Wait, no, I don't want to sit on the couch."

Mack walks past me to the couch, where he thinks we'll be sitting. Instinctively, I touch his biceps to stop him from walking away.

*Forbidden touch.*

Instantly, he freezes.

I freeze too, but I leave my hand there. I can't move it. His skin is lukewarm to the touch. The scales are smooth though, like it might feel nice to run the front of your nail beds down them. Scale ASMR.

The muscles in his arm are hard and defined like a human man's. Actually, more so. He's a hunk of solid muscle mass. Just . . . scaly too.

But I've touched him for too long, even though only a second or two has passed. He shakes away from my grasp.

"What the hell?" he asks, alarm dotting his tone.

Even I'm not that alarmed at the touch of another. I have Kate after all.

But then a feeling sinks inside my stomach.

I wonder when the last time anyone touched him was?

I move my hand like it's been scalded. One singular touch has thrown us completely off kilter. I bite my lip.

"I'm sorry," I mumble. "I just . . . the surprise doesn't involve sitting on the couch."

He lets out a big sigh. "What does it involve, then?"

"You really wanna know?" I ask, a little playful sound in my voice. The most flirtatious I've sounded in years.

I think he can't help but smile back because he does just that. His teeth are bright white, nearly luminescent. His tongue is pale blue. But otherwise, perhaps, a normal human tongue . . . I note that down in my brain bank about him.

"Fine, yes. Tell me how you've tricked me into coming over again."

I dig into my purse and then pull out some goggles, a sponge, and a washcloth. "I'm gonna clean your tank for you." I smile big, holding the items up by my face. "Surprise!"

***

It takes some convincing for Mack to let me into his tank. But my mother was an overbearing bitch, so I know how to be one too, when the occasion calls for it.

"Look at this glass!" I say, pointing like Vanna White at the tank. It spans most of the wall and almost all the way to the ceiling. "There are smudges everywhere! Did you grow up in a barn?"

Mack's jaw drops. "I'll have you know I keep things *very* clean in there. You might even call me fastidious! In fact, lots of people would look at this tank and say *Oh Wow, this Mack guy must have a cleaning fetish or something for how fucking clean this tank is.*"

I run my finger along the corner of the tank. I have rubber gloves on now, and I mostly just brought them for effect, but I hold out a finger to Mack. "Look at this. Look closely."

"I'm not looking." He crosses his arms over his chest.

I lean in and put my fingertip directly in his face. "Look, Mack. Do you see what I see?"

He turns his head away. "I have no idea what you're talking about. I'm pretty sure you're just a crazy woman who breaks into my apartment and harasses me sometimes."

I smile a little. It might not seem like it, but he's flirting, for sure. Weird flirting, but flirting nonetheless.

"Grime, Mack. This?" I push the finger a little closer to his face. "Is grime. And you know what? I don't approve of grime in my aquariums. I didn't spend seventeen months on the Freemont Aquariumaniacs Forum to let grime build up in someone's tank, did I?"

When he doesn't answer, I step even closer but drop my finger. He's much taller than me, almost unnerving in size, and I'm pretty tall.

"Did I?"

We're face-to-face. Definitely an aggressive posture. Even more so because I'm keeping my gaze on him, something I don't often do with many people. And he's keeping his on me. His pale blue eyes travel from my eyes, to my mouth, and back to my eyes. The muscles on his jaw flick ever so slightly, his gills rippling like butterfly wings in the wind, and right next to them, the flittering of his heart beat visible in his neck.

The sponge slips from my hand, landing softly on Mack's floor. My feet stutter a step backward, an almost imperceptible distance.

His voice is smooth and deep. "You win."

My knees shake beneath me. My chutzpah has been doused. I'm not sure why though.

*Relax, nothing's happened, Jules. Get it together.*

Nervously, I run my hands through my hair. But then I remember why I'm here.

*Because I'm becoming obsessed?*

No, because I want to help a friend.

Right. I can do this. Hell, I took a bus to get here! With the general public and everything.

I grab the hem of my shirt and pull it up my chest.

"No, stop!" Mack says, alarmed.

I pause midway through undressing. "What?" I ask.

"Why are you taking your shirt off?"

"You didn't think I was gonna wear my clothes in there, did you?" I raise my eyebrows, like *duh*.

"You can't just get naked in front of me . . . Oh . . ."

But it's too late, and my shirt hits the floor.

"I'm not naked. I'm in a swimsuit."

Next I unzip my pants, pull them down the length of my long legs, and step out of them. This time, I'm a little more bold. When they reach the ground, I kick them his way.

He looks stunned, and as if on autopilot, he leans down and picks them up. "Oh."

Although I'm sure all the color has been sucked right out of my skin, I refuse to be embarrassed. "I'm wearing just as much as you are," I point out, gesturing to his body. His tall, lean body. Sure, scaly too.

He also gestures to his body, running his hands up and down his chest. "Yeah, but I'm a little different from you. Wouldn't you say?"

I raise my shoulder. "That's true. You're not wearing a shirt. Are you suggesting I take mine off?"

Reader, I swear to you, his chin moves downward in a nod before he catches himself and circles off into an aggressive head shake. "No! Please. No, keep your top on."

I smile and give a cute little scrunch of my nose. "Okay!" I say cheerily, pulling the goggles over my head. "Gimme a boost?"

At first, his weight shifts to his back foot. *Is he going to run away?* Maybe I've really taken this way too far.

But then, he steps forward. Inwardly, I smile. And maybe outwardly, I'm smirking a little. I smother the look off my face when he approaches.

He kneels down, threads his hands together in a makeshift step, and clears his throat, giving me a cue that I should step up.

Daintily, I lift my foot. My feet aren't pedicured. Back when I modeled, I always had to keep everything so flawless and touched up. Normally, I don't think about it, but a brief wave of anxiety washes over me, my confidence faltering just a tiny bit at the idea that he might find my feet gross the way they are.

But then, as I place my foot onto the center of his hands, his white scaly body reminds me that *he's an actual fish creature.*

*He's not gonna give a fuck about my toenails.*

Before any more useless worries can swirl, I hoist my weight onto his hands, grab the top of the tank, and with his help, hoist myself over the top.

And then my entire world muffles.

It isn't like stepping into a pool where one part of my body feels the water first. Instead, it's like a baptism. The kind where a reverend dunks you full force.

I'm submerged, and the water is just slightly cool, like the soft breath of breeze or like the first dip of summer. Cool enough to cool down the heat on my cheeks or the flush that I've realized has brushed across my clavicle. Warm enough to prevent a chill.

Somehow, our encounter has gotten me heated up.

I hold my breath under the water for a few seconds, my hands coming out to touch the various plants that surround me. I blink, remembering

I'm wearing goggles. I press my hand against the tank wall, and there's Mack.

Right in front of me. It's jarring to see. From this perspective, he looks more man than fish.

I guess, in this case, I'm the fish.

What an interesting swapping of roles.

I smile under the water, my hair flowing above me like Medusa's snakes. I wave.

He waves back. His mouth is moving, but the words are nothing but muffled noise.

Right. I'm under water.

It's almost like I've forgotten.

I push upward, swimming the short distance to the top, my head breaking past the viscous surface. I pull myself up and rest my elbows on the glass edge, holding me just above the surface.

"What'd you say?" I ask, futilely wiping at the wetness from my face with the wetness from my hand. "I can't hear you under there."

"I said it's easier if I do the cleaning. I can actually breathe under there."

"You don't need to brag about it." I roll my eyes. "I can hold my breath for a *really* long time! You should time me."

He raises a hand in a stop motion. "Absolutely not, the very, and I mean, the very last fucking thing I need is for you to drown in my tank. Especially of your own volition."

I stick out my tongue. "You're no fun. *Look at me, I'm Mack. And I take everything way too seriously, wah, wah, wah.*" Then I turn to the side of the tank wall, next to the tall table where his laptop is perched. I mimic typing over it with my hands. "*Blahblahblah, this is where I type.*" I accidentally nudge the keyboard, and the computer comes to life, revealing a black screen with endless lines of code running down it. Then I pause. "Hey, this *is* where you type, isn't it? You're telling me this is where you were the whole time we were talking on the Aquariumaniacs forum?"

"It's true. How does it make you feel to know that?"

A little shiver runs through me because *that voice . . . so deep and smooth.*

I give him a suspicious look. "I feel like you're trying to distract me."

"Is it working?"

I pull the sponge out of the strap from the bottom of my bikini. This bikini is from college. That's where all my sexy clothes are from, pretty much. It's a string bikini with little palm trees on it. The straps have beads at the end, and they dangle at various intersections of my body. My hips, my neck. My back.

I finger one of the beads by my hip. "Nope! I'm going back under."

I dive back down, and this time, I'm determined to get to work. I pull out my sponge, and at first, I make a show of it, scraping the sponge along the tank, but then my arms start to get tired.

I travel back up to the top, my breath heavy. Although, I don't mind it this time, it's still not as heavy as it is when I wake up from a dream.

Mack stands there with his head tilted. Arms crossed over his chest. "That's all you're going to do? I could do that in my sleep."

"Nope! Just needed some air." Determinedly, I plunge back under the surface, continuing to scrub, scrub, scrub. I think we both know that the scrubbing does absolutely nothing to clean the tank, which is actually as spotless as Mack claimed. But . . .

Mack is watching me.

His eyes are on me.

And yet, I don't feel watched, if that makes sense.

Instead, I feel seen.

It's a new feeling for me. Maybe one I've never experienced before in my whole life.

I emerge again, but this time, I dip right back down. It's a performance now. A performance with an audience of one.

As I swipe at the large swatch of glass, it dawns on me how large the tank really is. I might be doing this for a while. My muscle spasms in my shoulder, and my lungs scream at me to go back to the surface.

A little voice inside me speaks, though. "Stay under . . . give in . . . disappear . . . what would happen . . ."

Curiosity. That never-ending curiosity. *Stay under . . . stay under . . .*

The burning in my lungs lessens. The cessation of oxygen is nothing but a bright relief in the center of my chest. But then . . . .

Black spots.

Inky, watery spots dot the light in my eyes.

*Oh, shit.*

I've stayed too long. I can't move my arms, my legs.

*Crash!*

Arms seize me.

And then oxygen hits me like a bomb.

"Jules! Jesus fucking Christ!" Mack's body is pressed against mine, his arms enveloped around my chest. "Breathe, Jules! Breathe!"

Our faces are mere inches apart.

My chest heaves as I gulp for every little molecule of oxygen.

And I'm aware of every single little thing around me.

"Were you trying to fucking kill yourself?" he asks.

I wipe the wet hair from my face and yank off my goggles. "I forgot . . ." I pant, gulping down air before I can get out the words. "I forgot about breathing. I forgot I couldn't breathe under water."

"You definitely can't. I think it's time for you to get out—"

"No!" I shout.

He's taken aback by the force of my declaration, and frankly, so am I. But every fiber of my being wants to be in this water right now. Maybe a little too much so considering what just happened.

"I'm fine! Stop!" I clear my throat and speak with a more even tone. "No. I came here to do something. And I'm going to do it."

We stare at each other for a moment, like a standoff. But I refuse to blink or look away.

Finally, Mack's intense stare softens. "Are you always this unreasonable?"

The way he asks tells me he's not mad at me anymore. In fact, instead, it feels a little bit like an invitation.

For what though? Flirting, perhaps.

I smile and teasingly say, "What's so unreasonable about me?"

He regards me with his pale blue eyes. His tongue flits out, wetting the middle of his full lower lip. He releases me and climbs from the water, but he doesn't jump back down to the floor.

Instead, he dangles from the side of the tank like it's nothing, hanging on by nothing but sheer arm strength. Then, the next words out of his mouth shock me to my core. "That bikini is pretty damn unreasonable."

My breath has settled by now, but I let out a fake gasp, hand to my mouth. "I didn't take you for a prude," I say. And I swing the little string that's fallen over my shoulder from the back of my neck.

"Not a prude. Just an observer."

I tilt my head to the side. "You know what I observe?"

"What?"

"Those in glass houses, um, *aquariums*, shouldn't throw stones. I'm wearing more than you are. You don't even have a top on." Then I incline my chin. "A little slutty if you ask me."

His eyes darken, light blue to gray, from a day sky to a stormy eve, and the look he's giving me is definitely the look of a man. Not the kind of look I've seen in a long time.

"Take it off," he says.

Adrenaline shoots through my belly at his words and then explodes through my appendages. My nipples harden beneath the small triangles of my top. It only took three words to make me come to terms with the effect he has on me.

But the old me isn't completely gone in this moment. I swallow hard. "I—I."

"I'm sorry." He shakes his head, speaking quickly. "I didn't mean it. I don't know what came over me. That . . . was completely inappropriate."

But I shake myself alive. "Shut up," I say.

I reach for the string at my neck. But I can't do it like this. Not out in the wide open air. Not with my eyes so clear.

I turn around in the tank and grasp onto the other side.

"Don't do it." His voice comes from behind me.

"Why not?" I call over my shoulder.

The strings at my neck slide out from their tie and spill over my shoulders. Then I snag the one at the back, tugging until it releases. I grab it and throw it over the top of the tank. The bottoms are next. I tug on the string at my right hip, tug at the string at my left hip, scooch until release, and then toss it out the tank.

"Please, stop." Mack's voice is a strained plea. "I can't . . . I can't . . ."

I hold my arm across my breasts. "Can't what?"

"I can't . . ." He pauses. "With you."

I can't even say exactly what he means by that, but his doubt spurs me on further. I have to prove it to him. Prove what exactly? *It. He needs to know.*

"Mack," I say with the most confident tone I can muster.

"What?"

"Get down from the tank and face me."

If I'm going to do this. I'm gonna fucking do this.

"Jules I—"

"Do it now."

Behind me, weight shifts, and I can hear sounds but only imagine what's happening. He drops to the ground with a thud.

"I'm on the ground. Now what?"

I glance over my shoulder, but there's nothing to see. I'm too high up to see Mack from here without looking down. "Good, now don't move."

I crane my neck toward the ceiling briefly, praying for strength from some god I don't even believe in because, holy hell, what am I actually doing right now . . .

And then I let go of the ledge, submerging my body back in the water.

I don't have my goggles, so when I open my eyes, all I see before me is a blurry, upright form. Maybe not a fish. Maybe not a man.

An outline with Mack inside. I know he's there.

We're living in different worlds.

I hold out my hands, pushing them against the glass. My body is bare to him. Not a stitch of clothing to cover me. The only thing between us is a see-through barrier, warping and refracting the light.

And yet, I'm on display. For him. Like a fish in an aquarium.

And I want him to see. I want him to see it all.

# CHAPTER 14

There's a crash in the water.

In a flash, Mack has scaled the tank wall and leaped in. His strength and speed are like a shark ready to attack. He grasps my body, and I grasp at his. My eyes snap open in the water, and even though his form is blurry, I see more clearly than I ever have in my entire life.

His hand comes behind my head, and my arms wrap around his torso. He feels different in the water. Warmer. Softer. But also so hard at the same time.

He presses his lips against mine. I pull him flush against me, my arms desperately grappling with the smooth scales, the long muscular contours offset by the soft flag of fins down the seam of his body. I move my hands up to his jaw, and it's almost a struggle with the way we're holding onto each other. I push into the kiss, my tongue finding his. Briefly, he swirls his tongue against mine, and a pleasurable tingle shoots down to the pit of my belly.

Before I can dive for another kiss, I'm rocketed upward, bursting through the water, Mack's large arms enveloped tightly around my ribs.

The blast of air is a shock to my system, and almost immediately, I'm gasping for air.

How long was I under?

Longer than I realized. But I didn't black out. I didn't even notice at all.

Due to Mack's abnormal strength, he's able to pull me over his shoulder from the edge of the tank and leap down to the floor. His neighbors must be so confused by the noise.

I would laugh at the thought, but I'm being encased in towels. Wrapped up tight like a sushi roll and carried to the couch.

He places me on the cushion, and I'm wrapped so tightly I can't even move my arms. I realize he's covering me. Covering as much of my body as he can.

Outside of the water, my nakedness feels different. I'm less protected. Less bold.

I think he understands.

He sits down next to me at the other end of the couch. Water seeps into the cushion from his slick body, like blood filling veins. His legs are spread, his elbows on his knees, and his head in his hand.

"Why'd you do that, Jules? Why'd you have to do that?" He looks up at me.

When his eyes are on me, I can feel every part of my body. Like an awakening from the deepest, drooliest kind of nap. I can feel so much of my body that my nipples still ache. And so does my pussy. An almost painful ache. I open my lips and consider lying, consider ducking my head back in my shell, cocooning deeper into my isolation.

But there's no denying who I am anymore.

So, I go with the entire self-evident truth.

"Because I want you, Mack."

***

"Are you trying to fuck a fish?"

I startle awake, my hands splashing in the water around me.

It's pitch black.

I'm naked.

I'm submerged.

Where's Mack?

But Mack's not here. Because I'm not there.

I'm in my apartment.

I shake my head to dispel the grogginess. "Kate! Get out of here!" My voice is thick with sleep.

"No way. I'm worried about you." She flips on the light, and I cover my eyes in shock.

"Too bright! Too bright!"

"Well, it's eleven in the morning. Guess what? It's bright out! Maybe you need to get used to it."

I almost feel hungover after my encounter with Mack two days ago. Heavy and sopping. Like a T-shirt that didn't wring out enough in the rinse cycle.

"It's not my fault I don't like the sunlight," I slur. Then I brace my hands on either side, lifting out of the tub. "I can't help what I'm into."

"Oh, yeah, that's for sure," Kate spits out in a staccato tone.

I step out of the tub, shoving my wet limbs into the green silk robe that I discarded on the ground earlier. It sticks to me like seaweed. Bad choice.

"Can you move out of the way, please?" I try to push past her, but she shoves a phone in my face.

"Do you mind explaining all *this* to me first?"

"Huh?" I squint at the phone and see a list of blue messages on her screen, all from me.

I grab it from her hands, and she follows me out of the balmy bathroom into the kitchen. "What's all this?"

"They're weird fucking messages you sent me at four this morning."

"Jeez . . . I don't remember doing this at all." I scroll through them.

*I went into his tank, Kate.*

*He watched me in there.*

*I got completely naked. I've never gotten completely naked for a man. I always leave something on. I've only slept with three people. I never even liked it before.*

*But I want to sleep with him.*

*I don't even know if he has a functional dick or not.*

*But I want to see it.*

*The next time I go there. I'm going to see it.*

Oh boy.

I rub my face with my hand. I'm sweaty and hot now because the silk has turned into saran wrap. I pick up my printed work assignment on the table and fan my face with it. "I'm sorry. I was on drugs."

Kate crosses her arms, her legs wide apart, her expression furious. Her dark hair is tied up into a ponytail, shiny and thick. Her olive skin is splashed with freckles.

"You're so pretty . . ." I murmur. It's like I'm seeing her for the first time. I always knew she was beautiful, but usually, when I look at the world, everything is dim. Today, it all seems exceptionally bright.

She points a finger in my face. "Don't try to butter me up. And don't lie to me either. You don't do drugs. I should know. You turn me down every time I offer."

I stomp away and plop down on the couch, rolling up the bat sleeves of my robe. "Fine . . . fine. Sit down. I'll tell you the whole truth and nothing but the truth."

I don't really want to spill my guts to Kate. But on the other hand . . . I *really* want to spill my guts to Kate. There's no one else in this world who would believe me. Or who I could trust. Or who would understand. But I know Kate will.

"So, you know how one of your boyfriends is a ghost?"

She gives a concerned look and fixes her ponytail but nods. "He's a shadow, but sure."

"And . . . you know how Mack is a fish?"

"Of course."

"And remember when you gave me the address to Mack's building."

Her eyes shutter closed, and she pinches her nose. "Yes . . ."

"And I went to see him . . ."

"Yes, and then you told me he didn't want to see you again."

I fidget with the silky hem of my robe. "Well, I went back to his house. A few times, actually."

"Jules! You can't keep going to strange men's houses without telling me! It's like girl code one-oh-one to always share your location. He could murder you!"

I collect my words before I say them because I know how insane I sound. "He's not a strange man. Or at least . . . he's not a man. Per se."

She leans in. "Yes, I'm aware."

I wince a little while saying the next words. "It turns out . . . that . . . I . . . may have . . ."

"If you're even going to say what I think you're going to say . . ." She shakes her head.

But I must.

"Ikissedthefishmonster!" I shout all at once.

It takes her a few seconds, and then she slaps the pillow next to her. "What the holy fuck?"

"I know! I know!"

She picks up the pillow and launches it at my head.

"Hey!" I fend it off with my hands. The pillow bounces off me and hits the ground.

Then she picks up another one, throwing that one at me too. "You're fucking a fish monster, and you didn't even tell me? What do I look like to you? A clown? A joke?"

"I didn't fuck him! I swear to god, I didn't fuck him. I said kiss! Just a kiss."

She pulls out her phone again, pointing to it menacingly. "Then what are all these messages about? Hmmm?"

I stand and put my arms on her shoulders. She's gotten to her feet, so I push her back down to the couch. "God. It's embarrassing. It's embarrassing on every level. I didn't fuck him. I just . . . *want* to fuck him."

"Wow. *Wow.* I thought you were just asexual—"

"Pretty sure I'm demisexual."

"Right, and you're fishmonstersexual."

"Don't call him that. I know I called him that, but nobody should call him a monster. He's not even close to a monster. He's . . . kind. Really kind."

Kate leans back into the couch. "You like this guy."

Suddenly, in my mind, I'm back in the tank, submerged with him, our lips locked together. "I do."

Kate opens her arms as if she wants a hug. "Well, who am I to judge other people's love?"

Then she leans in and wraps her arms around me, pulling on me so tight I feel like I might puke all over her. I let it go on for the count of three seconds, and then I wiggle out of her tight embrace.

"It's not love. It obviously can't go anywhere." My mind ticks away all the reasons why it's completely unreasonable for me to want to see Mack again. Even though I know I'll try. My spirits immediately dampen. "Let's change the subject. Why are you here . . . how'd you get in?"

Kate digs into her pocket and produces a single key. "I made this forever ago. I've had it for years. You don't talk to *anyone*. Do you think I'd let you die in this apartment all by yourself? Anyway. I'm here to remind you that next week is my birthday. And you . . . you agreed to *Little Mermaid* Drag."

"I didn't agree. I said maybe."

"Well, that's as good as a yes in my book. So, here's your warning. You better show up."

I wipe my hair out of my face and glance at Kate furtively.

But considering how brave I've been these last few weeks . . . odds are actually looking pretty good that I'll turn up. Miracles upon miracles. Still, I won't promise.

"We'll see," I say. I hold out my arm. "Here, take your phone back."

She grabs my hand, pinching at the skin. "What the hell is this on your skin?"

I look down.

There's a second green fleck.

# CHAPTER 15

*Jules: Question for you*

    *Mack: A question for me? Not surprising.*

*Jules: Can I ask it?*

*Mack: You already did. Kidding! Fine, ask it.*

*Jules: Have you ever been to the ocean?*

*Mack: It's only 20 minutes away.*

*Jules: Yeah, but, like, as you are now . . .*

*Mack: No, but I think about it.*

*Jules: Really?*

*Mack: Sometimes in my dreams. Yeah.*

*Jules: What keeps you here?*

*Mack: I have family.*

*Jules: You do?*

*Mack: Or I used to at least.*

*Jules: You have friends too?*

*Mack . . .*

*Mack: No, not anymore.*

*Jules: Your family knows then . . .*

*Mack: For the most part.*

*Jules: And what do they think?*

*Mack: It's complicated.*

*Jules: Sure, yeah. I get that. I do.*

*Jules: Okay, well, it's late. I guess I should get to bed.*

*Mack: Late? It's seven thirty in the morning?*

*Jules: Really?*

*Mack: Yes . . .*

*Jules: Shit . . . well . . . good morning.*

*Mack: Good morning.*

*Jules: Do you want some coffee?*

***

As soon as Mack opens the door, we're kissing. My hands wrap around his neck, and his arms pull me in, pressing my soft form into his hard one. His body is so different in the air as opposed to in the water. The whole experience is different.

The kiss is surprisingly fierce, but it's like we're locked in it in his entryway. His hands travel upward, cupping my jaw; his lips are soft, and his tongue searches for mine.

My hands . . . They're traveling everywhere. He doesn't have a shirt on, only the light blue swim trunks I've seen him in before. My eyes flutter open, and I catch a glimpse of my hand on his chest, my pale skin against his even more opalescent, shimmery scales . . . now looking more greenish blue than before.

I caress the tight, scaly skin across his chest. His entire chest is tightly contoured, as if I'm looking at a human skeleton stretched with muscles and covered in scales and fins. He pulls away when my hand reaches his neck, touching the slit-like openings at the side.

*Gills.*

"Sorry," I murmur against his lips.

I push up on the tips of my toes to press my mouth against his, but he breaks away, pulling back.

He rests his hands on my shoulders, his fingers gently rubbing in place, as if moving of their own accord. Nevertheless, he keeps me at arm's length.

"It's just too weird. Isn't it?" He leans forward and whispers the words against my hairline. "You . . . and . . . me . . ."

Spiky waves rush down my neck at the touch.

I bring my hand to his neck again, gently this time, my fingertips hovering over the delicate gills. "It's unknown. That's all. But the unknown doesn't have to remain that way. Will you let me?"

His nostrils flare. And then he swings his gaze downward, and I notice the clean half-moon line of his eyelids. No eyelashes.

I want to run a fingertip along that line as well.

Then he nods. "Yes . . . go ahead."

With his consent, very carefully, I glide my index finger along the line of his gill, following it as if it were a vein or a strand of hair. It quivers at my touch, the little slits fluttering as I run my fingertip along them.

"Does that hurt?"

The veins on his neck bulge. The muscle at the corner of his jaw flicks. "No. It doesn't hurt. You can't hurt me."

Emboldened, I trail my fingertips upward then, to his ear, then along his jaw. His cheekbones are high and prominent, more like the sharp corners of a shark than any other aquatic animal.

For the first time, it dawns on me that he's not just unlike other humans. In many ways, he's much more powerful. He can breathe both in and out of the water. He can heave himself up and over the tank without trying, even holding onto my body as well.

And for the first time, it dawns on me that he's not really a fish at all. He's not a human either. But he is a predator.

And yet, I'm not scared.

Instead, if my nipples and pussy are any indication, I'm excited.

My fingers trail along his lips, then over the high peak of his cheekbones, and then, just like that, we're kissing again.

He nudges me with a step, and I comply, one foot scraping backward and then the next, until we reach the couch, where he pushes me with enough force that I fall to the cushions, my back pushed against the armrest, my legs spread open, and my breath heavy with desire.

*I cannot believe what I'm fucking doing.*

This desire is new to me. Sure, I've masturbated before, but my body has never responded this way to any man.

*Except he's not a man, Jules.*

He follows me to the couch, positioning himself between my legs, hovering, slanted across the cushions. He's draped over me, and with an even closer view of his chest, I can vaguely see the outline of a beating dark purple heart.

Before my brain can make sense of that revelation, his lips are on mine again, and I'm melting into nothing but a puddle of clouds.

As he deepens the kiss, my hips rock impulsively and uncontrollably. I'm straining to press my pelvis against his . . . but he's out of reach.

I let my hands travel down the length of his back to grasp at his taut, muscled hips, but he growls softly into my mouth. Then, one by one, he pulls my hands off him and holds them over my head.

"Stay put," he commands.

And as my body responds to the directive, I'm dying for more contact. His chest doesn't even touch mine; a wave of air could blow right between us. Our only points of contact are our lips and his hands on my wrist.

I wiggle in his grip. "Let me go," I say.

And instantly, he releases me.

Instead of standing, though, I push against his chest with my hands, pressing his back into the back of the couch, his legs spread, and then I move to him, one leg straddling either side.

His chest heaves as our bodies cleave, the connection point directly at my core, rubbing against his cock.

I can feel it now. Hard and thick against me. And I'm . . . wet and sopping already.

His head falls back against the couch, and his Adam's apple bobs as he swallows hard. Because I'm rocking my rips into his, slowly but surely, rubbing his cock against my covered clit, little pulses of pleasure shooting through me.

"Look at me," I say as I continue to rock.

I pull my sweater hem upward and over my breasts. I'm not wearing a bra, so I'm exposed to him.

The look in his eye is almost deadly. Or maybe like he's going to die. I can't quite tell.

"Touch them . . ." I say, breathless. "Please. I need to feel your hands on me."

His mouth closes, the flick in his jaw returning. Then his fingers creep up over the waist of my jeans. They hover there, spread right at my belly button. I buck harder against him, and his body jolts, his fingers slipping upward. I'm pushing myself upstream, getting close to something.

An orgasm? From this?

I've never had an orgasm with another person before. Let alone from dry humping.

But the body . . . and the mind . . . want what they want. Little moans escape my throat involuntarily. I'm mewling like a cat.

"Mmm . . . mmmm . . . mmm . . ." I lick my lips. "Please . . ." I whisper.

"Please what?" His voice is hoarse.

I swallow hard, my eyes shut. "If you touch them, I think I'll come."

"Jules . . ." His fingertips are inching up my flat belly. Halfway there and then they stall. "This isn't right. We shouldn't be doing this."

He bucks hard against me, and a burst of pleasure propels me forward.

"Gah . . ." An animalistic sound comes out of me. "It's not right for you to make me come?"

"No . . . it's . . . not . . . that . . ." He winces as his mouth tightens, bucking his hips against me again. "Never . . . that . . ."

"Then . . . what?" It's almost like we're fucking. Except for the very most important parts.

We're in a simulated sex sequence. But it doesn't feel simulated to me. It feels practically like the real thing.

*It makes me want the real thing.*

"It's me." One more buck of his hips, one more roll of mine, meeting somewhere in the sweet, sensual middle. "Agh," he growls.

He drops his hands, letting them fall to his side. His head falls back, and his hips still.

I rub frantically against him.

"No . . . no . . . I'm so close . . ." I whisper.

He brings his hands to my upper arms, slowing my rocking until I still as well. "That's enough, Jules."

"Why?" I whine.

"Because I don't know what will happen if we go any further. I've never . . . I've never done any of this with anyone in so long. Not like this."

My head spins, drunk with lust, drunk with want and need and maybe something else. "You really are a monster," I hiss.

To my surprise, his body vibrates with a chuckle. I want to push my head against his thickly muscled chest so that I can hear the rumble deep in my ears.

*Jesus, maybe I really am losing it. Haven't I been worried about the same thing from the start?*

I'm sobering up now. Not so dick drunk anymore. Right. Right.

I'm not some kind of sex freak, I swear. I don't even usually like sex at all.

With some effort, I pull my legs out from either side of him and roll over to the side of the couch. My pussy and the tender flesh of my inner thighs are coated with moisture, slick and aching.

"What do you think's going to happen? Do you think your cum is going to poison me or something?" I look over to him. Oddly enough, a pinkish flush covers his body now.

And for the first time, I get an eyeful of what's below his waist. I could feel it before. But now I can see it too. The bulge.

It's large. Almost shockingly so. I couldn't tell so much when I was riding him, but now I'm really getting a good perspective of scale.

He's much bigger than any human man I've ever seen. How could that fit inside me? It doesn't seem scientifically possible. But then again . . . neither does he . . .

I lick my lips.

And my gaze lingers on him. He meets it.

Then abruptly, he stands.

"Nope. Nope. Nope." He shakes his head, pacing back and forth, his hand running the length of his smooth skull. "It's not happening. It can't happen."

"Oh, come on!" I whine.

I sound ridiculous. Hell, this whole thing is ridiculous. The fact that I never want to fuck any man and suddenly, here's this . . . person . . . creature, whatever you want to call him. And all I want to do is *all the things to him*, and I think he wants to do all the things too. But instead, he's too scared. The very laws of nature might be against us.

He's standing in front of his tank now. Bulge and everything. No shirt. Only shorts.

I remember that I, too, have my shirt hiked up, my own body exposed.

"Jules. This is dangerous, what we're doing. Not just because we don't know what would happen if I were to . . ." He tilts his head a bit, his voice lowered. "*Come* on you or inside you . . ."

I moan at the very thought. Again, his gaze darkens, and he shakes his head.

"But there are so many other things we don't know. I don't even know what I'll be in the next year or the next month. Hell, the next day. And you . . . you can't get tangled up in this. You're so . . ."

"Don't say beautiful," I clip out.

"Vulnerable" is what he says instead.

"I already told you I'm not scared." Which is only a partial lie.

"Maybe you're not. But I am."

I let out an exasperated sigh, crossing my arms over my naked chest. I glance down at my flesh, exposed to him and to me.

Like a camera flash, an idea lights up my brain.

"Just wait a minute. Wait, wait, wait. I have a proposal. Will you hear me out?"

He furrows his brows together. "I don't want to, but I'm intrigued. My curiosity often gets the best of me."

"You've already seen me naked, and nothing bad happened, right?"

He gives a cautious look. "So what?"

I lean forward a bit, dropping my arms to expose my breasts again. "So, get naked in front of me."

His hands go to the waistband of his shorts, lingering there. An involuntary response, no doubt. He's scared, I get that. I've lived my whole life scared. But also . . . These feelings. They're reciprocal.

He fingers the waistband along the cut of his waist. His muscles are defined and sinewy beneath his scales along his thick forearms, wrapping like cling wrap. "Haven't you ever heard of a slippery slope?"

This time, I let my fingers travel to my nipples, lightly circling one until it beads up, aching and pink. "You can't trick me. I'm a copywriter, and I write for science magazines. And one thing I know about a slippery slope . . ." I glide my finger from one nipple and then over to the other. Satisfaction surges through me when he bites his lip and winces in response. "It's a logical fallacy. A false argument. So go ahead, then. Get naked. Only look. I promise. I won't touch, there's no slippery slope here . . . unless you want there to be, of course."

Puns! I've got puns today. I have never openly expressed this side of myself before, and I'm ravenous for more.

But also, I do mean what I said to Mack. I'm not an asshole. I don't touch anyone without their consent. I know all too well what that feels like.

For a brief second, I worry if maybe I've pushed things too far. I'm new to these situations; I'm only working off instinct, and I have no way of verifying if what I'm doing is right.

But it must be. Because Mack drops his shorts, steps out of them, and kicks them to the side.

And there he is in front of me.

Completely bare. His body is so cut that I can barely see an ounce of fat on him. Just tight muscle, taut and lean down his long form, and opalescent scales now shimmering a little bluish green in the light.

And his dick is . . .

Ummm . . . glorious.

It looks like a human dick. *Mostly*, at least. It's the same shade as the rest of him but with more pink and red hues. And I can't quite tell, but there's something along the top ridge of the shaft. Is it a fin? Is it an appendage? What is it?

I want to get closer. I have to get closer. There's no way I can get this far and still leave with this one unanswered question.

I fall to my knees on the ground. Then I put my hands down and slowly crawl to him, my neck craned upward so that I can keep my eyes on him.

I'm out of line. I'm a filthy slut. I never thought of myself that way before, but my mother used to sometimes call me those names. "You're dressed like a whore. No wonder all the boys want to sleep with you." "Show the photographer how nice you look in your bikini. Pull up the straps a little tighter." She never knew which way she wanted to yell at me. Either I was a slut, or I was being slutted out.

But now, I want to be a slut in a whole different way. In a way that's about me. Never has being a slut sounded more like freedom.

I crawl a little closer toward him. "Just . . . let me . . . let me touch it. Suck it. Just one little suck. One tiny little suck." *So I can really know what's going on with you. So I can have you inside me once and for all.*

His eyes darken again. And this time, they really darken, not just in the sense that it looks like he wants to eat me. Now, it's more murderous. The whites of his eyes turn dark gray, the blue part going almost completely black.

My pulse pounds through my body. My knees ache on the ground.

I don't care.

At first, I think he might pounce on me. Push me to my knees in front of him and put me to work.

The degree to which I want him to do that startles me.

*Wow, I've really become a wanton.*

But, of course, he doesn't do that. Instead, he balls his hands into fists; the knuckles would probably be white if they weren't already.

He brings a fist to his lips and clears his throat. "Maybe you should—"

"Don't tell me to leave now," I say.

I know his moves at this point. We're all creatures of habit. Whenever we creep toward the edge of something, we push back. But I want to tip over the edge.

Then, in a softer voice, I say. "I'm sorry. I promise. No touching. I respect your boundaries. Swear on my mother's grave."

She's alive, but I still mean it.

He considers this, and then, my pulse leaps when he leans down, reaches out his hand, and curls a finger beneath my chin. He tilts my chin up so I'm looking up at him from down on my knees.

But I realize he's doing something else as well. He's holding me back.

He's not applying pressure or force.

It's all psychological.

He has me by the theoretical throat.

And I'm not moving an inch without his say-so. Slowly, he applies upward pressure beneath my chin, and I lift from my knees, coming to a standing position. I still have to look up to see him because he's so much taller than me.

But then I see what he's doing with his other hand.

A wave of dizziness and lust rushes over me.

Because his other hand is working his dick, stroking it back and forth, slowly it seems, but still moving with that familiar rhythmic motion. I can't see his dick with my chin angled as it is. I can only hear the noise of the scaly skin of his hand stroking against the skin of his cock. I can feel the bouncing movement. I can see his shoulder shake as he continues to jerk himself right in front of me.

Just out of reach.

But his eyes are on me. And mine on him.

"Look at me," he commands, his voice gruff when my gaze wanders to his hand. "Look at me while I do this. Because I'm doing this for you. Because of you."

I nod wordlessly. And I follow orders, keeping my eyes on him as my hand travels down below my belly as well.

"*Fuck. Shit. Fuck,*" he bites out.

His strokes quicken. Even though I can't see them, I can feel it.

And mine do as well, my fingertips circling again and again over my clit, wet and lubricated and sensitive to every touch.

"I have to see you come." He nods, and the desperate look in his eye is almost a mirror reflection of the one I'm sure is in mine.

I nod back, but I don't move any closer. He doesn't look below my face though. Not at my naked body or at my hand that is now working over my wet pussy.

"You . . ." He prompts me with a nod. "You have to come first."

I work my hand harder, the muscles tightening in my throat. His gaze becomes agitated.

"What did I say?" he barks out at me.

I move my hand faster, my breath uncontrollable. "I'm almost . . ." I eke out. "Almost . . ."

And then both our hands are working so fast that the only sounds in the room are the flowing water in Mack's tank, his hand pumping away at his cock, and my hand circling my clit.

"Now, Jules." His finger is still under my chin, but now he pinches it, directing my gaze down.

For the first time, I can see him, really see him and all his moving parts up close. His cock is unbelievably large. He wants me to look.

"Be a good girl for me and come."

The sight of his hard cock encased in his large hand hits me hard, as does the first wave of my orgasm.

"Come hard," he commands.

His words are what really does it. *Who knew he was so dirty? Certainly not me.* The only dirty talk directed at me before has been wholly unwanted. But now I would lick the cum off his dick if he called me a good girl again. I would crawl on my knees on a leash if he asked me.

The second wave hits me even harder, and although I'm trying to keep my eyes open, to keep them on his cock, to watch that hypnotic movement until its final culmination, I can't. I give into the little wave of death rushing over me. My eyes shutter briefly, my hearing muffled as if I've been dunked in water, although I can vaguely hear him still talking.

"That's right, that's a good girl. You're coming so . . . hard . . ."

The wave surges and then falls within me and then circles again and again and again until it relaxes back to a glassy pond. My body is boneless from the assault of pleasure.

When I come to, he's almost on the brink. My eyes go wide because I need to see it as well. I need to see him come too.

But he drops his hand from my chin and turns around, his hand flying furiously.

He's not going to let me see him come.

It feels like an insult, but I keep my distance.

Shortly after he turns around, he lurches forward with a hiss, groaning.

I see nothing else. Maybe he's hiding something. He'd probably say it's none of my business.

And besides, I'm now wrung out like a rag. Standing in the middle of this near-empty room. Half naked. With a creature. Who isn't human.

It's safe to say I've never done anything like this with anyone in my whole life.

After a few seconds, he's breathing hard, and then he turns back to me, wiping his hands down the length of his washboard torso.

Nervously, I glance up at the ceiling. "Well, that was unexpected, huh?"

But he just shakes his head. "Oh fuck, Jules. What's going to happen to us?"

# CHAPTER 16

I haven't visited the fish forum in days.

I used to do it almost out of compulsion, as a way to push down other feelings. As a distraction from the darkness in my life. The almost humdrum isolation that I've put myself in.

But now that I've been with Mack . . . after our . . . experience together.

Now, I can't seem to think about anything else. I haven't even changed the water in my tank. Usually, I do that about once a week. A cleansing ritual of sorts.

But right now, I don't feel the need to be clean.

If anything, I yearn for a particular kind of filth.

*Kate would be so proud.*

Still, normal life calls, and I have a deadline; one of my articles is due to my boss. *The multiverse again.* I'm honestly getting sick of writing about it, but nevertheless, I continue to renew my contract. So I can't fall back into the fantasy of our encounters, or I'll never come up for air.

*Maladaptive daydreaming* is the psychological term. I looked it up. But my therapist never mentioned it.

However, instead of finishing my assignment, my mouse is drawn to the browser. I click once, and before I can stop myself, I'm opening the Freemont Aquariumaniacs Forum.

I scroll, scroll, scroll through the list of new posts.

*How to tell if my fish likes me.*

*Is my fish lonely by himself?*

*I dreamed about sharks last night, and now I'm worried.*

Interestingly enough, there's no FishKiller1234 in sight. Maybe the mods finally banned his ass from the forum. Good thing he has that Facebook group for people to follow. Fucking asshole.

I keep scrolling, but nothing quite holds my interest the way chatting with Mack on this forum used to.

Of course, Mack has a way of disappearing on me out of nowhere. Like shutting down just when we're on a precipice. He did it after we sent the pictures on the forum.

He did it after I saw him IRL for the first time. Although I get that, it was understandable.

But hell, he disappeared on me even after we orgasmed together. Maybe he didn't physically disappear, but he was just . . . gone. His eyes blank.

*Jules, what's going to happen to us?*

The messages on the post pop up and roll down the screen in real time. My eyes follow the movement as my mind wanders.

Mack really does believe something bad will happen if we spend time together.

He thinks he can hurt me somehow.

I tap my fingernails against the clear counter of my desk. There aren't any coffee cups splayed out from the last few days. I've been spending too much time thinking about Mack.

And that's why I'm compelled to message someone else.

The very concept of Mack is riddled with complications. And I think I know someone who claims to have answers.

I open his profile and type out his handle: AverageJoeGuy

Our previous conversation is still available on the screen. My fingers fly across the keyboard.

*JulesLikesToSwim:* I think I'm ready to talk.

***

When AverageJoeGuy doesn't respond right away, I get antsy. Sometimes I forget that not every single person is chronically online like me, just waiting dead eyed in front of their devices for little notifications to light up their phones or their brains.

The dopamine hit my childhood could never give me. But I digress.

The day is fading as the sun sets outside my window. I know because I have the curtains open.

My palms and my fingers tingle. I scratch at the skin of my hands, the little skin tags now growing in number on my arm.

The antsiness builds in the base of my back, compelling me to jump right out of my skin.

What is this feeling? It's not like the usual anxiety I experience.

Instead of freezing, I'm agitated. Activated.

I think I want to actually . . . go outside?

I can't remember the last time I actually sought out the sun or the moon or the stars. Or the sea, as it were.

I get an idea.

I'm going to *go for a walk.*

I haven't gone on a leisurely walk for years now, maybe an entire decade. The last time I remember taking a walk was when my dad was still alive. He took me to the state fair. We walked around and around the grounds for hours.

He played one of those games with the plastic cups and the Ping-Pong balls. Won me a goldfish and then told me he was glad all that beer pong practice had paid off.

I had that goldfish forever, even after my father died. And then . . .

I'm already pulling on my jacket and squishing my sockless feet into my sneakers, which I had to harvest from deep in the wilderness of my coat closet.

I'm dressed and opening the door before I can even comprehend that I'm doing it.

I'm going for a walk!

My natural inclination is to walk up to George and order a coffee, but he isn't at the shop. So, I keep moving.

I keep my legs moving past the sidewalks, past the people. I even look around a bit at the dusky night sky. The fallen light of day is broken up throughout the street by street lamps and lights hanging from the buildings on the road. I hug my arms to my chest. Breathe in deep.

Something gets caught in my throat.

*Cough.*

I'm coughing now. Shit.

I hunch over, hacking my guts out. I put my flat palm against my sternum and try to relax my throat. Maybe I have some allergies. No big deal.

I haven't gone too far, at least a few blocks.

But when I look up, I'm not surprised where I find myself.

***

I wander through the lobby of Mack's apartment building, not for the first time. The copy of *Moby Dick* is still on the table. I wish they'd replace it with something better, a little more optimistic, maybe a little more fun. But then I think about all the similar kinds of stories, and I can't think of a single one that ends happily.

*The Little Mermaid*, perhaps? Technically, it has a happy ending if you go by the Disney version.

Except, I always wondered why Ariel would ever give up her fins?

Since I'm already in the building, I approach the elevator. As usual, no one's around, and I love this about Mac's building. How did he get so lucky?

I press the number five and watch as the steel doors slide closed. But just as I'm about to stand in blissful solitude, a hand breaks through the space, and the door halts, then slides back open.

My heartbeat quickens. *Fuck. Fuck. Fuck.*

Being locked in such close proximity with a stranger is jarring, especially after so many years of avoiding it. The person walks in. A woman, presumably. She's got long blonde hair, and she's petite, wearing a yellow sundress. The gold earrings on her ears are designer. I still have an eye for that kind of thing, even after being out of the modeling business for so long. She has money.

When she sees me, she gives a cute little smile.

"Thanks for waiting," she says.

My eyes shift to either side of the elevator. Is there any other way out of here? Of course not. So, I just nod.

The woman goes to touch the button but then pulls her hand back. "Oh. I see we're headed to the same floor."

I hold back the desire to roll my eyes. Again, I don't say anything, but this time a little hum comes from my throat.

*Mm-hmmm.*

Luckily, traveling five floors doesn't take too long, so the small room we're trapped in comes lurching to a halt in just a few seconds.

The door opens, and the woman looks behind her. "Hope you have a great day."

I just nod blankly. I have to get out now. She knows we're going to the same floor. There are also only five units on the whole floor. I step out of the elevator as slowly as possible, waiting for the woman to enter her unit first.

And then my heart sinks when I see where she's going. Past the doormats, past the plastic plant, past the conservative news listener, and right to Mack's door.

I meander, stalling, and attempt to hide behind the plastic plant while keeping an eye on her.

She knocks on the door. "Mack. Hey. It's Delaney."

She waits and then knocks again. "Mack. Open up."

For some reason, I can't fathom this encounter. I can't imagine there's any way he'll let her in.

But then the door bursts open, and she hustles inside, no sight of Mack except for the smallest flash of his arm.

Who the fuck is Delaney?

# CHAPTER 17

My knees are shaking, and my chest feels hot. This was a bad idea. A walk? Who am I kidding? I don't go for *walks*. Hell, I don't leave the apartment.

I squeeze my jacket tight around me and turn on my heel as quietly as I can. Instead of the elevator, I walk to the dark corner at the end of the hallway toward the Exit sign and force myself to trot down the gray, dank stairwell. It's even more alarming than the stairwell in my building. Older and creepier.

Whatever. I've got to get the fuck home.

Who the hell was that going to Mack's apartment?

My first thought is the letter that was left at his door with a woman's handwriting.

This has to be the woman. Has to.

I barely remember my walk home; my head is spinning a mile a minute. Why did I think Mack was only for me? And why did that appeal to me so much?

I don't even know him at all.

I just think I do.

When I round the corner to my apartment building, I run up the stairs. I'm out of breath by the time I make it to my floor, but then, down the hall, I see Jason.

*Shit, not Jason. Not now.*

But he's not even standing at his apartment. Instead . . . he's standing in front of mine.

I keep walking because although my fear rockets at the very sight of him, I just want to get the fuck inside.

I draw near and narrow my eyes to make sense of what he's doing.

It looks like he's fiddling with my door knob.

*Is he trying to break in?*

"Hey!" I bark out. "What're you doing?"

The shouting surprises even me. My anxiety is compounded by my anger about Mack.

Jason looks up quickly, guiltily, in my opinion.

"Jules! I was just looking for you."

"Why?" I say in my most deadpan voice. I halt in front of him, hands on my hips.

He fidgets a bit, touches the handle of my door for a second, then looks at me and drops his hand. "There was a moth on your door handle. But I killed it."

*Yeah the fuck right.*

"Great. I've gotta get inside."

But he steps in front of the door, blocking me from the entrance. "I thought you'd be grateful."

Any other day, my heart would be pounding now. Any other day, I'd do whatever I could to forgo some kind of conflict. But today isn't just any other day.

Instead, I fix my gaze on Jason, gravity tugging downward at the corners of my lips. "Grateful for what?"

He looks exasperated now. But I'm feeling exasperated too. "Grateful that I killed a possibly poisonous bug on your doorknob. Goddamn. I guess you really are all looks and no brain."

I glare at him. "Shut up, Jason."

He stares me down for a moment. I've never spoken to him that way before. I've never spoken to any man that way before. I always just take his annoying and rude remarks like I don't hear them, or I shuffle by with a nod.

My blood turns cold as he watches me. I almost flinch. But no. This time, I won't be deterred.

"Goodbye," I grit out between my teeth.

He stares for a moment longer. *Don't you fucking flinch.* Then he nods. "Yeah."

I'm relieved as he steps out of the way, slowly stepping back toward his apartment and then turning around. I wait until his door's shut before getting my keys out, my hands trembling around the metal, barely making it into the locks and turning the door.

When I'm finally inside, I crash on the couch.

My eyes are watering. I actually think I might . . . cry?

Over what though? A mere woman walking into Mack's apartment?

A confrontation with Jason?

Jesus, maybe Mack's on Tinder or something. Maybe there's a fish Tinder.

Fuck, why did I never think of that before? People have fetishes. It's a thing.

*Is it my thing?* Oh my god.

I pick up my phone, and I see a message from Kate.

*KATE: LITTLE MERMAID DRAG SOON DON'T FORGET! ALSO PEOPLE ARE SERIOUS ABOUT THESE COSTUMES SO DRESS TO IMPRESS. I'M GOING AS URSULA THE SEA WITCH BECAUSE SHE'S THE HOTTEST CHARACTER BY FAR*

As if. Right now, nothing could pull me out of this apartment. Not even wild horses.

I lie on my back, my head flopped to the side, my arm hanging off the edge with my phone dangling from my hand.

I don't have the energy to respond to Kate. I feel crushed.

Mack. He belongs to me. He's *mine*.

Yikes. Where did that come from? Maybe I need to call my therapist again. What would she have to say about this situation?

Maybe she'd agree with Mack. Maybe this thing between us really is toxic or bad or dangerous or something?

But then, my phone rings.

*Mackthefishguy*

He's . . . calling me?

Thoughts swirl a mile a minute in my head. What do I do? Do I answer? When was the last time I even answered a phone call? When was the last time *anyone* answered a phone call? In these days? In this economy?

The phone vibrates again in my hand, and I almost throw it.

*Fuck it.*

I pick up the phone.

"Hello?" I croak out and clear my throat.

"Hey . . ." His voice is soft. "Can you talk?"

# CHAPTER 18

"It's kind of funny. I had this feeling you would come over today. Show up uninvited, like how you do."

I'm pacing around the apartment, phone stuck to my ear and my hand behind my back. Like my mother used to do when I was a kid, except this was when people still had cords on their phones. She'd talk and talk and talk, and walk and walk and walk, expanding the spiraled cord until it was pulled taut and straight. When I'd grasp at the corner of her sleeve to get her attention, she'd wave me off, an irritated scowl on her pale pink lips, shaking her head.

But as I'm not attached to anything, I meander to my desk. My embarrassment piques at Mack's words because I did go to his home today. Uninvited, as usual.

But I won't let him know that. When all's said and done, he behaved pretty shitty to me, actually. Messing around with me and then freaking out and then, as usual, going radio silent.

That's no way to treat a person.

I plop down on my computer chair, the hinges creaking noisily. "Well, I didn't go to your apartment today. Because you basically hit it and quit it. Or don't you remember?"

There's a brief pause on the other end. "I'm sorry. That's not how I want things to be between us. You have no idea."

I lean back in the chair. "Then tell me."

There's a sigh on the other end of the line. I'm pissed at him, but I'm also elated to hear the subtle soft tones of his voice. Like a warm breeze on an open beach on the first day of summer.

"So . . ." he begins, and I can feel the hesitation in his voice. "So, I've been feeling pretty bad today."

"Okay . . ." I say slowly. "Me too. But why you? You go first."

"I—I uh . . ."

I wonder what he's going to say. That he's with another woman? That was his fish girlfriend? That he loves someone else?

"I saw my sister today."

"Your sister?" The words come out a little too loud, a little too surprised. I rein in my anticipation. I don't want to seem weird on the phone. "I didn't know you had a sister."

"Yeah. She's older than me. I'm the baby in the family. Or was . . . at least . . ."

"Oh," I say quietly. "Because of your *change*?"

"Yes. But it's complicated. I don't blame them for turning their backs on me. And Delaney, that's her, my sister, she tries, you know? She tries to understand."

"But they're your family. Why would they turn their back on you? It's their job to accept you."

The words come out of my mouth, but I don't even know how. Has my own mother ever accepted me? Although my father did once. Before he died. Even when I was young, he accepted me.

"I was taught never to talk about it, but my family is wealthy. Really, really wealthy. It's how I manage to survive, actually. I have a trust fund, and I'm able to keep track of it because I can access the internet, obviously. That's what keeps me going. That, and the fact that my dad owns the building I live in. He thought it'd be a safe place for me to hide. No one there but retirees. But I used to work. I just had to quit my job when . . . well, when things became a little too obvious. It was either quit or who knows what would've happened to me. I still freelance, but I don't know that I'll ever be able to work a real job again. I'm just glad my parents didn't take away my trust fund. Or I don't know what would happen to me."

"What was your job before?" I ask because I'm acutely curious about him. Both who he used to be and who he is now. And what that all means for me.

"I'm a programmer. I code. Always had a brain for patterns and languages and that sort of thing. I made pretty decent money. Still do with my freelance work, actually. But all that's kind of different now."

"So, are you and your sister close?"

There's a pause. "She tries. She really does. That letter on my doorstep the other day . . . That was from her. But she did come by to deliver another message today."

"What?" I ask.

"She wanted to tell me that my parents found a surgeon."

"A surgeon?"

"Yes, one who they think can, well, put me back the way I was."

"Is that possible?"

"He's discreet. Apparently, he does work on celebrities and billionaires, so it's in his best interest to keep his mouth shut. My family has money. So, I looked through it . . ."

A mix of emotions runs through me. "You're considering this?"

On the one hand, if Mack had surgery, maybe he could have a normal life again. Maybe he could be that guy in the framed picture on his wall. Be the guy he presented himself as on the forum where we met.

And maybe he and I would actually have a shot together. We'd be like two normals in a normal world, just doing normal people, normal world things. I know it's a selfish thought to even include myself in this discussion. I don't even know him that well. Although, that's not true. We've been talking for a long time. And we . . .

Well, we did what we did together. That counts for a lot for someone like me.

But on the other hand, maybe it would ruin him. Maybe putting him *back to normal* isn't the answer at all.

I like Mack the way he is. I like him exactly the way he is.

Gills and all.

Mack clears his throat. "I'm going to be honest with you. I did think about it."

"Oh." My tone falls. "I see."

"But I have some concerns. The surgeries . . . they're still pretty rudimentary. They don't quite look right. There's something uncanny about them, especially when they're meant to force someone back to the way they were. Plus, the scars . . . And I'd potentially have to continue the surgery process throughout my life. You know, if the transformations are ongoing. It doesn't seem like much of a way to live, does it?"

I don't know what else to say. I shake my head even though he can't see me. "That sounds awful. I'm so sorry."

"There's more. The company I've been freelancing for. There have been some discoveries recently . . ."

"What do you mean, discoveries?"

Mack sounds thoughtful. "There might be other solutions. But drastic ones. I just . . . I don't know yet. They sound crazy, to be honest."

"Everything sounds crazy."

"Yeah. I agree." He's quiet again. "You know what the worst part is about all this?"

"Tell me."

"It's not that I look the way I do now. If I'm honest with you, the way I look feels more like the way I am on the inside than I ever looked before. But that's not the worst part. The worst part is that I miss my family. I miss my friends. I miss having people over. I miss dinners. I miss parties. I miss live music. I used to love live music. I played guitar."

"Really? You're a musician? I had no idea. Where's your guitar? Maybe you can play for me sometime."

He chuckles. "C'mon, Jules. You've seen my apartment. There's nothing in there."

"But why not? It's not like you don't have the money. Or so I'm just learning."

"Once I became isolated enough, I threw everything away. Felt like I couldn't hold onto anything from my past life. Especially if no one I loved was going to be in it."

"They should be there for you."

Another pregnant pause. I can feel my throat tightening up. I'm angry. I'm angry for Mack. I'm angry that his family abandoned him almost completely. Money doesn't make up for love.

"Yeah, but life isn't perfect or easy like that. They're doing their best, and I don't claim to have handled this well either."

"But it's their job."

"I know. I know how bad it is. Believe me, I think about it every day."

I fidget as I sit on the phone with him, my fingers absently typing away at my keys, opening up the aquarium forums.

Mack is one of my very few friends in the world. But I didn't think I'd be one of his very few friends as well.

Then, an idea trickles into my mind. A crazy idea. A potentially dangerous idea.

But also, maybe a fun one.

"Mack. I have a very serious question to ask you."

"What's that?"

"How do you feel about drag?"

"Drag, like gender-bending, costumes, dress up, singing, that kind of thing?"

"Yeah, alcohol too."

"I guess I feel fine about drag."

"Then I have a proposition for you."

***

When I get off the phone with Mack, I stare at my computer screen. I've convinced him to go to the drag brunch because I've specified it's a costume party. Not a Halloween costume party. Not a spooky ghouls and demons type thing. Just a fun, good old dress-up party.

The perfect cover for him to go out in public again. The perfect cover for him to spend time with friends. See a live performance. Get out in the light of day. The very things he says he misses the most.

A part of me was shocked he agreed. But another part of me knows how much he needs this.

We all need to connect with humanity sometimes. Even me. A shut-in.

Speaking of connecting, I text Kate back and give her the 411.

*Kate: Mack?! You're bringing Mack?*

*Jules: Do you think it's a terrible idea?*

*Kate: No, I think it's a great idea! In fact, it's the perfect crime. There are crazy good makeup artists at this drag event. Like some of the best in the country. People will be asking him for a business card.*

*Jules: I hope you're right.*

*Kate: I know I am. In fact, I'm so right, I'm going to bring The Shadow as well.*

*Jules: Ghost boyfriend?*

*Kate: He's a shadow, but yeah. We'll just pretend he's in a costume too! How fun! This is really going to be a party. You're even coming out. And you're dating a guy? Are you kidding me?*

*Jules: We're not dating, don't be crazy.*

*Kate: Whatever. Don't care. Say what you will. Happy thirtieth to me!*

I breathe a sigh of relief at what I've organized. I'm extremely proud of myself. I know I owe Kate a better friendship. So now, I'm actually going to show up for her. The way a real friend should.

And I know Mack needs this too.

But even through this immense web of excitement, I'm still sitting in front of my computer screen, hours later, with the aquarium forum up on my screen when a notification pops up in front of me.

*1 message from AverageJoeGuy*

Oh shit, he responded. I almost forgot about him.

Quickly, I click on the message.

*AverageJoeGuy: We can't discuss this over message. We have to meet in person. But you're going to want to hear what I have to say. Meet me at 218 Way Street, Tony's Pizzeria. Friday. 2 p.m. Don't be late.*

I look at a map. The location is an hour away. Drivable. I'd have to rent a car or get a car service. But it's crazy to meet a stranger like that.

But I am crazy. And if AverageJoeGuy knows something that could help Mack, then I want to know what AverageJoeGuy knows.

I message back.

*JulesLikesToSwim: I'll be there with bells on.*

# CHAPTER 19

"Wow. You look . . ."

I'm standing in front of Mack in his apartment in nothing but a clamshell bra and a skintight sequined green maxi skirt. I have on a red wig, courtesy of Kate. Actually, all of it is courtesy of Kate.

Mack stands before me, staring. Like he can't believe his eyes.

I cup the bottom of the lavender clamshell, pushing up my cleavage, which has also been doused in glitter. "Tell me about it, Kate stuffed these things to the hilt. I look halfway pornographic."

Mack nods, then swallows hard. "That wasn't the word I was going to use, but wow."

I smile a little playfully. "What word were you going to use?"

He looks down at his feet, a little sheepish. "I was going to say you look breathtaking."

Heat creeps up into my cheeks. "Oh. Well, you look . . ."

"Like a fish dressed up like a man?"

I laugh because his outfit is a touch confusing at first but nonetheless clever. He's wearing an open white shirt with blue pants and a black belt. "No, I was going to say you look high concept. Everyone loves a high-concept costume. Especially drag queens, right? You're . . . Prince Eric if he became a fish for Ariel."

He smiles. "That's what I was going for. Do you really think people will buy it?"

I look at him. Take him all in. The honest answer is I don't really know, but I do know one thing. "It's all about framing. People see what they want to see. I learned that from my modeling days. Kate says you can pretend to be a world-renowned makeup artist."

Mack scratches his head. "Maybe this is a bad idea. What if someone starts asking me questions?"

But instinctually, I reach out and grab his hand, squeezing hard. I don't let him pull away. "Then you'll lie. Everyone lies. About all kinds of things. You're being scared over nothing. And besides. You won't be alone. We'll be together. We'll be together in this lie."

# CHAPTER 20

Mack and I order a car to the bar that's putting on the *Little Mermaid*–themed drag party. I think the cloak of darkness adds a little bit of a layer of safety to the whole thing. We're not in the light of day, and with me dressed up like Ariel next to him, I don't think anyone's going to ask too many questions.

Again, framing. It's all about the framing.

But naturally, I'm a little nervous too. Okay, a lot nervous.

When we step out of the car, my heart is beating hard in my chest. I look over at Mack. He turns to me as well. The sidewalks are crowded with people. It's a fun night out for the regular crowd.

No one's even giving us a second glance.

But then someone shouts "Hey! Cool costumes!" as we walk by.

"See?" I say, waving back at the person as if I go out every night of the week. "Nothing to worry about."

But I let out a big breath as well. And then I put a smile on my face. The prongs of agoraphobia prick and poke at my sides, but tonight, I have on a mask. The mask of a normal girl with her normal boyfriend at a drag show. And for now, that's all the cover I need.

The inside of the bar is spectacular. It's decorated to the nines in *Little Mermaid* paraphernalia. Seaweed is strung along the windows and the bar and the ceiling. There are clamshells as centerpieces, and everyone, and I mean *everyone,* is in a costume.

"Man, some of these people look more like a fish than you," I lean in and whisper in Mack's ear.

The greenish hue of his opalescent skin flushes a little pink.

And then a sprinkle of goose bumps runs down my shoulder when he leans in and whispers in my ear as well. "But none of them look as good as you . . ."

I shiver a bit. These feelings are new to me. And I like them.

"Jules! Oh my god! Over here!" Kate waves, her hand up in the air, sitting in a large corner booth surrounded by four men in costumes. Or at least, what look like men.

As promised, Kate is dressed as Ursula, the sea witch, with light blue makeup all along her décolletage, arms, neck, and face. She's wearing a long black skintight sweetheart dress, a beauty mark right above her lip. Her makeup and wig, though, look professionally done. I almost wonder if she had a drag queen do it for her. It's so good.

The men with her, on the other hand . . . I don't even know what to think.

I tug at Mack's sleeve. "C'mon. Let's go."

We slide into the booths, and Kate leans over and gives me a hug. Then, she does the same to Mack. His eyes go wide.

I haven't told Mack that Kate knows. Kate won't tell a soul. But it doesn't surprise me at all the way she accepts him.

"Oh em gee, I'm so incredibly glad you guys made it to the party! It wouldn't be the same without you. Anyway, so let's get the introductions out of the way, Jules, Mack . . ." She gestures toward the four men sitting down the curved row of the booth. "This is Ere, Dante, Gabriel . . . and

. . . well, the man at the very end. He goes by Shadow. You can just call him that."

"Wow, guess I'm not the only weirdo here," Mack whispers in my ears, and I let out a giggle because . . .

These men . . . are *different.*

Ere looks like a regular man though. With dark hair and a sexy gleam in his eye, he's dressed as a classic Prince Eric. Not the high concept we're going for with Mack. Dante . . . well, something's a little suspicious about him, but I can tell he's supposed to be King Triton. He's shirtless, wearing a crown and what appears to be a large fake Santa Claus–like beard. There's something off about the crown, but I can't quite figure it out. Still, he's a hulking chunk of man. Next is Gabriel. He's dressed like the seagull. Wings and everything on his back, which look particularly real.

"Wow, those wings are really . . . immaculate, Gabriel," I say.

His face lights up immediately. He has a happy, innocent glow about him. "Thank you so much, Jules," he says in the most earnest voice I've ever heard. "I grew them myself."

"Okay then. Great work."

Next to Gabriel is one more of Kate's boyfriends. He's definitely dressed to the theme, but there's no telling what he looks like. He's wearing an eel mask, but his eyes glow an eerie light blue through the eyeholes. On his body is a green suit.

He doesn't look particularly prone to talking, so I turn to Mack instead.

But Mack's already looking at me. And we're making the same face at each other. Like, *Who the hell is that guy?*

I let out a laugh. "Wow."

But also, something strikes me when I see Mack's face. His eyes, they're different than they were. Now he looks . . . happy.

Really happy.

And in the depths of a place I never usually feel, happiness surges through me as well.

The lights change in the building; they lower and then burst, and disco balls glitter the room with flashing colors.

"Ladies and Gentleman, please welcome your favorite mermaids to the stage . . ."

The music blasts as the drag queens strut onto the stage, each in their own version of Ariel. The pink dress. The yellow dress. The ship-wrecked scrap of white with a sash made of rope.

The energy in the room is palpable. The excitement is so thick with joy you could practically suck it down with a straw.

"Get down on this floor and dance!" one of the queens commands.

Beneath the table, I feel a hand rest gently on my knee. Then a whisper at the shell of my ear. "C'mon. Let's do this."

***

I'm drunk. I don't know the last time I was drunk. I'm drunk off scotch on the rocks, I'm drunk off the signature Mermaid Margarita, I'm drunk off the life force of this room.

The lights are flashing now, the music loud, the drag queens mingling with the crowd and dancing with everyone.

Mack's hand is hard against my lower back, our bodies pushed against each other. My drink sloshes in my hand, arm in the air, as we jump together to the music playing at the highest possible volume.

Kate is surrounded by her men, all of them in a circle and touching her in various ways. She looks ecstatic. And she is, in fact, ecstatic, I know because she took some ecstasy. She gave me two tablets as well.

"Here's a little present from me to you for coming out tonight," she said in the women's bathroom.

"Shouldn't I be giving you the gifts? It's your birthday." And I hadn't even gotten her anything.

"Psh." Kate waved her hand. "Fuck convention. Who gives a fuck?"

She dropped her pill under her tongue, but I'm not so brave. Instead, I pushed the little tablets into one of my clamshell cups.

And now Mack and I have been dancing fools out on the dance floor with the other aquatic creatures. I've never felt more alive.

Mack pulls me against him, his mouth against my ears. "Let's get a drink." The timbre of his voice vibrates all the way to my nipples. "I think I need a break."

I'm surprised because of how strong he is, but then I realize he must not be used to being out of the water for so long. I wonder if he's uncomfortable.

I nod and gesture to the tiki bar outside. "Let's go to that one. I could use some air."

Because if I'm honest, I don't have the best lung capacity to begin with. It's not like I'm running on the track every Saturday morning. As usual, I'm out of breath. The dancing is taking it out of me as well.

Mack grabs my hand, our fingers intertwined, and then he squeezes tightly. He takes the lead, pulling me through the crowd, his body tall and hard ahead of me, protecting me from the jabs of elbows and hip bones from the rowdy dancers all around us. A shark through a school of fish.

When we make it to the tiki bar, the outside air feels particularly cool, but my ears are still ringing from the sound. I wipe sweat from my brow with the back of my hand.

There's no sweat on Mack, but he leans forward and brushes the side of my mouth with his thumb. "Some of your lipstick is smeared."

I put my finger to the same spot and rub there, his thumb and mine touching. "Here?"

He rubs again. The feeling of his skin isn't rough like most human men. It's unbelievably smooth. My eyelids droop from the smooth slide of him against me.

"I got it," he says.

I turn to the bartender as we take our seats at the bar and hold up two fingers. "Two Mermaid Margaritas, please. Can you make mine the spicy kind?"

The bartender, dressed as Sebastian the crab in all red, nods, flipping out the plastic cups from below the bar and working on our drinks.

When he places them in front of us, he chews on his lips, eyes on Mack. "Your costume is amazing," he says.

A little flush breaks tints Mack's skin. I hope the bartender doesn't notice.

But the bartender is eyeing him closely. "The details. The craftsmanship. The artistry. Truly remarkable."

Mack takes a sip of his drink, Adam's apple bobbing. Then he scratches the side of his face. "Thanks."

"And you've even done your hands. How'd you manage to get this texture? Do you mind if I touch?" the bartender asks, eyebrows raised.

"Uh—" I interject, trying to come up with an excuse. "The paint might smear if you do!"

But I shut up quickly when Mack begins to unbutton the cuff of his white sleeve, rolling it up to expose more of his scaly, muscled arm. "No, I don't mind. Go ahead."

He holds his heavily muscled forearm out to the bartender, who slides a finger along the scales.

The bartender shakes his head in some kind of amazement. "You did your full arms. Wow. Gorgeous work. I would never even be able to tell. My friend works in special effects, makes fake skin and shit like that all the time. Is that what you do?"

Mack pulls away and unrolls his sleeves, pulling at the cuff again. "Something like that. A man's gotta make a living somehow, right?"

At that, the bartender smiles. "Oh honey, with cheekbones like that, I'm sure you could make a living any old which way. I don't even need to see under the makeup to know you've got something good. I'd go under the sea with you, if you know what I mean."

The light strikes Mack in such a way that I can't help but stare. It's true; his cheekbones are severe. His coloring is eerie. And then there's the fin that falls down from his neck to his throat. Like a beard. It doesn't seem so crazy anymore to think he's handsome. I'm not the only one who sees it.

Mack lowers his head and chuckles a little. "I'm flattered. But I'm not on the market."

The bartender looks at us both and then winks. "I get it. Have fun tonight. This round's on me."

"Thank you!" I raise my drink. When the bartender turns to help another customer, I tip my drink toward Mack. "Cheers."

Mack meets me halfway, and our gazes connect as our glasses clink.

"I once heard if you don't make eye contact when you cheers, you'll have bad luck," I say.

Mack's eyes twinkle. "Hopefully, this means good luck from now on."

My cheeks warm, and a pleasant buzz travels through my limbs. I'm not even worried about the crowd around us. The cover of a costume is protective, for both Mack and myself. I cross my legs gingerly; the material of the skirt is stretchy but still extremely tight. The very end of the skirt is ruffled to imitate a flipper.

I lean forward to fix the ruffle that's gotten stuck in my sandal, and when I straighten back out, my wig has fallen just a bit.

"Oh shit." I push it back on my forehead. I laugh. "Am I straightened out?"

"Here." Mack reaches toward me, and with a delicate touch, he brushes the hair out of my eyes, tucking it gently behind my ears.

When he moves away, I mimic the motion, tucking the hair behind my ear again. "Thanks."

"You're welcome."

Then the sight of his little fin beard catches my eye. It looks so soft in this lighting. I wonder what it feels like. I lean forward and reach out my hand, dragging my fingertips down the length of the blueish-green strands.

Immediately, Mack's eyes go heavy, rolling back in his head. "You shouldn't . . ." He swallows hard. "You shouldn't touch me there."

I let go, brows raised, hands up in the air like I'm being arrested. "I'm sorry. It just looked so . . . enticing for some reason. I didn't mean to hurt you—"

But he closes his eyes, wincing. "It doesn't hurt, it's just that . . ."

"What?" I ask because everything about this man is truly a mystery.

"It's just that it's kind of an . . . erogenous zone. For me. I mean, it turned into one."

My jaw drops. "What do you mean an erogenous zone?"

"This is embarrassing."

"Don't be embarrassed. I've never been more interested in a piece of information in my entire life."

He takes a beat, then straightens up. I notice he's shifting around a bit in his chair. I glance down to see what's going on in his pants, and there's definitely some tentage happening. "It's basically another dick. But it's hidden in these fins."

"Don't fuck with me, Mack. I know I'm drunk right now and miles from my actual home that I never ever leave. But don't fuck with me. I can't take it."

He smiles a little sheepishly and scrubs his hand down his face. "I'm not fucking with you, Jules. I'm telling you the goddamn truth."

I lean in, my voice a whisper. "You can, like, fuck with it?"

He shrugs. "I don't know. I've never tried it out."

"But if I touch it—"

"If you touch it, I like it."

My eyes go wide. "This might be some of the craziest information I've ever learned."

His eyes glimmer. "Just imagine what it's like on my end of the equation."

"Will you let me touch it?"

Again, he shifts in his seat. "You can't talk to me like that. Not when we're out here."

I stare at him for a moment. I'm staring directly at his chin. He knows what I'm doing.

"Oh, come on," he says. "Don't do that. I can't take it. You're gonna turn me on."

"Would that be such a bad thing?"

"It would be in public."

The pause between us is nine months pregnant, so I clap my hands together, smiling big. "Fine. Change of subject. This is cool, isn't it?" I gesture toward the inside, where the music is bumping loudly and throngs of people are dancing for their lives in extravagant makeup in costume.

I think I spot Kate making out with King Triton in the middle of the dance floor.

Mack lets out a big exhale, the tension between us punctured. He drinks from his cup. Mine's almost empty.

"I can't even describe the feeling. It's like I'm living my old life again, except better. And you were right, there was nothing to be afraid of."

"See!" I say and playfully whack his arm. Then I get an idea. I lean in close, so close that I can see the small, fine lines that disseminate each little scale on his face. "Hey, do you wanna make this night even better?"

He leans his head back, arm on the bar, at ease with himself and the environment around him. "What . . . exactly did you have in mind?"

I reach into my clamshell bra, and his eyes darken. I have to wiggle around on the stool a little at that look because I didn't even mean for it to be sexual, but now I'm a little happy that it is. I fish into my cleavage and acquire the two small pills from Kate.

I open my hand, the pills in my palm. "Which do you choose . . . the blue pill or the red pill?"

"You only have red pills."

I smile and pop one under my tongue. "Then I guess we know your answer."

***

The street is glowing. No, it's not glowing. It's glittering. No, it's sparkling. It's diamonds. It's made of pure gold and silver. It's a precious gem.

And I . . . am high as fuck.

I've got my hands tight on Mack's arm, but my legs are stumbly, one unsteady foot in front of another. I'm glad these sandals don't have heels. I used to wear heels all the time, back in my modeling days. But when that was over, I never put a pair on again. I'm unsteady enough as it is.

Mack is propping me up and propelling me forward. I can't tell if he's as affected by all the drugs and drinking. But his pupils are now wide and black. The light blue of his eyes is barely visible at all. Shark-ish.

Next to us, taking up the entire alleyway, is Kate and her four boyfriends. In fact, the biggest one, Dante, a.k.a. Triton, is carrying her like a princess past the threshold while she kicks her legs up and down and sings songs as if nothing weird is happening at all.

"Oh my god, you guyzzzz . . ." she slurs. "We have to do this again! We have to do this all the time. Don't you think so? Mack, c'mon. Tell Jules we have to make this a weekly thing."

The dopamine coursing through me is greater than any kind of rush I've ever experienced before. "I think you might be right, Kate! Maybe it's time I start coming out more." I squeeze Mack's arm. The fibers of his shirt are the softest thing I've ever touched in my entire life, the muscles wrapping around his bones the hardest. "Mack too."

We approach an intersection, and Kate waves her hand. "We have to turn here now! Are you guys good to get home?"

"Yes, I can bring Jules back. It's no problem," says Mack.

Kate puts her fingertips to her lips and kisses them, then throws them out our way. "*Bezos, bezos. Ti amo. Je vous adorez.* Byyyee!"

I wave my hand. "Bye!"

Then Kate and her crowd of men disappear into the darkness, leaving just me and Mack on the road. One foot in front of another, each footstep lighting up the pathway like that one Michael Jackson music video.

"I don't want to go back to my place," I say and tilt my head. "Wow, I've never said that before. I don't want to go home at all. Look at the stars. They look like glitter strewn across the sky. Kind of like this glitter on my clavicle. Do you like it? Tell me you like it." I'm baiting him a bit. It's gotta be the ecstasy, or maybe the ecstasy is just bringing out my true nature. The one I usually hide away.

Mack breathes in deep, his gills fluttering in his neck. His entire image flashes in my vision. An image of who he was and an image of who he is. I can see both.

And I know which one I like better.

I can't even blame that on the drugs. I just have to come to terms with the fact that I'm a freak.

A freak who wants to fuck a fish guy.

I nudge his arm when he doesn't answer right away. "Do you? Do you like it?"

He nudges me back. "Don't ask me questions like that unless you want them to lead somewhere."

"I want them to lead somewhere. I want them to lead everywhere." I bite my lip and glance up at him.

The pressure of his body against mine feels like a million hugs.

Then he halts suddenly, and I would've face-planted right on the street if it weren't for his firm grip.

"Whoa. Look on the ground, do you see that?" He points to a hidden corner near a brick wall.

I hold my wig hair back with my hand, squinting as I sway a bit. "That? That little brown bug down there?"

Mack undoes my grip on his arm but holds me by the shoulders, ensuring I'm steady before letting go. "Hold still, just for a second." He crouches down. "That's not a bug."

"What is it?" I ask.

But I can't focus on what he's looking at very well because everything is glowing in a beautiful hue. Including Mack. There's a golden halo engulfing his entire body.

When he stands back up, he holds out his palm to show me the little creature in the middle. "He's a rainbow land crab. Definitely not from around here. Wonder what he's doing so far from home?"

"He still looks like a bug to me," I say, but then I narrow in on him, his little brown and red body, only about an inch wide.

"To be technical about it, all bugs are crustaceans, but not all crustaceans are bugs. He lives in the water."

"You found a little sea bug!" I exclaim. "How cute! A little sea bug for a seaman!" My hand goes over my mouth. "Oh my god, do you hear what I said there? Seaman. Get it? Like semen?"

Mack rubs his chin, as if he can't believe how corny I am. He shakes his head but then holds out his free hand after dipping the little crab into his front shirt pocket. "C'mon. Let's go."

I point ahead as if I'm a sea captain. "Back to your place!"

And in my body, I've never felt more alive.

# CHAPTER 21

As always, Mack's building is quiet. "Does anyone even live here?" I ask softly as the elevator doors close on us.

"My dad owns the building. All the residents are retirees. If you don't count me, that is. Although I do feel retired from life in a certain kind of way."

"Your dad?" Memories of a conversation with Kate swim through my brain. "Your dad is John Vasser? Real estate tycoon?"

Mack nods. "That's the one. For better or worse."

"'Til death do us part!" I throw in the non sequitur.

Mack Vasser. Jules Lowe. Mack Vasser and Jules Lowe.

I'll have to do the math on our names later. For now, I glance up at the elevator ceiling, the warm glow of the drugs still coursing through my system. I've never done ecstasy before, but is it really supposed to make you feel this way?

Like you're floating on a cloud?

Like you want to live forever?

Like you're . . . madly in love?

Oh god, even under the drug spell, my hand comes to my mouth. *Relax, Jules. Just enjoy the night for what it is.*

By the time the elevator doors open, I'm already a million stories high.

I'm not sure if Mack is feeling the same way. Not sure if the drugs are doing the same thing to him as they are to me.

We tiptoe through the hallway because even with the cloak of *Little Mermaid* disguises, it'd be better not to see a neighbor.

Mack's steady hand unlocks his door, and when he opens it, we enter silently. He walks to the corner of the room where there's a very small tank next to his larger one. He dips his hand into his pocket and gently lets the small crab scurry into the tank.

Then he makes his way back to me.

We're standing in front of the door. I wonder if he'll grab me again like he did before when we made out in front of his door in a furious flurry.

But he doesn't. Instead, he swallows hard. The irises of his eyes are almost completely black. *Shark.*

"I'm feeling a little . . ." He pulls on his collar. "Different . . ."

"Different how?" I ask, my mouth gone dry.

"Like I wanna do things to you. Lots of things. Lots of different things."

I bite my lip and nod my head. "Uh-huh . . ."

Anticipation nips at my skin, scaling up and down the sensitive nerves beneath. And yet, I don't make a move. I've been making most of the moves.

It's his turn.

"Like if I don't touch you right now, I'll die. Like if anyone else touched you, I'd kill them."

"So you said . . ." But my voice is no more than a wispy breeze.

My whole body tightens as he lifts his hands, his fingertips drawing near my skin. They land softly in the middle of my sternum, in between the pushed-up cleavage of my purple clamshell bra.

My body's reaction is quick, nipples tightening to hard points. Then, a sharp inhale of breath as his fingertip glides along the sparkly skin.

His head is tilted as he traces the upper swells of my breasts. His expression is less human than before. Maybe it's the drugs making his pupils so big. Maybe it's the predatory, nonhuman part of his brain taking over.

Or maybe it's just the fact that he's not all human at all.

But whatever it is, I'm both his subject and his rapt audience.

"What are you doing . . ." My voice trails off when his finger hooks into the intersection of my cleavage.

As if he's experimenting, he pulls me forward from the juncture, simultaneously pulling the top away from my breasts and yanking me toward him.

His expression doesn't waver. Still, straight mouth. Widened, dark eyes. Curiously tilted head.

The feeling of being on display is not new to me; it's a feeling I've hated throughout my life. But I've discovered I like being on display for him.

His fingers drop, my skin cooling in their wake.

With aching slowness, he circles me, swiping my hair from my back over my shoulder, the touch tickling and soft.

Then, there's another yank from behind. I yelp at the motion.

He's undone the strings to my clamshell bra.

The cups fall from the slope of my sensitized breasts and clatter to the ground.

The balmy apartment air wafts past my naked nipples. My body feels heavy. Achy.

This time, he can't ignore my physical presence.

His breath caresses my neck, a slight tingle telling me he's behind me. At my back, just barely touching.

Then he circles back to my front.

Again, he glides his hands down from my clavicle, each hand on either side, sliding his fingers downward, over the slope of my breast all the way to my nipple.

I whimper when his fingertips hit the bump of my areolas and then spring off them.

"No . . ." I murmur because his touch disappears.

I breathe a sigh of relief when his fingers reenact the same motion, but this time moving upward from the bottom swell, touching the underside of the nipple instead. He flicks each nipple back and forth, as if testing something, watching the dark pink flesh bounce with his manipulation.

My tight skirt already has my legs pressed together, but I clamp my thighs even harder. The anticipation is making me wet with need.

I'm like an insect under a microscope, and he's zooming in.

He's got me squirming.

And then he drops to his knees.

At first, he uses his hands, sending them up my belly. Then he leans his face in.

My breath catches.

He rubs his cheek along the taut skin of my abdomen. Then he grabs my breasts, pulling me down just enough so that they're at his eye level.

He cups both with his hands, and finally, the moment I've been waiting for. His mouth closes over one aching nipple, his tongue flicking out to the very, very tip.

"*Oh fuck, Mack,*" I exhale.

The motion he makes with his tongue is dizzying. Bursts of acute pleasure bordering on pain shoot down my belly to my clit.

He draws the nipple in his mouth, sucks hard, and then pops off.

Finally, he looks up at me, like he's flicked back into another gear, his mouth swollen, the flush running down his shoulders. Then, while maintaining eye contact, he rubs his face against my breasts.

The sensation wipes across me like a damp cloth wiping chalk from a slate, soothing the aching and throbbing with his mouth but at the same time, doubling the near-painful ache in my pussy.

He rubs his face and then lifts his chin and rubs that along the surface of my skin as well.

His tongue slides out, gliding a trail down the bottom swell of my breast, down to my belly button.

And I realize what he's doing.

*His special parts in his beard.*

He's rubbing them against me.

Maybe it's the drugs heightening my sensations, but when he hooks his fingers into the waistband of my skirt, pulls it from my hips, then past my thighs, to my knees, and finally to the floor, and then rubs his cheek and chin against the waist of my G-string, I almost pass out.

"Mack." My hand falls to his head, and he grabs it, roughly rubbing it up and down his face, all the way to the fin beard at his chin, where I can *feel* it.

"Oh shit," I murmur, but my hand involuntarily fists the area.

A little nub hidden under the long strands of the opalescent fins. But it's large enough that I can stroke it with my fist, rubbing up and down and up and down.

Mack pushes my hand away and then proceeds on his own path.

He doesn't pull the G-string from my body. He simply pulls the scrap of material covering my pussy to the side, and he pushes his face into the Y intersection of my legs.

He breathes in deep and his gills flutter.

I squeeze my eyes shut because the sensation of his touch is so powerful that the folds of my pussy are quivering against his mouth.

He rubs again with his face, his chin, his cheeks, the whole time his hand holding the material of my underwear to the side.

Then he brings his index and middle fingers to my labia, pushing on either side of the skin and exposing my clit to him.

He does it again and again in a little pulsing fashion, until the very motion builds an orgasm.

While he's pushing down the pads of my labia, he slides out his tongue and gives me one long, slow, tantalizing lick from the base of my slit all the way to the sensitive buzzing tip.

The vision below me is too forbidden, too unbelievably dirty and strange and hot to possibly be real. Sweat beads at my hairline. I grab the wig from my head and throw it to the ground, shaking my hair out.

I'm getting a little lightheaded from standing. Black starts to spot my eyes. My posture is swaying.

And then, for a moment, I lose all consciousness.

A flash later, when I come to, my eyes snap open.

We're in the water. A change in space and time as if guided through a portal.

My senses swim back to me from the distant shore.

Mack is holding onto me; we're at the surface of his tank. He hasn't even taken off his clothes. His shirt clings to him, white and clear, stuck to the contours of his frame. I can only see the shadow of the pants below the surface.

"Hold onto the ledge," he says as he sinks below inch by inch, roughly throwing each of my thighs over either of his shoulders.

He dips below the surface, but his head is between my legs.

My head falls back, and I can't see anything. All I can do is feel as Mack's mouth is now on my clit. He's kissing it under the water. I've never had any man go down on me before. The very few men I ever let touch me were fast and rough. Wham, bam, thank you, ma'am, as the saying goes.

But Mack is making a meal of me.

I can feel the pleasure senses of my clit sparking, but Mack is holding back with his gently planted kisses.

I circle my hips in the water, which is difficult given his grip on me. Me, with my arms perched on the ledge, my head hanging over the top, my breasts just barely floating at the surface.

And him, with my thighs wrapped around his neck. His face buried in my pussy.

He so effortlessly keeps himself afloat. I guess that's the benefit of a fish monster going down on you. He can hold himself up in the water. He can hold me too.

And most important of all. He can hold his breath for . . . an indefinitely long time, it appears.

"*Agh*," I let out a surprised cry when Mack's tongue flicks out and over my clit. "*Fuck.*"

I tighten my thighs around his neck again. I'm not even worried that I'll hurt him. All I can think about is chasing the orgasm.

"*You can't hurt me,*" he told me before.

We're testing that theory now.

He begins to lick me in earnest, the lapping of his tongue and the pressure of the moving water on my clit almost more than I can bear.

I circle my hips against him as much as I can despite his grip on me. I'm practically humping his face, and I just don't care. I want what he's giving, and what he's giving is a tongue swirling against my most sensitive, vulnerable private areas.

And I want him to have it.

"Oh yes, oh yes, oh yes . . ." I chant rhythmically like a prayer.

The pressure rises in my belly, and I tighten every muscle in my body.

I'm so close. I'm so close to this moment.

And then he stops.

"What!?" I yell out. I almost laugh, but the noise coming out of me is one of pure frustration. "Why did you—" But then I swallow my groan at the next sensation.

Because something . . . and I think I know what, has pushed inside me.

It's not as big as a dick. It's a little wider, more rigid, but short.

And he's fucking me with it right now as he licks my clit.

My moans become choked and strained. I ride my hips into his extra appendage to the same rhythm as his tongue circling my clit.

The impending orgasm building in the base of my stomach might quite literally suffocate me under this acute, near-pain pleasure.

And yet, I still want, *no*, I need more from him.

I bring one of my hands from the ledge and hold it against his head, pressing him into me hard, riding his face in every single way I can.

His hands are squeezing the flesh at my hips so tightly I wonder if I'll have a bruise there tomorrow.

I hope that I do.

I want the evidence of his presence to stay on me even after I leave. So that when I do inevitably leave, there is proof that he exists. That he's always here with me.

Now, we're moving in tandem, my hips, his extra appendage pushing in and out of me. It's like I'm getting fucked with the first third of a dick, my pussy clenching for more, but also his tongue is forcing an orgasm from me regardless.

The push and pull of desire and fulfillment is overwhelming.

So overwhelming that with one final plunge, my hips straining to get closer to him, the orgasm I've been swimming toward comes crashing into me.

"*Oh god . . . .*" I moan as my voice crescendos because Mack doesn't slow. He grasps me tighter with his hands, fucks me harder, licks faster. "Oooooh god . . ." This time, there's no mistaking it.

"Ah! Ah! Ahhhhh . . . ." The orgasm rips through me, up from the sensitive spot of my clit and all the way through my legs and arms, hitting the back of my throat.

My eyes roll, lids close shut.

The climax has hit, and now I'm tumbling down shore with tiny little snaps of my hips, lapping up every single second left of all the sensations.

Finally, my body slows and then stills, and I slump completely, my thighs slackening from their tight grip around his neck.

He's still going . . . the fucking, the licking, the grasping.

But I put my hand on his shoulder, tapping him.

His movements still as well, one final push into me, one final lick, and then he pulls away.

The emptiness is okay though. I'm so incredibly spent that I don't even have the words.

He emerges from the water, head breaking through the surface.

I'm nearing some kind of absolute meltdown, just trying to hold it together.

I might be the only person in this world to have ever experienced what I just experienced.

He grasps me tight against his body, his arms wrapped around my back.

We don't say a word, but somehow so much has been said already.

No one could do that to me except for him.

And he knows it too.

Then, floating in the water, safe within his grasp, I rest my head on his shoulder.

# CHAPTER 22

I wake up with one gentle breath. My eyes flutter open. I look around, but all I can see is the white, wet material of a man's shirt. My cheek is pressed against the material. My shoulders are dry, but everything else below is wet. Wet and naked.

I kick my legs in the water. They're weightless. Relaxed.

Mack's eyes flutter open as well.

We've been in the tank the entire night.

"How'd you sleep?" he asks, his voice hoarse.

There are shadows beneath his eyes. Silvery gray little smudges I've never seen before.

I, on the other hand, feel like a brand new person. A newborn. A baptized saint.

"I slept like a baby," I say.

When we leave the tank, even fewer words are exchanged than were the night before.

Mack simply towels me off, one limb at a time, the rough fibers of the towel scratching along the length of my skin. Then he slides his fingers beneath the straps of my G-string and slides the wet, tiny scrap of fabric down my legs. It sucks to have to step back into my clamshell bra, but

Mac gives me a T-shirt to wear over it and a pair of light blue shorts. I push my sandals back on my feet.

"Thanks for taking care of me," I say, fumbling with the hem of his T-shirt.

I bring it to my nose and breathe in. It smells like sea air and something else, not quite identifiable. Something otherworldly that doesn't belong here.

Mack tosses the towel over his shoulder. It reminds me of a move by a professional swimmer, his motions so graceful and easy, his muscles so bulging yet defined. "Thanks for taking me out. I almost felt like I belonged for a moment. I almost forgot."

I perk up at that. Because it's true. He did belong last night. *We* belonged. *We belong.* "See! There are places where we can be together. Safely. Last night proved that to us. We can live in this world together." I gesture with my arms wide, but I'm only gesturing to the confines of his apartment. "Right?" And while my voice might fall, I'm hopeful. Optimistic. Excited. All new feelings for me.

The corners of Mack's lips lift only slightly. A sad kind of smile. "Sure."

"What do you mean sure? Don't you see? Everyone was all dressed up like you last night. We can go to every drag party the city has. You're kind of in drag, right?"

But he shakes his head. "You know better than that. This isn't a costume, Jules. I can't take it off. This is who I am, not what I wear."

The distance between us stretches again. Always the constant snap back and pull of the rubber band. So close, but so far away.

I blink my eyes, imploring him with my gaze. "Don't go silent on me, okay? I swear to god, I'll freak out if you do. If you just suddenly ghost me after this. If you act weird or distant. I'll stalk your apartment. I'll come here every single day and pound on your door."

He leans forward and kisses me on the forehead. "Promise. Promise on my life that I won't."

Before I turn to leave, his voice stops me.

"Wait, Jules, one more thing."

I pivot back around on my toe, expectation brimming. "Yes?"

He walks to his small tank and picks up the crab, coming back to me with the little creature in his palms. "I think he belongs with you."

# CHAPTER 23

I stagger home with my mind completely distracted, partially destroyed possibly.

When I get inside my apartment, the first thing I do is gently drop my new little aquatic friend into the tank.

"I think I'll name you Bug," I say to him.

He scurries away into a dark little hidey-hole created by rocks in the corner of the tank.

I stare at the tank for a bit, like I've always done. But this time, I don't need it to help me breathe.

I'm clear and open.

So much so that a yawn overwhelms the back of my throat. *Fuck*, I'm tired.

I slouch off to my bed, falling into the hug of seafoam green sheets, and drift away.

***

When my eyes crack open, my bedroom is black, darker than it's ever been, even with the blinds drawn. My heavy eyes adjust to the pitch of the room. Air swirls above my head like a rushing waterfall. Is my ceiling fan running on high, or are my ears broken? Is this a dream? Or is my consciousness active? But a light breaks through at the corner of my room. My eyes adjust again to the change. It's coming from my aquarium. My no longer empty aquarium. My now living aquarium. I squint, pushing my hair from my eyes, peering through groggy lids. My limbs weigh a million pounds.

I shake my head because a narrow but bright circle of light emanates from directly in the center of the tank. A black shadow crawls along the illuminated curve, almost frantically, excitedly, like it's looking for something. Or sending a message. Like a lighthouse flashing the attention of boats. Or Morse code. *What is it?* The circle crackles, fiery and electric, the bright color flushing from orange to green to yellow. Or maybe I'm hearing things, seeing things. Inside the circle is nothing but a black swirl.

The shadow crawls along the line of the curve again, and it dawns on me what it is. It's my crab. But what's he doing with this weird orb? What is this thing? He's like a spider in a web.

Although my brain insists on pushing my body out from the bed to inspect what's happening, to clarify that I'm hallucinating, to confirm that there is certainly a reasonable explanation for what I'm seeing—sleep paralysis demons, perhaps— my body protests. My toes resist the wiggle. My back sticks like a magnet to a metal board. My eyes weighed with the heaviest exhaustion.

*Have to get up. Need answers.*

But my body has other plans. My lids close shut, the contours of my limbs are enveloped by the mattress. And in another moment's time, I'm once again surrounded by darkness of a different kind.

***

I'm back in the creaky chair in front of my computer. The screen glows. The blinds are drawn. My robe has been collected from the floor, arms pushed through, sash tied tightly. I'm alone again. Naturally. Well, except for my rainbow crab.

This morning, after waking up in a disconcerted haze, I crept over to his tank, groggy and confused from my dream from the night before, and peeped over the cover. I couldn't find him because he was hidden away in the nooks and crannies on the floor of the enclosure.

But in the reflection of the light from the window, a thin line of a circle, like a sunburst, glimmered for a moment against the glass. I shook my head to clear my vision and drew the blinds, then looked back into the tank. No more glowing circle. I let out a breath, and the tiny crab inside creeped out for a moment and then halted, his small primitive compound eyes still and focused on me. I looked back. And then I had the strangest feeling that he was trying to say something. A talking crab? All things considered, it wouldn't be the craziest thing to happen to me this week. My adrenaline spiked, but just as I opened my mouth, he hurried back into the nook of a dried sea barnacle resting on the bottom of the tank.

"Hello, Bug," I called into the tank to the hidden crab. "You still look like a little brown bug to me."

He didn't acknowledge his christening, but I felt good about it.

And then I had no choice but to shake off my fugue state and get back to work.

While my world has been officially blown open by so many things, the power of cunnilingus notwithstanding, a girl still has bills to pay.

I crack my knuckles and straighten my keyboard on my desk and then type away, pushing the weird dream out of my mind, the weird image of that fiery, electric circle.

*The multiverse is not only an interconnected, ever-expanding conglomerate of contained systems, it is also, Theodore Lake theorizes, interconnected as a web. Much like the World Wide Web, which is connected through a series of servers and fiber optic lines, undersea cables, and satellite links all over the world, so are universes interlinked by a mysterious set of veins and threads. Lake also theorizes that each universe link exists parallel to but also exempt from the space-time continuum.*

I lean back in my chair and then jerk to the right, glancing over my shoulder. An unnerving sensation takes over me.

I've spent more time out of my apartment these past few weeks than I have in years.

And it's having an effect on me.

In fact, my apartment is really spooking me out.

I have this feeling like I'm being watched, like there are eyes on me from somewhere floating in the distance. It's a new set of anxieties for me, but I brush them aside. Now that I have Mack in my life, my excitement continues to trump almost all my issues. Anxiety, stress, agoraphobia even. My therapist would be proud.

"Oh, yeah, honeymoon phase," Kate texted yesterday. "But you can only ignore reality for so long. Problems don't just disappear. You have to solve them."

I shook my head at that because the girl has *no* idea what she's talking about. Did *she* experience underwater cunnilingus? Methinks not!

I finish up the final paragraphs of my copy and send it along to my boss. Not a moment later, my phone alarm dings out throughout the silence of my apartment. I practically jump in my seat.

While I might be getting out more, I still startle easily. And today, I'm really pushing my limits of travel because I'm going to visit AverageJoeGuy at a pizzeria an hour away.

My weight on the chair may as well be a thousand pounds, though, because part of me wants to blow him off. I don't want to meet a stranger, especially not one from a random internet forum. I don't want to potentially rain down on my good mood after my night out with Mack and Kate and her boyfriends. However . . .

AverageJoeGuy knows something I don't. I just have this suspicion. My intuition is pinging like neurons through the fibers of a cell. Maybe he can help Mack. Maybe he knows a solution to Mack's very curious *situation*. If nothing else, maybe he'll offer more information.

And if he doesn't, well, I've added a spike to my keychain, and I'm not afraid to use it.

I tramp over to my closet, swinging the door open while peeling off my robe. Another day where I have to wear normal clothes. Another day where I cosplay as a regular girl. This closet gets so little use I may as well dust it off.

I pull on jeans and a forest-green sweatshirt in the dark, flipping my hair out from the collar.

And then, after I've slipped on my shoes and tucked my little stabby keychain into my pocket, I order a car.

***

The car ride, for the most part, has been mercifully silent. A middle-aged man named Hank is in the front seat humming along to some yacht rock while I sit in the back. Of course, I don't spend very much time in cars anymore.

It's nice though. I can totally zone out and watch the scenery go by. We're near the ocean, so occasionally, we cross long strips of island connectors, water surrounding us on either side. I wonder what the water's temperature is.

I glance at the time on my phone. Hank is making good time. It seems like I might arrive without any incident at all.

I'm proud of myself for not spiraling into complete terror and anxiety until I catch Hank's eyes in the rearview mirror, glancing at me one too many times. My body tenses up. My palms break into a cold sweat.

Men are so predictable.

I make a point to disrupt the accidental eye contact, turning my gaze solely to the window, but Hank starts talking anyway. "Hey, you know who you look like?"

I bite my tongue so I don't roll my eyes. "Medusa?" I ask.

He plows right past my joke. Of course he does. "No, no, no. You look like that one actress. The one who was the mermaid? With the hair? You know the one."

I *do* know the one. Of course I know the one. I weigh my options of playing dumb or just playing along with the conversation, and I come to the conclusion that playing dumb will just prolong my suffering. "Daryl Hannah. From *Splash.*"

"That's the one!" Hank says, excitement in his voice.

I think the conversation will end, but of course, then it doesn't. Of course Hank can't leave it there. "Do you think she had a pussy somewhere in those fins?"

*And there it is.*

In my modeling days, men used to do this to me all the time—sexualize every conversation, push to make me uncomfortable in every possible way—and I'm still not used to it. In fact, I'm so taken aback that my body begins shaking.

I'm stuck in the car with this man. I can't get out. Nowhere to go.

I clench my spiky keychain hard. In my fantasy mind, I'm stabbing him right in the side of the neck with it. Carotid artery. Blood spurts.

Dead.

But then he flicks on his right blinker, and we're turning into the parking lot of the pizzeria.

*Fuck. Exhale. Big breath. Let it go.*

Although, it's a good lesson for me. Don't trust men. Never trust the men.

I tumble out of the car the second it halts, mumbling a thank-you and slamming the door shut. I don't turn around to see if Hank is watching me. I'm ready to get to the next obstacle of my day.

The pizzeria has an outdoor seating area, and that's where I'll find *AverageJoeGuy*. Luckily, there's only one table with anyone sitting there.

Except there are two somebodies sitting there.

Hesitantly, I walk up to the table. "Are you . . . ?" I start to ask.

"Jules Likes to Swim?" one man asks.

He's got a plate with a stack of pizza on it in front of him. He's an older man, maybe in his fifties, lean and tall with a head full of salt-and-pepper hair. He's wearing a suit, which gives him the air of someone with importance. It's funny how influential appearance can be. He has a jovial look about him, though, with a smile on his face.

He reaches his hand to the empty chair across from them. "Please, please. Have a seat. I'm Dr. Hammer. This next to me is your friend, Average Joe."

The man sitting next to him is much smaller in stature, his build a little frail. But that's not what strikes me about him. Instead, what strikes me about him is the glaze over his eyes. A little red like he just took a rip off a bong or something. But he smiles at me as well.

"Hi Jules. It is Jules, right?"

I pull out the chair, the legs scraping along the concrete, and gingerly sit on the hard metal seat, crossing my legs.

I need to take a breather, but we're outside in a public space. *I'm not in danger.*

"Hi. Nice to meet you."

"Pizza?" Dr. Hammer lifts the box in between us.

I shake my head. I'm so nervous I couldn't possibly eat something right now. Joe doesn't have anything on his plate either.

"Ah, just as well. I'm sure you're counting your calories. Maintaining your figure. And you probably want to get down to business, don't you?"

"Yes, please." I lean in a bit and lower my voice.

"About the fish monsters," provides Dr. Hammer.

I nod again. "Yes, but do we have to call them that?" Although, even I have referred to Mack that way many times.

"What would you prefer? Fish Freaks? Fish Mutants?" His eyes glimmer at that, and he lets out a hardy laugh as if he's said something funny.

Joe, sitting next to him, laughs too, but it's weaker.

I'm starting to think these two have a really weird fucking dynamic. But if he's legit, I've gotta know.

"Forget it. What do you know about them?"

Dr. Hammer chomps into his pizza, his teeth slicing through the greasy, cheesy flesh and bread. He chews loudly. "I know how to fix them."

"Oh great . . . so you're a surgeon. You want to do a hack job on them?" I think about Mack's brochure from his sister. About the kind of doctors who offer special, discreet services. "I've heard about your kind of surgeries. I'm not interested in learning more."

But Dr. Hammer shakes his head, dabbing at the corner of his mouth with a folded napkin. "Surgery? My dear girl. I'm not one of those body mechanics. No, I deal with more sophisticated materials." He reaches into the side inner pocket of his jacket and pulls out an orange, translucent pill bottle filled with little blue pills, the kind you get at pharmacies. "I deal in chemistry, of course."

He sets the pills in the middle of the table. "Go ahead. You can take them."

My gaze lingers on his face, but his expression doesn't crack. So, hesitantly, I reach for the bottle. Curiosity killed the hermit. I pick up the bottle and shake it around a little, the sound reminding me of maracas. But there's nothing remarkable about them. They look like regular blue pills. No label or anything.

"How do I know any of this is real?" I open the bottle and take a futile sniff inside. For better or for worse, it smells like nothing.

"That's why I have Joe here with me. That's why he's on the forums."

"What do you mean?"

Dr. Hammer turns to Joe. "Would you care to explain to the young lady, please?"

Joe's eyes shift. "Uh, yes. Of course. Dr. Hammer *cured* me. You see, I used to be a *freak*. Just like we talked about on the forums."

I lift a brow. There *are* more Mack's out there. Although, I don't like the way Joe says *freak*. Mack's not a freak. He's special. But also, I know that many people don't think like I do.

"Like a freak how? What happened to you? If you don't mind me asking."

Joe smiles faintly. "My body changed. It was slow at first. Scales taking over my skin. Orange scales. A bright, vibrant orange. Too bright to even hide, which I did try to do at first. Gills cutting through at my neck. Fins bursting through my flesh. But then my family and friends started to notice. Here, take a look."

He pulls his phone from his back pocket and scrolls through it, landing on a picture and flashing the screen. My eyes go wide at the picture. There he is. Kind of like Mack but different. He's not as hard cut as Mack; he's not full of sinewy muscle and pearly scales. Instead, he's a little chubbier but brighter. He's right, the orange on the scales is unmissable. But also. Kind of beautiful. Vibrant. Like a jewel.

I nod, and he puts the phone back.

"That wasn't the biggest issue though. There were other changes too."

"What do you mean?"

"Shifts in my personality. I didn't want to do the same things anymore. I didn't want to be around the same people. I felt like I was being called somewhere else . . ."

"Like the ocean?" I ask.

"It's a maladaptive desire," Dr. Hammer interrupts. "Antisocial behavior. That's what we call it. Joe here had it pretty bad before I came along. He was even getting one of those"—he flips his finger beneath his chin—"*fins* right here. Isn't that right, Joe?"

"They were on my back and shoulders too. It was . . ."

"Terrible," Dr. Hammer interrupts.

I cross my arms over my chest. "So, you just took the pills and then . . . voilà? No more fish scales? No more fins?"

"The effects of the pills are slow but cumulative. For safety's sake, they're never meant to be taken all at once. Taking too many at once could be fatal, too harsh on the system. The process might be painstaking, but slow and steady wins the race," Dr. Hammer muses.

Joe's eyes are turning even redder now. He seems pleasant enough, but something is just a little bit off about him that I can't put my finger on. "Yep, that's right. I'm a totally normal person again. Just look at me." His face breaks into a toothy smile.

I nod and fix my face to hide, instead of reflecting, the nerves bubbling in my belly. "And there are no side effects to these pills?"

Dr. Hammer shrugs his shoulders. "Well, you have to take them every day for the rest of your life, but it's certainly not a surgery. Plus, the effects are undetectable. Exactly as you once were. Just as good as before. Isn't that right, Joe? All better now."

Joe sniffs a little and rubs at his red eyes. "That's right, doc."

I pick up a napkin and hand it to him. "Are you okay? Are you crying?"

Joe laughs, weirdly high pitched. "Ha, ha, ha. No, crying? Me? I just have allergies. Really bad allergies."

"He has allergies," Dr. Hammer repeats. "The pills don't fix those, unfortunately. You have to understand, Jules. I'm not one of these extremists on your forums. I'm not trying to eradicate the fish people. I'm simply offering solutions. A return to proper form. That's all."

"Hmmm." Again, I pick up the bottle. "How much?"

Dr. Hammer smiles. "On the house. I do what I do for the great care I have for the safety of our society, not for monetary gain."

I tilt my head. Could this actually be the solution for Mack? It seems like Dr. Hammer is telling the truth. I can't imagine this is all an elaborate hoax. What purpose would it serve? Also, my feelings of optimism have been growing since I met Mack. And maybe that's okay. Maybe this is the solution. Changing him. Or . . . changing him back. Not just so we can be together. But so he can have the life he wants again. Friends, family, parties, playing the guitar . . .

Dr. Hammer's voice interrupts my thoughts. "Might I ask, Jules. Is this for you or a loved one?"

"A loved one." I tuck the pills into my purse.

Dr. Hammer reaches out toward me, his fingers pinching the cuff of my sweater and pulling it up over my forearm. "Are you sure about that?"

My eyes widen at the sight of my skin, the eerie blue veins. And now, in stark contrast against the paleness, a smattering of dark green bumps all up and down my forearm.

"Have you had trouble sleeping lately? Feelings of suffocation or drowning? Do you find yourself waking up in strange places? Like the bathtub, perhaps? How about night terrors that you can't remember? That's your body changing, Jules. Your lungs mutating and pushing upward, three little slits preparing to slice through the human skin of your neck and extract oxygen from water. It would be such a shame if someone with your beauty was to . . . *turn*."

I glance up, shock spiraling through my brain. I look at my own body so infrequently, hide away in the dark so often, cover up in every way that I can . . . But those aren't bumps, are they? They aren't skin tags either.

They're scales.

"Excuse me. I have to go." Abruptly, I jerk my arm out of Dr. Hammer's grasp and push my chair out from the table, a well of not only emotions but sickness bubbling up in my stomach.

*Fuck, I'm gonna vom—*

I rush away from the patio and run to the grass outside, puking my guts out in the bush.

Huffing and puffing, I'm bent over.

I take a moment, then I pull my sweater sleeves all the way past the middle of my palms.

What's happening to me? *What the fuck is happening to me?* When was the last time I even looked in the mirror?

I wipe my mouth with the back of my hand and straighten out, running my hand through my hair and pulling down the hem of my sweater.

Whatever's happening doesn't matter anyway. Because I have the pills. I have the pills.

Mack can take the pills. And . . . so can I. If I must. If I have to. If what's happening to me is really happening.

I walk to the end of the sidewalk and pull out my phone to order another car, the pills rattling in my bag.

One thing I know for absolute certain though . . . Mack can't know about what's happening to me. He'll think it's his fault, that he's infected me somehow. And who knows? Maybe he has. But I can't risk it. I can't risk losing him. Not when we're so close. Not now. Not ever.

***

By the time I get home, my entire nervous system is shot. I feel like I've run a marathon. Which I've basically performed the social equivalent of today. For me at least. I trudge up the spiral staircase, running out of breath before I get to the top. Then I push the heavy emergency door open to peek into the hallway.

No sign of Jason.

I don't think I could take it.

I trudge some more to my apartment, keys in hand, but then my heart drops.

There's a Post-it note on the door—familiar loopy handwriting.

*Dear Juliet,*

*Since you're so hell-bent on ignoring me, the woman who's sacrificed everything for you, I had to stop by in person. I don't know where you could possibly be hiding. But you need to call me. NOW!*

The note isn't signed. There's no sweet closing "Love ya!" or anything like that. But it's obviously from my mother.

*Fuck.*

I snap the note off the door and crumple it up in my hand. On a regular day, I'd be hard pressed to answer her calls. But on a day like today? I push my door open, step inside, and toss the crumpled paper into the waste bin. Not a fucking chance.

# CHAPTER 24

I'm getting ready to go out. I've been messaging Mack, and we're going to have a totally normal date night together. I've showered and everything. All the rest of my worries are being temporarily pushed out of my mind because, dammit, I just want to see him.

My phone vibrates with a message, and I check it in the darkness of my closet. I've been hanging out in here alone for a few minutes. Haven't so much as turned the light on.

*Kate: Now that you're an outside girl, do you and Mack wanna get drinks with me and the guys tonight?*

*Jules: Sorry but can't. I'm seeing Mack at his place. Ordering pizza.*

*Kate: Come to us instead.*

*Jules: I can't . . . we're . . . doing stuff.*

*Kate: Oh, I see! Has my little Jules finally experienced her first sexual awakening?*

Awakening is putting it lightly. More like my first sexual bomb exploding. But I don't need to specify that.

*Kate: We love to hear it.*

I flip on the light and double-check my outfit in the mirror. I can't believe I'm using this mirror in my closet again. Excitement and nervousness invade my psyche like goats grazing on a never-ending field of bushes.

I should be happy, right? I have good news for Mack. Amazing news, in fact. News that could change the course of his life.

And my life. I think.

I'm wearing a black long-sleeve shirt with little cutouts for the thumbs. I can't have any accidental skin slippages.

I'm not sure how the whole thing will work given my dynamic with Mack. I guess there won't be any hooking up. No matter how tempted I am to jump in the tank with him.

The thought of the scales crawling up my forearms makes my heart leap. *Don't get in a tank, Jules. You're not a fish, Jules. You're not a fish monster, Jules. You were a model, for god's sake. And that's how Mack knows you. That's the way he likes you. That's who you are.*

Things were going so well for me. Leaving my house. Wearing regular clothes. Attending social engagements. Having . . . hell, having orgasms with another person!

I'm not going to let the anxiety get the best of me.

And with that, I hurry out the door and down the spiral staircase.

I make it to Mack's apartment in record time. I'm getting so good at this outside stuff; it really is impressive.

As usual, when he opens the door, nobody's there, but I rush in and find him behind the door, pulling him into an aggressive hug.

"I have so much to tell you!" I say, but he speaks at the same time.

"I'm so happy to see you."

I blush a little, picking at my hair and tucking it behind my ear. "Really?"

He puts his hand on my back, leans forward, and his lips meet mine in a kiss. Already, feelings are broiling beneath the surface of my skin. Deep, exciting feelings. "Always."

Two pizza boxes sit on the kitchen counter. I've never even been that far into Mack's apartment. We never seem to make it past the tank. I meander over to it. Everything is clean, immaculate.

He's wearing a different pair of blue shorts and pulling a T-shirt over his head.

"Are you getting ready to go somewhere?" I ask.

It's kind of a funny question because even if he were getting ready to go somewhere, certainly he couldn't just pull a shirt on over his chest and call it a day.

I tip the lid of the pizza box and look inside. Normal pizza. Not sure what I expected. Maybe I expected Dr. Hammer to, *poof*, appear in the air out of nowhere. My stomach blips a little bit when I think about the pills in my purse. How do I bring it up? What do I even say?

First, maybe we can just enjoy our time together. After all, my stomach is grumbling.

"Should we sit on the floor to eat this?" I ask.

Eating pizza together is such a mundane thing to do, yet Mack's apartment doesn't have many mundane items like chairs or a table.

Mack slides the boxes off the counter, balancing them on his hand, and points to his window. "I thought we'd eat out there."

"You have a balcony out there? In this city? Guess you really are rich." I tiptoe to the window, but there's nothing outside but a steep drop to the ground.

"No, there's a ladder. To the roof." He walks toward the window and pushes the wooden sash upward, a waft of fresh air drafting into the balmy room. "C'mon. I'll show you."

The metal ladder is similar to a fire escape, flat against the brick of the building. Except it runs all the way up to the roof.

"You want me to climb up this ladder?"

"You scared?" He steps out onto the first step.

From my perspective, it's as if he's balancing on air out the window.

I inch closer. "Yes, always."

"What's the worst that could happen?"

"Death?"

He chuckles and hops up a step with total ease. "Is that all?"

"Don't be so glib." I pout, but I lift my leg over the window sill, my foot hitting the metal step. "Not everyone's afraid of heights, but everyone's afraid of falling."

My feet are a little unsteady, but for all my fears, it turns out he's right, and I'm not scared. I almost giggle as I climb each rung because it's kind of a weird irony.

Higher above, Mack moves up the ladder effortlessly, the boxes balanced perfectly on his hand the entire time.

But when we reach the top, the giggle dies on my lips.

*The view.*

The view in front of me is utterly unbelievable.

Mack hops to the ground, sets the boxes down, and offers me a hand as I hoist over the edge and onto the brick floor.

"Wow," I whisper. "Did we just enter an entirely different universe?"

Because in the center of the large space of the roof is an enormous pool. Surrounding the pool in a larger perimeter is a wrought iron fence. And covering it all is a large glass dome.

There's a door that he opens with a key, and then he gestures for me to enter.

But every inch of the space, and I mean every inch, is completely filled with flowers and trees and plants and bushes. It's one of the craziest greenhouses I've ever seen. Or maybe it's closer to a biodome. Or its own planet, really. Its own universe. Colors explode among the scenery: green, red, orange, pink, blue. Where the stairs dip down into the pool, there's even a table and chairs nestled into the middle, untouched by the water.

"You like it?" he asks. He locks the door behind us. "Here, come this way."

I follow deeper into the labyrinth of plants, letting my hands run along the large palm-like trees that brush us as we walk. "Like it? It's *The Secret Garden* out here. Holy shit, it's so beautiful." I touch a fuchsia-painted hibiscus, the smell wafting beautifully through the air. "I've never seen anything like it."

He hands me a rose, pale pink with a dark green stem, thorns sharp and aggressive. "My dad helped me do this. Helped design it. Brought in all the plants. I maintain it now though. But mostly it maintains itself. My dad and I don't talk anymore, but I know he's thinking about me sometimes. Every once in a while, he'll send a plant."

I shake my head, my eyes wide. I genuinely can't wrap my head around what I'm seeing. "Why don't you live here? It's so much bigger than the tank you have downstairs. It's like an apartment in and of itself."

Mack steps into the water and down one step, and then he pulls out both chairs, gesturing for me to sit, and places the pizza on the marbled sea glass table. He waits until I sit to open the box and offer me a slice. I take it, still thinking about my most recent experience with pizza, but for the moment shake it out of my head.

He takes a bite, so I follow suit. "Yeah, I know what you mean. I literally dreamed about this place before I built it into existence. But it's not really practical. I can't have things delivered here. I'd always be going up and down the ladder to get to the apartment, and the more I do that, the higher the risk I'll be seen. Not to mention, drones monitor the area quite a bit, and I can't hide everything in the dome. I don't need the CIA or the FBI watching over me."

I bite into the pizza. Greasy and hot. "No, I get it. My neighbor's a cop, and I swear to god, sometimes he listens by his door, just waiting for me to come out. I hate it. Constant surveillance. But I don't know, for this place? This place might be worth the risk."

Mack nods. Then he shrugs. "I guess I just need my life to be bigger than this. The tank is contained. I know that it's not really what I want. This place . . . it's so close to something real. To something free. But just not quite there. In a way, that almost hurts more."

I chew and swallow. I'm not sure what it means, but also, in another sense, I feel like I know exactly what he means. "So, do the other residents know this even exists?"

He holds up the key. "Maybe, but it's locked. My dad built it, so I'm the only one who has access. Plus, they're all old, a lot of them unable to climb a ladder anyway. It's kind of my own private oasis."

I snort at what he's saying. The way his life has been so privileged. Even now, even though he's being punished in so many ways simply for existing in his body, he's still protected in other ways. It's an interesting conundrum. "Pretty crazy how I would actually probably hate you if you hadn't grown scales all over your body."

Mack tilts his head, a confused smile on his face. "How do you mean?"

"You're a total rich kid. I mean, damn, even beyond this dome, look outside, look at this beautiful sunset. I've never dated a man who could take me somewhere like this. It's crazy. Meanwhile, I've been working since the day I was born."

He gives a gentle kick under the water, splashing my ankle. "What do you mean you've been working since the day you were born?"

I finish off the crust of the first piece of pizza. Eating a little bit has whet my appetite, and now I'm ravenous. I like the feeling. I go in for another slice. "Oh you know. My mother has barely ever worked a job a day in her life. She was always relying on me to bring home the money."

"But as a kid?"

I shrug and chew messily, enjoying the freedom. For some reason, I don't think Mack will judge me. "I modeled throughout my childhood and beyond that, right up until my young adult years. And my modeling paid all the bills. Put the food on the table. Kept the lights on. Paid for the pack of Marlboros my mother used to smoke every night. And the Botox she'd get injected into her forehead."

"No kid should be responsible for their parents like that. I guess I don't know anything about that at all since my family comes from money. They would never expect me to do something like that."

I lift the pizza in a cheers gesture. "Yeah, but they still turned their back on you."

He nods. "That's fucking true. But without them, I'd surely be dead."

I purse my lips together at the statement, and we sit in silence as it falls like a brick. "I'm glad you're not dead."

"Me too."

I nibble on my lip, thinking about the note I found on my door the other day. "My mother . . ." I say softly. "Well, she's around. But I'm pretty sure she hates me. She hates that I don't model anymore, that she can't pimp me out to older men. That's how she used to always get the jobs."

Mack knits his brows together, shaking his head. "Fuck, Jules. That's terrible."

"Yeah, and I still talk to her. Can you believe it?"

"Family is complicated like that. But sometimes we hold on because we don't know if we have any other choice."

I give a rueful laugh and kick the water so that it splashes on his ankle this time. "Yeah, and sometimes you have to know when to let go."

He laughs too. That smooth, deep sound. "You certainly have a point there."

# CHAPTER 25

Beyond the horizon, the sun sets cotton candy pink, blood orange, and periwinkle gray. Mack and I finished our pizza a while ago, the boxes still open on the table where a few slices languish. I've never had the biggest appetite, but the excitement of the recent events has me starving for more and more.

Now, I'm stuffed. But also, I want more of something else.

Mack and I are sitting at the edge of the pool, our legs dangling over, splashing our feet into the water. I've taken off my pants, so I'm in my thong and my long-sleeve shirt. He's just got his shorts on, but he may as well be naked.

Even though he's wearing shorts, maybe for some kind of modesty for what he feels is for my sake, I can still get an eyeful of his cock. *God, I wish I could tell him about the scales. I wish I could tell him about the green that's been sprayed across my arm.* But if I do that, he'll probably never touch me again. Or he'll freak out. Or he'll ghost me. Our relationship is so tenuous in so many ways, hanging on by a mere thin hook.

There's silence between us. He doesn't seem to mind the silent moments we have that seem to make other people uncomfortable. He knows how to let a moment sit when it needs to.

And it gives me the continued bravery to reach my hand out and grab his. He squeezes my hand back and places our clasped hands on the hard muscle of his thigh. Keeping hold of him, I rub up and down his scales.

The feeling is one I've only ever felt on him before. His leg is both textured and smooth. Cool and warm. Everything at once. It's satisfying just to touch.

He shifts a little when I let our joined hands trail a little farther past his shorts. Closer . . . and closer . . . and closer.

I've seen his cock, but I still haven't ever touched it. He's kept it away from me.

But I've been thinking about it a lot. Maybe too much. And even if messing around with Mack is what's giving me scales, the damage is already done. I might as well go all in.

*Plus, the pills, Jules. You have to tell him about the pills.*

I will. I swear I will.

But I don't want to ruin the romantic moment. Not yet.

I let my finger catch on the hem of his shorts, even with our hands still clasped together. I give it a little tug. "Come closer to me."

His eyes glimmer a bit at the touch. And he abides, scooting over until our hips touch. "Like this?" he asks. "Close enough?"

"Not quite enough." I roll up on my knees and move in front of him, in between the spread of his legs.

I unclasp our hands and rest both of mine on his thighs, pushing my weight into them, my knees and the tops of my feet flat against the concrete ground.

He was afraid of the consequences of our hookup, and this will only prove his fear true. I'm a little afraid of the consequences of our hookups too, but for a person who's been living in the desert to experience water for the first time . . .

They'd be desperate for it too.

His hands creep up behind me and come to either side of my ass, squeezing the bare cheeks. His eyes glimmer darkly. "Take your top off. I need to see you."

I bite my lip. *Agh.* What do I do? I want to take it off. But I can't risk it. There's too much he might accidentally see.

So, I switch strategies. "This isn't about me, Mack . . ."

I let my fingers linger at the waistband of his shorts, just below his belly button. I pull the material away from his skin and then let it snap back.

He lets out a short groan. "What are you planning?"

But I'm already leaning over him, my face level with the fly of his shorts. "I think you already have an idea."

He leans back a bit, an unsure but torn look in his eye. He wants this. I know he does.

I keep moving forward. I have to. I pull down the zipper and almost moan out loud when his cock springs out. I've seen it before. Yes, but now it's right there in front of me. Right by my mouth. It's flushed a pinkish red, but the scales are the same, smooth and almost shimmery.

It's weird, but my mouth is watering. I've given blow jobs before . . . forced to, more like. But I've never absolutely, completely, in the deepest depth of my soul, yearned to give one before. Never. Never in my wildest dreams.

I dip down, letting my mouth circle the head. It's large. Mack's cock is larger than almost any cock I've ever seen, and I wonder if he was born with it or if it were the mutation. I'm still not sure if it will even fit inside me. I'm barely getting my mouth around it.

But I manage.

And as soon as I do, his head falls back, and a hissing comes out of his mouth, but his words are a near groan. "*Fuck, Jules.* Your mouth on my cock. *Fuck.*"

His hips buck just a bit, and more of his length is fed into my mouth. I nearly gag but swallow instead. As if the only thing I want in this world is to take as much of him inside me as possible.

His skin doesn't taste like the skin of most men. Instead, his temperature is cooler, the texture smoother, the taste mild, clean, and a touch salty.

I like it.

I like it a lot.

I dive for more even though my mouth feels so completely stuffed, but I've got to see what I can accomplish. The fact that he's letting me do this is remarkable. I get him halfway down, and I'm almost choking.

He reaches out a hand and brushes back my hair, then fists the hair at the back of my head, holding me there. "C'mon now, Jules. Don't stop now. You can take more. I know it."

The shock and dirty words go straight to my pussy, and I clench my thighs together. Also, he's right, and I relax my jaw more and dive even deeper. This time, I'm bobbing up and down and up and down on his length, a fraction of a centimeter more each time. My throat is making obscene glugging sounds around his dick, but I couldn't care less. All I want from him . . .

*Is everything.*

I'm humming around his dick, rubbing my thighs together, ass in the air like I'm some kind of porn star. But again, with Mack, it's different. It's different than with every other man.

Finally, my throat has opened, my jaw stretched as wide as it can go, and I'm practically gulping down his cock, but I've made it. I've made it to the base, my mouth pressed against the smooth, flat, taut skin. The V-shaped muscles are so defined, pointing downward on either side of his cock. It's like an arrow directing me.

"Shit, you did it. You took the whole thing. Fuck, you're such a good girl."

He holds his hand to the back of my head, holding me in place, and I blink my eyes a few times. They're watering now, but I open them wide so that I can see him looking down at me. I can see him, watching me, taking his entire cock in my mouth.

It's the hottest thing I've ever done, and if one year ago someone would have told me this story, I would've called the fucking cops on them.

His cock is filling so much of my mouth that I'm drooling, but I'm still holding in place for one more second, and then his hand releases my head. I don't want to let go, but he pulls me off him, and I breathe in deep.

But I dive right back in. Taking most of him again, then bobbing up and down.

"Fuck, fuck. Fuck. You're beautiful when you suck my cock, Jules. You're so fucking beautiful." The words come out of his mouth like a hiss. But they're all I need to work my way to the finish line.

This time, he can't hide his cum from me. I want it. I want it all. And I'm going to do whatever I can to get it.

As I bob my head up and down over him, I can tell we're getting closer, but the jerking movements of his hips, sometimes pushing into me and hitting the back of my throat, sometimes just short and urgent, feel like he's holding back.

He's let go of my hair and is leaning back now, his throat tight, his eyes closed, his chest heaving. My eyes strain to get a good look at him from down on my knees, but I can make out the ever so slightly dark bluish outline of his beating heart beneath his opalescent scales.

One more deep dive, and then I pop up, sucking hard on the head of his cock, and that seems to really do the trick.

"Oh fuck, I'm gonna come. Oh fuck . . . pull it out . . ." he says, his voice almost a whisper, frantic and needy. "Pull . . ." He swallows.

But when I keep swirling my tongue around the head, then take the rest in, rinse and repeat, I can tell he's not thinking about pulling out.

His hips lift from the ground, and he grabs my hair again.

I'm sucking as fast and as hard and as deep as I can.

And then, his body freezes. I keep my eyes open as he tenses completely, eyes rolling back in his head.

With short little jabs into my mouth, he lets out a loud groan. "I'm gonna come, Jules, I'm gonna come in your mouth. Do you want it?"

I nod, humming around his dick.

And one more time, he tightens up, and then hot liquid bursts down my throat, circumventing my mouth since he's pushed so deeply inside.

Moisture is now building between my thighs, and my nipples are hard. I've never been turned on before giving a man head.

Mack gives one more small thrust followed by another burst down my throat. "Ahhhh . . ." Mack hisses.

He holds it for a moment and then slowly pulls out of my mouth, curling his finger beneath my chin.

I think he's probably worried, but he doesn't say anything. Instead, he pulls me into his arms, tightly against his chest, and squeezes hard. Then, I can feel the gulp from his throat next to me as he swallows hard.

When he speaks, his voice is harsh. "I think I love you, Jules."

I rub my hair against his chest, my heart fluttering. I'm out of breath, and my jaw is numb, but I've never cared less. His cock is still out, exposed and still hard even though he just came, pressed against my hamstring as I sit on his lap, my side pushed against his chest.

Over the horizon, beyond the dome, the pinks and oranges and grays of the sun have nearly faded into a murky navy blue.

I fiddle with the loops at the end of my shirt sleeves, the shirt that covers the dark green scales all over my arms. I look up at him anyway. "I think I love you, too."

He rubs my hair with his hand, then kisses me on my head, sending a rippling of goose bumps down my neck. "But I have to tell you something important."

# CHAPTER 26

Mack lifts me up from the side of the pool and carries me to a grassy area surrounded by a patch of sunflowers. They're enormous, maybe three or four feet tall. I realize he's brought me here because the area is lit up, whereas the rest of the city is going dark right now. He and I are just awakening.

I sit on the grass, crossing my legs, and he sits next to me. Absently, he reaches out and hitches his finger into the side strap of my thong, running his finger back and forth along the length. I'm still wet from giving him the blow job, but I still can't risk him doing anything to me and taking my shirt off.

He continues to slide his finger back and forth until it starts to tickle a little.

I giggle and slap his hand playfully. "What're you doing? That tickles. Get to the point. Tell me that something important. I have something important to tell you too."

His fingers stop, resting where they are, hitched to my underwear. He rubs his other hand down his face, shaking his head out at the same time. "You understand what I do for my job, right, Jules?"

I shrug. "Sure, you're a coder or something, right? Freelance?"

"Something like that. I take jobs here and there. But more recently, I took a gig with a company that has been doing some really interesting research."

"Research?"

"Yes, about . . . this will sound crazy, but research about the universe. More specifically, the multiverses."

"Oh . . ." I whisper because I'm already mighty familiar with that kind of company.

"Anyway, I've been working on code for them to . . . find something. Locate something nearby. And other things all over the world."

"What are you talking about? Find what? Locate what?" But from my own work, I already have an alarming idea of what he's referring to.

Mack pulls his hand from my hip and rests his hands in his lap. "Portals."

That catches my attention. "Portals? Like portals through the multiverse?"

He tilts his head. "Yes, how did you know?"

I shrug. "I might be a little familiar with the company you work for. In fact, I might work for them too."

"Really? I had no idea you wrote code."

"I don't. I write copy. Which makes a hell of a lot more sense than what you're talking about. How can you write code to find portals? How is it even possible?"

"It's complicated. It's kind of like *The Matrix*, actually. And I've been getting so close lately to answers, but I've been struggling. I've written so many goddamn lines of code at this point that I dream about it, see it on the back of my eyelids when I close my eyes. But no luck. There's always a bug in the code. Every time."

I can feel he's leading up to something, so cautiously, I speak again. "Okay . . ."

"But last night, I finally did it. I had a breakthrough. I had some crazy clarity, and it was like my brain was functioning on a whole other level, like I was seeing straight for the first time in my entire life. And I worked out the bug. And I was able to use the code to identify a portal location. Potentially, at least. The first one ever located. That I know of, of course."

"Okay . . ." I repeat, but my voice is higher pitched now, alarm bells ringing in my head. What is he implying?

"And it's twenty miles away. Right off Station 22, directly past the *No Swimming* sign and then a hundred meters in."

"What?" I scoff. "A portal to another universe? Twenty miles away. So—so, what are you getting at? What's that have to do with you? Or me? Or us? Or anyone?" Although my stomach is sinking because I think I do know what he's getting at.

He scratches his head, sighs a little, then glances up at me. "I've been having dreams, Jules. Visions, almost. The same dreams that inspired this whole place. I've been seeing it when I close my eyes."

"So? So you have a really active imagination? Some of us are just like that. It's the whole reason why I have terrible anxiety."

He shakes his head. "This is different. It's like I'm receiving a message from the universe. Clear as day and as loud as a blow horn. I think I'm supposed to go to the portal. I think maybe . . . this?" He waves his hand down his body. "This change that I went through? It's because I don't belong here anymore. This isn't the world I was meant to thrive inside of. It's the universe's way of letting me know that it's time I move on."

"But . . . but what about your parents? Your dad? Your sister?"

*Me? What about me?*

His voice gets quiet. "Yeah. I know. But I can't live in this small bubble anymore. I can't suffer just for them. Hide away for the comfort of others."

I run my hands through my hair. He's not looking at me. I can only see his profile against the dead of night, his severe cheekbones and the sharp point of the fins on his ear . . . the long fins that frame his chin . . . I shake my head. I say it anyway. "And me? What about me?"

I feel like I don't deserve to ask the question.

But the question has to be asked.

He puts his head in his hand. "You? I love you."

"And you want to leave." My voice is accusatory now. "And not just *leave* but like *leave leave.* You don't want to just move to Arizona or something. You want to leave the universe. We would never see each other again."

There's a beat before he answers again. "You could come with me."

My eyes go wide. "What?"

"I'm sorry. I shouldn't have said that. It's not right for me to even put the idea out there. It's too much to ask of anyone. It's not your fault that I am the way I am. In fact, I've been thinking about it. And you're better off without me. I think we both know it."

"No," I whisper softly, shaking my head, a desperate plea in my voice. "No, you can't . . . no, you can't say that." But how do I convince him? "I have to ask you something. Can I ask a question? Will you answer?"

"Yeah, of course. For you, of course."

"If you could stay here, if it was possible, if you could safely live here. With me. Would you do it?"

"Jules." He shakes his head. "I think I'll die if I stay here. I don't think you understand."

"Okay then, wait, wait. Before you say that." I hold out a hand, waving it frantically. "I have to tell you something else, okay? Don't freak out. You have to promise me you won't freak out."

His eyes widen at what must be my very disturbed expression. "What? What's going on? You look terrified."

"I have something, something that will change you back. You can look how you used to look. You don't have to go to the portal. You don't have to live isolated anymore. Your parents . . . your parents will . . ." I almost say *love you again.* But I know that it's wrong. I know that the argument I'm making is faulty in its own right. And yet, there's nothing else I can say.

Surely, he'll listen to me. Surely, drugs to change him back to his old human form are more reasonable than *portal jumping to another universe.*

The tender, sore muscles in my throat constrict at the thought.

I can't lose him.

I just caught him.

Mack shakes his head. "I already told you I won't do the surgery. It's not worth it, and I don't want it."

"Not the surgery. I have something else. Something more effective. And safe too. Pills."

"Pills?"

I nod frantically, then stand, rushing to my phone, which has been discarded in my pants near the pool. "Hang on, I'll show you."

I return and sit, flipping through my pictures until I find the one of Joe. He sent it to me after we met. The before and after. "That's Joe. I met him from the forums. He had the same transformation as you. And now look at him. Look! He's totally back to who he used to be, not a gill or a fin in sight."

Mack takes the phone from me and stares at the photos. His mouth opens and closes, as if he can't get the words out. Then, he hands the phone back to me.

"There are more . . . I always thought there were more of us . . ." He stares off into the horizon, not looking at me, his head shaking absently, his eyes blank.

"See! You can do this. *We* can do this."

But he shakes his head. "That's not how this works."

"B-but why the hell not? It's the answer to all your problems. To all our problems."

He grabs my hand and holds it in between us. "It's not, though. It's only the answer to one problem."

"But we could stay together. Don't you want that? You just told me you love me. How could you say that to me and then just . . . vanish."

"I do love you." He squeezes my hand hard and brings it to his lips. "And you're better off without me. Because I can never go back to who I was. Even if the drugs turned me back, I'm already too far gone for this world. Something inside me has changed. Do you get that? Can you understand that I'm fundamentally not the person everyone expects me to be? Actually, I don't even know if something inside me has changed. I think something inside me has just come out. Something inside that has always been there, no matter what else is on the outside. And I can't just put it away like it never happened."

I swallow the ache in my throat. Tears bite at the corner of my eyes. "That can't be right though. The drugs work. I saw it with my own eyes. Maybe they'll make you feel good in your old body. It could happen. At least think about it. Take them for a little while, see how you feel? You never know until you try it!" I'm pleading. Desperate.

He takes a breath. "You don't understand. I don't have much time. The portal doesn't exist in location alone. It exists in time as well. It will only be open for a period of twenty seconds on an exact day. And after that, I'd have to write more code to figure out its next location. And I might never figure that out again. This is likely my only chance."

The air between us now is stark and bare. I'm raw and ragged, the ripped-off edge of a rag. I'm scared I'll lose Mack. And I can't understand why he won't just take the drugs. It's the only reasonable solution. And reasonable solutions are always the best ones.

Instead, he wants me to hop dimensions with him. Instead, he wants to hop dimensions *without* me.

"What happens if you don't make the portal in time?" I ask quietly.

"It turns into a temporary black hole right before closing back up. I'd probably die. But at least it'd be a quick death. A death of integrity means more to me than a life of cowardice."

"And it matters so much to you that you're willing to risk everything? Even being sucked up by a black hole just because your timing's a little off? What kind of shitty portal is that anyway?" The burning intensifies. Tears are welling up. I sniff away the sting.

"I risk everything either way, Jules. I may as well give myself a chance at something or die trying."

I nod to myself, and a tear overwhelms the bottom lid of my eye, fleeing down my face and splattering on my arm, a small, darkened, wet stain on an already black shirt.

I have to change his mind. I have to do whatever I can to change his mind.

He can't leave, and I can't go with him.

I could never go with him. Deep down, I'm a coward. And I've always been a coward. Just because he's brave doesn't mean I am too. And it's time to come clean.

"I have to show you something," I whisper.

He looks over at me, a frown on his face.

I unhook my thumb out of my sleeve and yank the material up, exposing the skin and scales on my arm. I stretch my arm in front of him, the green scales glistening beneath the light. "It's happening to me too."

He looks at my arm and then back up to me. He grabs my forearm and runs a finger along the glimmering dark green scales that freckle up its length. "I did this to you, didn't I? I knew it. Fuck, Jules. You should've never touched me. You should've never let me . . . never let me touch you. I'm contagious. I'm a disease."

I shake my head. "If I'm being honest about it, like if I'm totally one hundred percent being real with myself, this started even before we met. I just didn't know what it was. But now, I guess . . . the process is beginning. And it didn't start because of you, Mack. It started because of me."

He lifts his gaze and catches my eye. His next words are hopeful. "Then come with! You can become whoever it is you're supposed to be. We can leave together and find our very own universe. The one where we belong. Just imagine it, the ability to spend the rest of our lives together as we are. Whoever it is we are. Just as we are. Without worry."

But I shake my head and pull my arm away. "You can't promise any of that. We could die instead. You said so yourself. I don't think sentient bodies react too well to black holes—it doesn't take a theoretical physicist to understand that much. Besides, none of this is even provable. It all exists in someone's imagination. It all exists in some code you wrote on your laptop." And I know that because I've also been writing about it for the past several months.

Mack nods. "I know. I know it sounds crazy. But this is more than just science to me. Yeah, it's just some theory. And sure, it's just some code. But it's code that came from my brain. And I believe that we're all connected to the universe. If the universes are connected, then so are we." He swallows hard. "Besides all that, I just feel it in my heart. I know I belong somewhere else. And that somewhere else is calling to me stronger than the moon calls to the tides."

I can't relate. The only place that has ever called to me is the confines of my apartment. I'd locked myself away in there for so long that I stopped hearing the sounds of the universe long ago.

I pull my sleeve back down and hug my chest. "Or we could take the medicine. And go back. Live a safe life. A happy life. A life together. With you. Me. Our families. Imagine it, the things we could have together. A house, a fence, two point four children."

"And if the same thing that happens to us also happens to our kids?" he asks, brow raised. "What then?"

I blink quickly. The tears are streaming from my eyes now, and I don't even know why. "Then we'll give them the drugs too, I guess. Mack, I don't know! Don't say stuff like that."

Because it's one thing to drug myself up for my own physical changes. It's one thing to stuff and maim and cut off my own true self.

But would I do it to my own children?

Would I betray them like that? The way my mother has always betrayed me?

Would I betray Mack like that?

Mack grabs my forearm, and at first, I recoil, but then I let him pull me back against his hard chest. He presses my head against his heart, the methodical beats pumping against my ear. "I guess we're at a stalemate."

# CHAPTER 27

*S**talemate.* Nowhere to go. Nothing to prove.

I spend the next thirty hours at Mack's. We climb down the ladder, order pizza, collect it, climb back up the ladder, and lie in the middle of the greenery off the side of the pool, under the sun or stars or moonlight. Together, just the two of us.

We don't talk about what's to come, but there's a tacit and silent understanding that the end is near for us.

We act like there is no black hole of inevitability chasing at our heels. Or rather that we're chasing. One of us, at least.

Like there's nothing weird or different about our relationship than with anyone else.

Not while we're hidden in the green grass and the sunflowers and the stars.

But, of course, we both know that there is.

"I'd understand," he says, our bodies side by side, flat against the soft blades of grass, the clouds floating lazily above like disconnected gods from another realm. "Of course I'd understand."

"Understand what?"

"If you took the medicine. You're not nearly as far along as I am. I don't even remember what it's like to be a human anymore, I've been changed for so long, so indefinitely. I don't remember the man costume I used to roam around in. But you . . ." He lets his hand touch my belly, turning to his side. "Maybe you're different."

The tears from earlier continue to plague me. I sniff loudly as they slink down the outward corner of my eye into the hairline by my ears. "I don't want to talk about it right now. Let's just lie here instead."

And I think I would've stayed forever, except that now I have a crab at home to feed. So, I stand to leave, telling Mack I'll return soon.

By the time I hightail it back to my building, my eyes are puffy and heavy. My body is drained like a dried-out fish. And I feel like I've tumbled from a mountain, falling rock by rock, all the way to the deepest depths of the sea.

I'm drowning in this shit.

And then it gets worse.

*Ah fuck.*

Jason.

He's dressed in uniform, so that means he has his badge and gun and baton and his dumb little matching shirt and pants. God, I hate him.

But he's standing right in front of my apartment door. A barrier as usual.

Also, he's looking at me with an expression that makes no sense. A scowl? But why?

"You haven't come home in two goddamn days," he says to me as I approach. He's breathing heavily, nostrils flared. The base of his palm is cuffing the grip of his holstered gun.

"What?" I dig into my bag, fishing around for my key. I clutch it hard when I find it. "How do you know I haven't been home?"

"Because I-I know stuff like that. I'm a police officer. Trained to notice the comings and goings of those around me."

"Kay," I mumble.

I halt in place, just waiting for him to move, but he keeps talking, his hand still on the grip of his weapon.

"A pretty woman like you isn't safe around here. Haven't you seen the protests going on around downtown?" Then he pushes out some air. "People are pissed. They're heading to our neighborhood soon, and I'll be joining for reinforcements."

"What are you talking about?"

Jason scratches the side of his mouth with his index finger, his gaze narrowing. "There are monsters out there. *Fish monsters.* And we're on a mission to get rid of 'em."

The blood drains from my face. Fuck. I stiffen to maintain my composure; my eyes are puffy as is, my skin dry and tired. I don't even know how I'm staying on my feet.

When I don't respond, Jason sniffs loudly. "You should let me protect you, I wouldn't want to see anything happen to an innocent girl like yourself. I think you owe me at least that much."

I scrunch my face. "Owe you?" I would no sooner employ Jason for protection than I would a toaster in a bathtub.

He frowns. "You can't just walk around here looking the way you do and expect me not to notice. You're a prime target, especially with all these fish monster shenanigans going on around us. One of them might snatch you up. Eat you alive. I see what happens to women like you on the street. Believe me, you don't want to end up like them."

My jaw drops. "Looking the way I do? Like a human?"

"You flaunt your body. I see it. Everyone sees it. And if you wanna do that, that's fine, but then don't come crying to me about the conse-quences. Suddenly, you're out and about all the time. Coming and going all hours of the night and day. It's wrong. You're going to get yourself into trouble, get tangled up with the wrong kind of people."

How the fuck does he know? The feeling of being watched. That familiar agoraphobic fear. Reassured. Confirmed. Right in front of my door.

My hand tightens on my keychain with the spike. I almost want to touch my fingertip to it just to feel its sharpness.

But also, I don't need a confrontation with Jason. I fucking hate Jason. And if he knew about what was going on with me, who knows what would happen? Nothing good. Probably something fatal. He might get the rest of the police force involved. What if they found Mack? What would they do? I'm ready to spiral right down the drain.

But instead, I purse my lips, close my eyes, and offer a tight smile. "Can you move? I have to feed my crab."

# CHAPTER 28

I'm in my apartment, writing my last assignment. When I'm finished, I'll collect my items and what's left of my dignity (wasn't much to begin with, if I'm honest) and drive back to Mack's. I would take my work to his place, but it's so barren, and besides, I don't want any distractions while we're together. Especially not any distractions with protestors and police officers. I want to stay in the bubble. Don't cross any lines in the time we have left. I've rented a car because time is of the essence.

And we have seven days.

Seven days, four hours, fifty-five minutes until the portal opens and Mack jumps into the ocean and out of this entire universe. At least, that's the plan.

Who knows where he'll actually end up? A black hole, a deep, dark pit? Evaporated? Dead. My stomach churns acid when I even think about it. So, I just won't think about it.

Mack was right when he said we were at a stalemate. We're completely stuck in our positions.

Mack can't stay here anymore, and I know that. His transformation has blossomed from the inside out, and he's no longer a being fit for this world. And I get that too. He deserves to live where he'll be accepted. Where he's not hidden away. Where his family can't be ashamed.

And me . . .

Well, let's face it. There was a reason I fired my last therapist. Because she didn't manage to fix me. And that's because I'm unfixable.

These last few weeks of leaving the apartment—trying new things, falling in love, having sex, being brave—are nothing more than a blip in my timeline. Every time I leave my apartment, I risk the hurt and pain of the outside world. And I'm not ready to be a walking target or a raw, exposed nerve. I want to hide away instead. Revert to the old me. The only way I'll stay safe.

Maybe that makes me a coward. Maybe it doesn't matter.

If I take the pills, everything can go on as normal. Miserably, oppressively normal.

I like it that way.

Except for the part where I'll sacrifice the love of my life. Except for that one small, insignificant, teeny, tiny detail. But who's keeping score?

I flip on my computer screen but then jerk around, looking over my shoulder. I shiver, and goose bumps coat my arms.

There's that eerie feeling again. The feeling that I'm being watched.

Maybe I'm off kilter from all the craziness that's been going on. I don't know.

I push the thoughts aside and begin typing.

*In the end, researcher Theodore Lake can only posit educated guesses based on theory. Do portals exist? And if so, when or where do they exist? And why do they exist? And if scientists do create the technology to locate portals, can the human body withstand the impact of interdimensional travel? These questions and more remain as we continue our research on this very important topic.*

I push oxygen through my lips, leaning back in my chair when I'm done. Again, I'm not going to think about it.

*Don't fucking think about it!*

Once I've sent the assignment off, I feed the crab and check the features of his tank. Water temperature and pH, plant distribution, food varieties. I can't tell if he's happy or not. It's hard to say because he's only about an inch wide and half an inch off the ground, but still, I care about his comfort. He might just be a little bug, but he's a little bug who's far away from home.

Once he's sufficiently cared for, I run into my closet and change, choosing another long-sleeve shirt. I close my eyes so I can't see the shimmering forest-green scales on my forearms. My hands tremble lightly. I'm nervous because we've got to make the most of this time together, but all I can seem to feel is bone-crushing despair.

I wonder if, after he's gone, I'll still read our text messages.

*Jules: I want to see you every day, okay? I want to spend as much time together as possible.*

*Mack: So do I.*

*Jules: And we can just pretend. We can pretend nothing's happening. We can play house. Make believe that everything's okay.*

*Mack: We can pretend.*

This is what he's agreed to. But deep down, there is no pretending.

Before I run out the door, I grab the orange bottle off the table, uncap it, and dump a singular blue pill into my palm. I throw it into my mouth and force a dry swallow. I almost choke it back up, but I will it to scrape down my throat.

*What's done is done.*

I hustle down the steps and make my way to the coffee shop, keys in hand.

I haven't seen George in forever, but now, it dawns on me that I've missed him, that my feelings for him have grown into a warm kind of affection. That's a new sensation entirely.

When I approach, he offers me a kind smile. "Black coffee, Jules? You're usual?"

This time, I smile back. "No, actually. Two waters, if you can."

He nods, reaches behind his counter, and pushes them across to me. "It's good to change it up every now and then."

"Yeah, I guess so." I pay with crumpled bills, grab the water, and then turn around. But something stops me midturn. I spin back on my heels. "Hey, George."

His eyebrows go up. I've probably shocked him since this is the most I've initiated a conversation. "Yes, how can I help?"

I push the hair from my face. "I just wanted to say . . ." I clear my throat. "I just wanted to say thank you. For that time you checked in on me. I never showed any appreciation for that, which was really shitty and selfish of me. But it was thoughtful of you to think of me. For you to care at all. When most people wouldn't."

My cheeks heat up at the same time cold waves flip in my belly. It's not easy for me to talk to other people this way.

But George offers another kind smile, the sides of his eyes crinkling. "I just want you to be happy, Jules. I have a daughter . . ." Then his smile falls. "Had a daughter."

"Oh." I lower my eyes.

Sometimes, the unspoken communicates more loudly than the spoken. The silence in between the words.

Then, I do something I've never done before. I reach out my hand and place it on top of his.

We stand like that for a few seconds until I speak. "I'll see you later, George." Then I freeze and pivot one more time. "Hey, by the way . . . what does your sign say?"

George closes his lids briefly, then glances at the sign hanging off his counter imprinted in Arabic. "It's a quotation from an Egyptian writer, Naguib Mahfouz. It says *Fear doesn't prevent death. It prevents life.*"

# CHAPTER 29

We float in a pool of our own despair; we float in a pool of sorrow. And also in a pool that belongs to Mack. Or his dad, more specifically.

It's just the two of us, naked as the day we were born. The stories of the constellations above. The mysteries of the water below.

And in the thin line between existence and nothing is us, floating on the very viscous surface.

"I want to give you a gift. Before I leave," Mack says, making a small little splashing noise as he turns his head to look at me.

I turn as well, and water caresses the side of my face. I study his distinct features because I don't want to forget them. I study his face because I know, somewhere deep down, that even though it will slip from my grasp, it belongs to me and me alone. I study his face because this might be one of the very few last moments I get with him. I want to say all these things to him, but this isn't our agreement. It's not the goodbye play we're acting out now.

Instead, I ask, "What's the gift?"

His hand floats to my hair, fingering the floating blonde waves gently in the water. It's almost as if a part of me is reaching out to a part of him across the void. "My inheritance," he says plainly.

I choke on a wave of water splashing into my open mouth. "Excuse me?"

"I want to give you my inheritance. And the apartment. And the dome. Every earthly possession I have pretty much belongs to you. I can't take it with me when I go. And who else would I give it to?"

I shake my head. "I-I . . ." My voice breaks. "I knew we said we weren't going to let the despair take over. But that makes everything too real. I don't need the money, Mack. Maybe the apartment. And the dome. To remember you by. But no . . . I don't want the money."

"Don't be a martyr. Money is what saved my life. And it can save yours too. I want to know you'll be safe when I'm no longer here."

"Just give it to someone else. Give it away. Burn it if you have to."

"You really don't want it? It's a lot. It's enough that you'd never have to lift a finger for the rest of your life. I want to take care of you, even if it's from afar."

I think about my fantasies, if you can call them that, the ones I used to have, locked away in my room alone, everything delivered to my doorstep, safely locked inside. But no, I can't take his money. It doesn't feel right.

"Someone else can use it more than I can. Lemme think on it for a day, okay? I'll come up with something."

"If that's what you want." Mack trails his finger down the side of my cheek, leaving a wet line behind it.

The talk of money and the trail that Mack will leave behind when he's gone poke at me like a pin to the gut. I'm desperate to change the subject now, so I grab his hand and yank him toward me. Immediately, he straightens up, and now we're standing in the water.

He pulls me to his chest.

I want to cry, but instead, I laugh. "Wanna mess around?"

***

*Two days to go.*

Mack's body is pushed into the white couch, and my body is straddled on top of his. We're making out furiously, and his hands are roaming my tits and my belly and hips like they're traveling the line of a map. This is all we've been doing for the past six days. No one has the right to fucking judge me. How else am I supposed to spend my last moments with the love of my life?

It's better that we stay out of the water. The water creates way more temptations. Turns me ravenous with need.

The land keeps us grounded. Literally. Figuratively. Metaphysically.

When I begin to move my hips, grinding my pelvis into his erection, he groans into my mouth.

"You're so perfect," he says against my lips. "You're everything to me . . ."

But everything isn't quite enough, is it?

Then he takes my mouth again, and I push harder, willing his cock to penetrate me through the thin fabric of my thong. But I know it can't.

Another thing we've agreed to is no sex.

It just isn't worth the risk. What would happen if I became pregnant? The odds are small, but they aren't nonexistent. I'm not raising a child on my own.

But the restraint is acutely painful.

"Fuck, I want your cock. It's so big and hard, I want you to shove it in my tight pussy and let me ride it until you shoot your come deep inside me," I bite out, grasping at the base of his neck with my fingers, riding him so aggressively that the whole couch is scooting.

My wanton behavior has gotten worse, not better, since this count-down. There is no room for embarrassment. No room for holding back. Because there will never be a chance again. So, if I'm going to be disgust-ing and vulgar and slutty, I'm doing it all the way.

"*Fuck Jules,*" Mack groans. "You make it so hard. You make it so fucking hard."

Maybe he's talking about his erection. Maybe he's talking about something else.

But my movements stop when an unfamiliar vibration sounds in the middle of the room.

"What's that?" I look over and see that Mack's phone is lit up with a message.

But who would message him? He talks to literally no one except for me.

He snaps his hips, bouncing me on top of his shorts again. "It's nothing, don't worry about it."

But then his phone vibrates again.

I am worried about it. I'm worried about everything.

He rolls his head back, then reaches over to the armrest where his phone is and silences the notification.

"Well?" I say expectantly. "Who is it? Is it your parents? Your sister. Have you even told Delaney about your plans?"

He rubs at his brow, then scrubs his hand down his face. I take special note of the little webs in between the valleys of each of his fingers. Webs I'll never see again.

"No, it's not any of them. It's . . . it's some stranger. I don't even know how they got my number."

He lets his index finger ride up the middle of my sternum, then he absently drums one of my nipples.

My vision wavers, eyes growing heavy at the touch, but I shake myself back to reality. "Wait, you can't hypnotize me like that! Why is a stranger texting you?"

In any other circumstances, a text wouldn't be strange. But these aren't normal circumstances. And he's evading me on purpose.

He sighs, and the corners of his lips droop ever so slightly. "People text, happens all the time."

I narrow my eyes. "You're lying. You're hiding something." I haven't known Mack that long, but the time I've spent with him has been so achingly intimate that I find myself reading his every little microexpression.

He pauses, a flicker in his jaw. "Fine. I've been getting threatening texts."

My lips part in shock. "What!"

He rubs his hands up and down my arms. "But I didn't want to tell you because they don't matter. They're just nonsense, and they don't mean anything. Even if they did, what difference will it make in two days? None of this matters in forty-eight hours. None of it. I didn't want to worry you. Or spoil our time together. We agreed." He squeezes my arms gently on either side. "Remember?"

I suck my teeth, feeling both irritated and terrified. Jason. He said there were protests, people who are out there in the world right now looking for others just like Mack. People who want to do him harm.

"What do the threats say?"

"Is this really how you want to spend our last days together, Jules?"

But I can't let it go. The worry will not release from my chest. "Just tell me, and then I'll let it go, I promise."

Probably a lie. But I have to know.

"They said they're coming for me and that when they find me, they'll shoot me down."

***

I creep heavily up the stairs to my apartment. I'm exhausted, but what's new? An invisible clock counts down in the corner of my mind during everything I do.

At night, Mack and I curl up together, either on the steps of the pool or on his couch or in his tank, where he holds me so tight I worry I won't be able to breathe.

But when I'm with him, I always can. The nightmares. The dreams. The breathlessness. Always gone with him.

But I must return to my apartment. I need the reprieve from the intense, acute emotions. If even just to check in. Mainly, I don't trust Jason. He's been acting so weird. Not to mention the little crab in my care, whose importance has increased tenfold in my life now that Mack is leaving.

When I open the door from the stairwell to my floor, however, I have instant regrets.

Because it's not Jason who's waiting for me.

It's my mother.

*Fuck. Double, triple, quadruple fuck.*

I wish I had taken care to open the door more quietly because then I could just turn around and make a run for it back down the stairs.

But she's already turned her head, spotting me in the entryway beneath the Exit sign.

"Excuse me!" She waves her hands over her head like she's directing airplanes. "And where the hell have you been? You think you're too good for your mother?"

I steel myself internally even though my insides are roiling like a hurricane.

*She won't understand, and you can't tell her.*

Even if Mack didn't look the way he does, even if he weren't disappearing through a portal in just a mere few days, even if there weren't people in the street protesting his very existence closing in on our town, even if I weren't also maybe one of those monsters too, even if all those things weren't true . . . I still wouldn't tell my mother about what was going on.

By the time I make it to the door, she's got her hands on her hips, and she's tapping her foot impatiently against the floor.

"Hey, Mom." I fumble with the locks but eventually shove the door open with my shoulder.

Before I can even step foot inside, she barges in.

"Come on in," I mumble, putting my bag down on my couch. "What can I do for you? Oh, c'mon, Mom, do you have to do that in here?"

She snaps open a pack of cigarettes and lifts one out. It hangs from her fuchsia-painted lips as she flicks her lighter, the end of the narrow cylinder now stamped with a fading pink. "What?" she says after lighting the tip of the cigarette. "It keeps me skinny."

Of course that's what she cares about. And it's true that I do get my looks from her. She's also tall and lean with blonde hair, now naturally streaked with gray, but she dyes it of course. She's had work done as well, some of it good, some of it not so good. When I stopped footing all the bills with my modeling gigs, she started getting the uneven Botox and the not-so-good migrating fillers, which give her a permanent stank face.

She inhales deeply, then blows out a gray billow of smoke right at me. I wave my hand, shaking my head and coughing.

But she keeps talking. "I have some news for you, Jules. Bad news."

More bad news. I'm worried I've grown numb to it at this point. "Okay, well, what is it?"

"I have cancer."

The words shake me, but she says them bluntly. She also takes another drag off her cigarette.

"W-what?" I stutter out. I look around the room, like I'm looking for an exit door or something. Like there's somewhere I might be able to escape to. "Are you going to be okay? What kind of cancer?"

I don't know what else to ask.

"Bone." She shrugs. For someone with cancer, she's being nonchalant. "The doctor says there's a fifty-fifty chance the treatments will work."

Even though I don't summon them, tears immediately sting the corners of my eyes. I shake my head, hands coming over my mouth. "Mom! You can't smoke if you have cancer. Put that out!" I lunge for it, but she flicks her hand away.

"Don't you get all self-righteous on me, Juliet. You've always thought you were too good for everyone else. What's it matter if I have a cigarette or two? You die doing what you love, or you die doing what you hate. Either way, you die."

I put my hands on my hips, defiant. "You could try just a little bit, you know? For me? Your daughter?"

She waves her hand. "Don't be so needy. And don't make everything about you. This is *my* cancer diagnosis. Why don't you do something for me for once?"

The words jolt me. So much of what I've done my whole life has been for her. I wasted my childhood, my teen years, my early adult years. All to keep her safe. At the expense of my own safety.

And I wish I could have the nonchalance to not care. But I still care. Even when she never does.

I don't have anything to say back, so I shake my head. "I have to feed my crab," I say quietly and walk over to the tank across from my bed.

My mother follows, a billow of smoke in her wake. She leans forward, squinting, while I carefully administer the frozen krill and dried fruit and pellets. The little crab runs up on his rock, snapping at the food.

"Crab, huh? Remember that fish you used to have."

I glance up at her. "Yeah, the one Dad won for me at the state fair."

She chuckles and takes another drag off her cigarette. "You were obsessed with that thing. You cried and cried and cried when I told you that fish died."

I fold my arms over my chest. A makeshift hug. Sadness pierces my sternum at even the mention of my dad. It always does. "Of course I did. It was the last thing from Dad before he passed away. It meant the world to me."

She waves her hand. "Oh, you're still just as dramatic as you ever were. I flushed that stupid fish down the toilet. That's how he died."

Shock runs through my system. "Excuse me? You said you found him floating at the top of his tank."

"Same thing. Same difference."

"It is *not* the same thing. I loved that fish. Why would you do that? What could have possibly possessed you?"

My mother glares at me, then ashes over the edge of the aquarium, little gray flecks now floating at the top. Quickly, I grab a net to fish them out.

"I had to! You were so obsessed with that fish, it wasn't healthy. You just spent all day in your room with that thing, moping and crying. Moping and crying. What was I supposed to do! I had auditions lined up for you."

"My dad had just died! Are you kidding me? I was *sad*, Mom. Of course I was moping and crying."

She shrugs. "Oh, please. You were eight. Like you even knew what sad meant. Besides, it worked, didn't it? You came out of your room. And you even booked your first shoot. So, you're welcome for throwing away your stupid fish. Imagine being so ungrateful to your mother who birthed you. Who sacrificed everything for you . . . *who has cancer.*"

"Do you even have cancer?" I ask.

My hip is cocked, my leg pushed out. She and I are standing in exactly the same stance, a future mirror image. But as much as she believes it, I am *not* a reflection of her. It's amazing I even came from this woman's body.

I think about my own body. About the scales on my arms. They're fading a bit now, just a tiny bit. Disappearing touch by touch, the bejeweled green dulling and flaking.

I could never show her. She would never accept it. She could never accept me in the first place, whether or not I take the medicine. Whether or not I stay beautiful.

And no one stays beautiful forever.

Like a hedgehog, the stark realization makes something inside my body turn in on itself. Like I want to hide again, like the armor on my outside wants to protect me again. The brave Jules of before, the one who found love, the one who walked the streets of the city, she's gone. She disappears like a puff of smoke against the wind.

I'm not safe anywhere. But I'm less safe outside than anywhere else. Now more than ever, this is true.

My phone begins ringing in my pocket.

There's no way I'll answer the phone in front of her.

"You've got to leave now, Mom," I say, rubbing at my eyes until the inner corners are raw.

"What? You're kicking me out? Your own mother?"

I push her out by her shoulders.

"Get your hands off me!" she yells, trying to shake me off, but I'm physically stronger than I used to be.

And the sound of the phone ringing in my pocket is pricking my anxiety.

Finally, with one more shove and a slam of the door, she's gone.

I don't have time to decompress though.

My head is spinning now. This information has dropped on me like a ton of bricks. But I can handle it, right? As long as there are no more surprises. As long as there's not one more thing piled on top of this wobbling Jenga tower I call my life.

But then I dig the phone from my pocket to see a familiar face on the screen requesting a video call.

I answer it. "Joe?"

# CHAPTER 30

*AverageJoeGuy.* He doesn't look right. He never looked right, but especially now, he really doesn't look right. His face is pale white, and his eyes are red and glassy. And there are tears. Those are definitely tears streaming down his face.

"Hello? Joe? Are you okay?" I ask when he doesn't start speaking right away.

But he shakes his head with jerky motions to the right and to the left.

"No, you're not okay?"

"Dead," he says, his voice strangely flat in tone.

"Dead?" I ask, alarmed. "Who's dead?"

"Everything's dead. All the things. Gone. Empty. Dead. Inside."

I scrunch my face, trying to make sense of what he's talking about. "Dead inside? Is someone dead inside?"

He nods his head. "The pills."

I look over to the table where my bottle sits. "What about the pills?"

"They'll kill you. But not on the outside."

"The pills will kill you on the inside?" I try to clarify.

He tries to talk, but his lips are trembling, tears rushing down his face now, which is beet red, as if he just ran a marathon. "There's nothing left of me."

"Well, can I . . . Can I help?" I'm stuttering, but what else can I do?

He shakes his head, the flat of his hand coming to wipe at the wetness slick over his face. "Too late for me. I've been on them for years now. Too long. Much too long. But . . . but it's not too late for you . . ."

My voice is frantic now. "Joe, can you come here? Can we meet again? I need to know more—"

"The protests . . . they're coming . . . tomorrow . . ." Then, his image disappears abruptly, the phone tumbling to the ground, nothing but a horizontal line of black on the screen.

"What do you mean tomorrow? Joe!"

But then the line disconnects.

He's gone.

One more thing.

All it takes is one more thing.

And something inside me just fucking snaps.

***

Mack is blowing up my phone, but I'm not responding.

Because now I have new suspicions.

Maybe I've caused the threats.

He's in danger because of me. Danger during a time when he's most vulnerable. Just days before the portal.

I'm at my computer now. I tap away impatiently until I'm back on the Freemont Aquariumaniacs Forum.

FishKiller1234. Who is he, and where did he go? I type his name in the search bar, but no account comes up.

But his old posts are still there.

I click through them all, *blahblahblah, kill all fish monsters, blahblah-blah, they walk among us.*

Then I see a link. The links to his Facebook group. I click on the link, hoping it's not actually some kind of hidden virus.

Luckily, it's not. Instead, it actually brings me to a Facebook group.

*Godly People Against the Fish Monsters*

The group has tens of thousands of members, which blows my mind. The posts are aggressive in tone.

*I don't want my kids exposed to these fish freaks.*

*As parents, it's our moral duty to eliminate all the fish freaks. The children are in danger!*

*Kill all fish monsters!*

A chill runs down my spine. Apparently, the anti-fish-monster brigade is real and growing.

I scroll a little bit until I run into an album showcasing a protest outside what looks like an apartment building. The people are holding signs with many of the same violent phrases.

And then, I freeze in place. A familiar face in one of the pictures.

Dr. Hammer.

*Eradicate all Fish Monsters* his sign reads.

My mind flashes back to the time I met him at the pizzeria.

*I'm not one of these extremists on your forums. I'm not trying to eradicate the fish people. I'm simply offering solutions. A return to proper form. That's all.*

But that's exactly what he's trying to do. And I was too stupid to even see it. And now Mack is in danger, no doubt because of my stupid choices. How else could someone find him if not through me? Am I being followed? Has my phone been tapped?

I scroll through the page, and the dates and locations are listed on the side panel for future protests. My nostrils flare when I take in the information.

Just as Joe said, they'll be here soon. In my town.

I'm trying not to spiral too hard. The absolute self-hatred coursing through my veins isn't new, but it is renewed.

If I stay away from Mack, then he can escape. As long as no one traces him to me. Someone already has, but there's only a little bit of time left.

And if I take the pills, I'll die inside.

If I don't take the pills, who knows what kind of danger I'll be in? Who knows the danger I might put others in?

And then . . . and then there's the portal.

Maybe a better person than I would be brave enough to go. Maybe a better person would jump at the chance to follow the only love they'll ever have in their entire life.

But I'm not a better person. I'm a coward.

I'm a coward, and my own mother doesn't even love me. And she won't love me when I turn. And she won't love me if I don't.

Dr. Hammer wants to eradicate us?

*Not if I eradicate myself first.*

What's the difference anyway between dying on the outside and dying on the inside? My outside and inside have never been particularly con-nected in the first place.

I pick up my phone, swallow hard, and type my last message to Mack. If I don't go to him, he can't come to me. He can't be seen out in broad daylight. It's too risky. Especially not with the protestors out. And he's too close to the portal time. So, I know what I have to do.

*Jules: I love you. You're the only one I've ever loved. You're the only one I ever will. But it's over. And it's better this way.*

Dr. Hammer said to never take all the pills at once.

I stumble over as if in a drunken trance to my table, pick up the orange bottle there, and dump every last pill down my throat, coughing and hacking as I chew the bitter dust.

A few minutes later, everything disappears.

# CHAPTER 31

Something is wrong. Very wrong.

*Bang, bang, bang, bang, bang!*

My eyes open, but I can't see. How much time has passed? Where am I?

I wipe my mouth, and drool is crusted over my cheek.

I stretch my hand in front of my eyes, and I see it as if it's a stranger's arm. As if I've never seen it before. I tilt my head, closing my fingers into a first.

Nothing.

Not a single sensation or sound penetrates the daze.

Numb. Like an etherized patient pinned to a table.

*Bang, bang, bang, bang, bang!*

The loud banging continues, but my brain doesn't accept it. It's nothing but a tiny little buzz in a distant universe. Muted and dying.

I stagger to my feet, my perspective swaying back and forth, my knees weak.

Then I spread out my arms and let my head fall back.

And I spin my body in a circle.

All around me, movement is happening, but I'm not really here. No one is.

I'm gone.

*Goodbye.*

The door swings open, and a person I recognize is there. But he's not a person . . . no . . . he's something else.

His mouth moves big and wide, but no sound reaches my ears, just an ever-muted, ringing hum.

He dashes around my apartment, but I'm still here in the middle. Spinning, spinning, spinning.

He's got the pill bottle from the table.

And then memories trickle in from the back of my brain like a little mouse sneaking in through the cracks of a wall.

I took those pills.

I took all of them.

Because I wanted to eradicate myself.

My eyes begin to well up . . . but I can't do anything but spin in slow circles. Wetness falls from my face, clings to my skin, drops to the floor.

And then I drop too.

***

I come to with my head above the toilet, gasping for air, my guts splashed into the bowl.

"Jules, can you hear me? Jules?"

The voice is echoey at first but then slams into me with crystal clarity.

*Jules, come back to me. I swear to god, Jules. Come back!*

I sit up fast as a rocket. "Mack. Oh my god. Mack."

He's holding my hair and rubbing my back. His brow is furrowed, and his eyes are drooping just at the corners. I know that look. Sadness. Despair.

"Thank god you're fucking back," he says, grabbing me ferociously to his chest, squeezing me so hard I'm worried he'll break my ribs.

But my pulse leaps as I begin to piece together the events of the night.

"What are you doing here?" I say, but my voice is merely a moan, my elbows pushing against his arms. "Can't be here. Crazy. The protestors."

I fist up my hands, hitting them as hard as I can against his chest, although there's no room, and I can barely feel anything around me.

But he covers me like a blanket, sitting on the bathroom floor. "I didn't have a choice. I had to come."

"Didn't people see you?"

"Yes." He rocks me back and forth. "I don't care if they did."

I lean into him, my breath easing now. They saw him, but he's here, and he's alive. "I vomited up all the pills, then?"

"All of them. What the hell were you thinking?"

I sigh. "I was thinking . . . What's the point of feeling anything at all if I can't feel it with you?"

He tightens his arms around me. "Come with me. Please. Come with me."

But I shake my head. "If I had more time. If I could . . . overcome this fear inside myself. It's too much . . ." I hiccup as I talk. "And you're in danger, you're in danger here."

"No one's coming for me now. No one's coming for me now."

It's a lie. They are.

He shushes me gently against my hair, rocking again. "I'll find you again. No matter in what universe. Or in what time. I'll come back for you. This much I promise." He brushes my hair from my face. "I found you in this world. I can find you in any other world too. It's not the end."

I turn my head to him, wanting to kiss him. Hell, I want to do everything to him. And by the way his eyes narrow in on my lips, it's clear he wants to kiss me too.

"No! Don't kiss me, I just threw up!"

He pushes his forehead against mine and lets out a chuckle.

At first, I'm too raw with my emotions to laugh, but then laughter finds me as well. And soon, we're laughing together, shoulders shaking.

"You're the one. And no matter where I am, no matter where you are, it'll always be you."

I swallow hard and nod.

Then, my head swivels to the side. "Mack. Did you hear that?"

# CHAPTER 32

The unmistakable sound of clomping boots comes from my living room.

Mack and I freeze in place. My eyes go wide.

I don't dare do so much as breathe too loud.

Because someone is definitely in my apartment.

And . . . odds are good, they're here for Mack.

We're in danger.

Before there's even time to plan, the bathroom door swings open, and towering over us is . . .

"Jason?" I ask. "Jason, what are you doing here? And," I say, my voice cautious and slow, "why do you have your gun out like that? Jason, put the gun away."

I inch my body in front of Mack's, although I don't know how I can expect to hide a person so much larger than me.

My heart vibrates in my chest.

"Who the fuck is this fucking freak? There's a whole host of people outside right now that wanna see this guy dead," Jason says, shaking his gun in Mack's and my direction. "Including me."

"Let me explain. It's not what you think," I say, slowly exerting pressure on my ankles and knees so that I can try to stand.

The truth is, I actually have no fucking clue how I could explain all this away, but if I can buy some time, maybe I can distract him enough to get Mack out of here.

"Sit the fuck down!" he shouts.

*Okay, or maybe not.* I put my arms up, stumbling back and falling to the floor.

"I know exactly what this is all about. I've been watching you, and don't you fucking lie to me. I know the fucking truth. I put cameras in your house, Jules. And I saw him . . ." He shakes his gun toward Mack again. "I saw this fucking *freak* walk in here like he fucking owns the place! Touching you and . . . and . . ."

"You put cameras in my apartment? Jason, what the fuck?" The reactionary words come out of me before I can stop them.

Jason scowls. "Yeah, that's right. I can do whatever the fuck I want in this city, and what're you gonna do to stop me? Call the police? I've got the law on my side. I got a key to your place too. I've been coming in and out of here for years now. Keeping an eye on you. And everything was going great until . . . until you started *leaving.*"

It never occurred to me that my locks were only keeping me locked in. They weren't keeping others locked out.

I shake my head and grasp Mack's hand when I feel him shifting to move.

I know Mack is strong, but there's not a chance I'm going to let him try to take on a crazed man with a gun.

"Okay, that's a lot of information to process," I say, trying to keep things light. New strategy. "Why don't you put the gun down, and we can talk about it?"

But Jason shakes his head. "Nah, we're not gonna talk about shit. Move the fuck out of the way, Jules. Because I'm about to blow this fucking monster's head off. You'll thank me later."

Then, Mack touches my hand, giving me the most imperceptible shake of his head.

He's going to fight.

"No!" I shout.

But he's already jumped into action, his muscles rippling as he springs into the air. The graceful arc of a shark taking out his prey.

He lands on Jason, and they slam to the ground, a struggle for the gun.

Shots fire, and I fall to the ground.

I lift my arm from over my eyes. He's hit him.

"No . . ." I whimper.

He's laid out. Blood splattered. Mack with a bullet right through his chest. Jason with his gun.

I always knew he would use that gun.

I'm shivering. Shattered inside.

But I'm not fucking going out this way.

"Jason." My voice is like nails on a chalkboard. "I'm gonna fucking kill you."

When I stand as if I have no fear, he looks surprised. He wasn't expecting that. He lifts his gun, hands shaking, but then he thinks better of it, drops it, and runs.

"You're not getting away!" I yell.

I run past the table and grab something off it. Before Jason can even get to my door, I leap on top of him, colliding with his body, my arms tight around his neck like a vise.

I really am stronger than before.

It's the transformation. I know it is.

I tighten my hands over the little keychain I grabbed from the table, the one with the spike.

He trips off balance, and I kick the side of his ribs until he's on the ground.

The next moves are purely on instinct. There's no time to weigh the pros and cons of my actions.

There's only life or death.

And I choose life.

But for him, it's going to be death.

With all the force I can muster, I swing my hand back and then bring it down against the side of his neck, hitting hard. The tip of the spike on my keychain punctures his neck. I yank it back out. The sensation makes me sick, but blood spurts from him.

"Ugh . . . ghmmm." He makes gurgling sounds, a rattle, actually.

I'm out of breath. I stare at the keychain in my hand.

Fuck. But it doesn't matter. None of this matters. What matters is Mack. Mack bleeding out on my bathroom floor, filled with bullets.

I snatch up my phone from the table and give one little goodbye glance toward Bug, my crab in my fish tank. *I hope I see him again someday but somehow I doubt it.* I rush back to Mack in the bathroom. He's trying to get up, but he can't. Red blood trickles down his wounds, his thigh, his shoulder . . . his heart. Visible. God, it better not be his fucking heart.

I'm no longer afraid. I'm not a coward. I'm going to save him.

I kneel down to him. "We have thirty-five minutes and"—I look at my phone—"twenty-three seconds until the portal opens."

He weakly shakes his head. "It's over, Jules. We'll never make it in time. I'm not gonna—"

I tuck my arm under his and heave myself off the floor. "Shut up, Mack."

He stumbles as he holds onto me, but I get him standing on both legs. Well, almost. He can't put weight on the right one from the bullet in his thigh, but he's still stronger than an average human.

And so am I.

I trudge through the living room, past Jason moaning on the ground.

"Close your eyes," I say to him as we pass by.

"Jules . . ." he breathes. "You'll get hurt if you try this . . . it's . . . not . . . worth . . . it."

"If you keep talking like that," I say, pushing us through the door of my apartment and dragging him toward the exit stairs, "I'm going to have to throw you into a black hole."

I've taken this spiral staircase so many times I can do the steps with my eyes closed, internally counting each number. My muscles are aching, and my chest is heaving. The dark green scales on my arms are brightening now. Something inside me is coming alive.

When we make it to the outside air, I brace myself for the crowd that's gathered down the street. People with signs tacked to wooden planks, bobbing up and down with their feet against the pavement. People with their angry fists in the air, chanting about purity and men and women.

*Fuck. We're gonna die.*

"You're not gonna die," I whisper. "You're not gonna die."

We're still hidden by the overhang of the exit at the side of my building, the alley narrow and dark, George's shop in view.

George. I think of all the times I've seen him. His gentle smile. His relentless kindness.

I wish I could do it all differently. If I could, I would.

But it's too late for that. Now is the time for forward movement.

My brain does the math on the quickest route to my car, which is parked on the side of the building, just the other side of the alley from George's shop.

"Now or never."

Mack gives a faint nod, his breath heavy in my ears, his body even heavier against my shoulders.

We emerge out into the open.

Eyes turn on us, and people make strange faces as if their brains are computing what it is exactly they're looking at. I know it's only a matter of seconds until they realize.

"Almost there," I pant. "Don't look at them."

We trip down the curb, and the car is in sight.

"Whoa, what's that?" A man points to us.

"I bet it's a TikTok thing," someone says.

"That's not a TikTok thing, that's a fish monster! Fish monster!" another person yells.

"Oh, shit." I almost fall. I'm trying to move my legs as fast as they can go.

We need to get into the car *now.*

A man with a sign catches my eye. He's making a run for it, and others are coming up the street behind him. I won't be able to protect us. Not either of us.

"Get the fuck out of the way!" I elbow someone off us and reach the passenger door.

The man is running full force. This is it. He's going to take us out. No matter how quickly I drag myself and Mack into the car, we'll never make it.

"I'm gonna kill you, you fucking fish monster!" The man's voice breaks through despite the loudness of the crowd.

I stop in place and turn to face him, freeze really, because I see one deadly branch of fate sprawled out before me.

He's almost here, and I close my eyes, lean my head in toward Mack's near-lifeless body, and prepare for the worst.

But then . . . nothing.

"Go! Go now!"

My eyes pop open at the voice.

"George!" I exhale. "Oh my god!"

George has the man by the arms, holding him back like a bucking bronco. "Hurry!"

I nod, clawing at the door until I find the handle. I help Mack fold into the car. My arms are numb from holding him up. His pearly opalescent coloring is turning a pale white. The blood running down his body is stark in comparison.

I catch George's eye one more time before I shut the door. He gives me a nod, and I give one back.

Then I face the front window.

"Don't die on me now," I say to Mack. "We've got twenty-nine minutes to go. Can you hold on for twenty-nine fucking minutes?"

The car engine revs awake, and I stutter on the pedal, pushing against the people who've gathered around to stare in the windshield.

But I mean fucking business, and I'll run them the fuck over.

"Get out of the way!" I scream, slapping at the horn as though if I hit the steering wheel harder, it'll beep louder.

*We're running out of time.*

And the people part like the Red Sea as I plunge through the crowd.

***

I don't need to use the GPS to know where we're going. My sense of direction has always been keen, especially because my dad used to draw maps with me as a kid. We'd walk around somewhere and then draw out all the places we went.

It's the only thing I have left of him now, and it's certainly coming in handy.

He won me that fish at the carnival, and now I'm going to return it to the sea.

"You're gonna cost me a fortune from the rental car company in cleaning fees," I say to Mack.

I've got one hand on the wheel, one hand pushing my balled sweater against his wound. He's barely conscious. His breathing is shallow, and his eyes are rolling back in his head.

The car in front of me isn't going fast enough, so I switch lanes, and a horn blares by us because I didn't check my rearview.

"Shit." I swerve back into the other lane and then hit the gas again and speed around two more cars.

I continue this way, swerving in and out, my eyes on the fluttering in Mack's neck, just to make sure his breath is still there.

This other alleged universe better have some really good healthcare.

Or maybe he'll just be magically healed.

All I know is, if he's going to die, it's not going to be in this universe, where he doesn't even want to live.

One more swerve, and then a cop car lights up at the side of the road.

"*Motherfucker*," I swear under my breath.

*Please don't pull me over, please don't pull me over.* But what a futile prayer.

*Woop Woop!*

Sirens.

*Shit, double shit.*

I catch my eyes in the rearview mirror, the pale blue iris surrounded by dark smudges, the skin puffy like pastries. I barely even recognize myself but not because of my physical appearance. There's something different about me completely.

Who am I? What am I even doing?

I've changed. From the inside out.

The cop car is gaining on me.

There's no denying I'm the target. After all, I'm driving like a fucking maniac.

"Pull over to the side of the road," a robotic voice calls from a megaphone.

Mack's head lolls to the side, dropping away from me.

"No!" I shout. "Stay awake!"

He's still breathing. He's still breathing.

I look at the clock on the car.

Seven minutes until go time.

The exit is in one mile.

All I have to do is get there. The water is within walking distance from the exit.

Then run a quarter mile into the water.

I'm so close.

The sirens are wailing now. Another cop joins in since I haven't slowed down.

Surely, this is the stupidest, most reckless thing I'll ever do.

But I refuse to be a coward anymore.

Exit in half a mile.

My eyes glance one more time in the rearview mirror . . .

And then, I fucking floor it.

# CHAPTER 33

By the time I make it to the exit, everything flies by in a blur of green and black and blue. Another cop car has joined. Sirens wail behind me.

I'm off the exit now and flooring it on a side road.

Thirty more seconds, and we'll be there.

Twenty-nine. Twenty-eight.

If we make it, my life is over. If we don't make it, my life is also over.

The cops are on my ass.

I lean on the horn, roll down the window, and shout "Get out of the fucking way!" as I pummel through the grassy shoreline that leads to the water.

People jump out of the way. I've lost the cops when I drove into the bushes, but they'll catch up soon enough.

When I shut off the car, I have three minutes to go.

I topple out the door and rush over to Mack's side.

"Stay with me, Mack! Stay with me!"

His eyes roll back, but he's still alive, even if just barely. Blood covers everything—the seat, his shirt, his shorts.

I yank him up with every single shred of strength I can muster.

I have to go in with him and fast.

I count in my head as I trudge through the sand, kicking off my shoes as I go.

Behind me are the sounds of the cops. But everything's a blur.

Two and a half minutes and my feet hit the water. Mack's dragging and stumbling beside me.

The water is shallow until it's not, and I stumble before plunging beneath the surface. I'm swimming one handed now, Mack against my chest.

One minute.

I'm pushing hard. I was never a strong swimmer . . . until now. I guess turning into a fish has its advantages.

I push all the air out of my lungs, but the need to inhale is gone.

I swim three meters to the east and then course correct slightly north.

I don't know what I'm even looking for, but even in the murky water, my vision has cleared.

Ten seconds and I scream under the water when I see it.

A whirling electric circle spinning in the middle of the ocean. Like a goddamn ring light.

The same whirling fiery circles I saw weeks before in my dreams.

*Push, Jules. Push. Push.*

I'm so close I can sense the electrical pull. The portal is within reach.

And then, suddenly, blackness blankets my vision, slimy strips slapping against my face.

Shit, what was that?

Something's stuck on my sleeve, plastered against my face and body.

It's seaweed, sticky and thick like plastic wrap.

It slips around my arms and splatters over Mack's face.

*No!*

I slap it away, but more and more keeps coming.

I swim harder, even though Mack is deadweight in my arms, and blood trails us like shark bait.

Three seconds . . .

Two . . .

I reach my hand out.

The electrical ring is barely at my fingertips, just one centimeter more. I'm stretching every muscle in my arm to get there. I'm straining every fiber in my body against the water.

And then, just as I'm about to make contact, it sparks out. Like an old-timey television.

*Zzzt.*

I drop my arm. I almost lose Mack as well.

*No. This can't be.*

*No. This wasn't how it was all supposed to end.*

I've missed it.

I've missed the portal.

At least I won't die a fucking coward. At least I'll die with the only person I've ever truly loved.

But it looks like I am going to die. We both are.

And then everything explodes into black.

# CHAPTER 34

"Hey! We need a medical unit! We've got two hoppers here. Looks like one's in pretty bad shape."

"Yeah, well, what's new?"

My eyes flutter between consciousness. My brain perceives the words, but they're quiet and far away. I try to move, but a hand touches my shoulder.

Wherever I am, I'm not in the water anymore.

"Mack . . ." My voice is hoarse, raspy, painful.

A voice responds, but it's not his. "Don't try to talk. Someone get the doctor, please!"

My consciousness wavers, and the heavy, dull wave of sleep pushes me back into the ether.

***

*Beep. Beep. Beep.*

The beeping sound registers first, and then, with a start, my eyes pop open, and I sit straight up.

"Holyshitwemissedtheportal!" The words come out like a garbled yell.

Around me is all steel and white plastic. Sterile. Cold. But clean.

"Well, good to see you're up. Your friend is still working on coming back to us."

The voice comes from behind a cracked door, and then the door opens wide.

"My friend?" I ask.

Frantically, I look around to get my bearings on my surroundings.

But my mouth drops when everything registers. We're in a room similar to that of a hospital room. Except the walls are glass, and on the outside is water as far as the eye can see. But not just water. Greenery too. Plants and flowers are growing everywhere.

Just like in Mack's dome.

*What is this place?*

"Yes, we kept him in the same room as you. Figure you two had a tough journey getting here. I know those portal hops can be . . . harrowing for some. Of course, it depends on where you're coming from."

The person before me has a woman's voice, but she's . . .

A fish. Well, not a *fish* fish but a fish-like person, just like Mack. She's tall and lean, and her eyes are a sharp green. Her scales run up and down her body in a shimmery deep slate.

My hands rush over my body. I'm in some kind of hospital gown, and I'm hooked up to some kind of machine.

"Portal hops . . ." I murmur.

Then the woman pushes open the curtain next to me, and there's Mack, lying on a medical bed. His wounds are wrapped. His chest expands and falls. His eyes are closed as if he's fallen into a deep, deep slumber.

My heart races at the sight of him, and tears immediately threaten my eyes, which I wipe at, sniffing hard.

He's alive. Somehow, he's alive.

And we're here together. But where is here?

The woman bustles around me. "I'm happy you're up now. You passed out and then woke up in some kind of fugue state, thrashing and wailing on everyone, so we thought we just as well might wait a few minutes until you were in your right mind. We'd never seen anything like it."

"B-but how are we here?" I put my hand to my head, and my hair is dripping wet.

How much time has passed? It might as well have been a lifetime. Maybe I'm dead. Can a dead person still feel?

The woman goes to the end of my bed, checking vitals or whatever it is medical workers do. She flicks off the dried strands of seaweed from my hair before speaking.

"I can't tell if you're joking or not. You jumped into the portal, and now you're in a new universe. I know your universe is a little more rudimentary about everything, but surely you knew what you were doing."

I shake my head. "No, but it's not possible. We . . . we didn't make it. We missed the jump, we ran out of time, the portal sparked out! Everything went black."

The woman tilts her head and looks at me curiously for a second. "Hmmm . . . well, that's very odd. Never heard of something like that before. Lift your arms up, will you?"

I comply as she checks different junctures of my body and presses a stethoscope against my chest, when a little creature crawls out of my hospital gown and onto my clavicle.

"Bug!" I shout when my brain recognizes the creature because I'm overjoyed to see him.

He came with us. He must've escaped his tank. My heart surges at the small return. Who would've taken care of him without me there?

The woman scoops the crab gently off my skin and puts him in the palm of her hand. "Oh! We've been looking for this little one. Well, that explains everything, doesn't it, then?"

"You've been looking for my crab?" I run my hands down the length of my arm, admiring that it's now entirely covered with emerald-green scales.

"Well, that's not a crab now, darling, is it? That's a bug."

"I know he's Bug, I named him that. But bugs and crabs aren't the same thing. Believe me, I've had this conversation."

"No, darling. He's a bug in the portal. We've been trying to locate him for months. Once he gets in there, well, he makes the whole operation go all wonky, if you know what I mean. One tiny little bug and it's like none of the code works that holds our entire universe together. But seems like he did you two a favor and kept everything open a little longer for you than usual. A little late for our portal appointment, were we? Naughty, naughty." She shakes her finger at me, her eyes glimmering. The crab crawls up her arm to her shoulder. "I guess we could say he's a *feature* and not a bug, then, how about that?" She chuckles to herself.

"A bug in the code," I repeat. I'm too amazed to come up with any other coherent words.

"Welcome home, little fella." She rubs the top of his little shell. Then she looks at me. "Well, I'll be off, then. Do you need anything before I leave? The doctor will be out and about doing rounds in a bit."

"Yes! Mack. I need to know about Mack. Is he going to be okay?" I gesture toward his sleeping body.

The woman smiles and puts her hand on mine. Her fingers are almost completely webbed together, the thin flesh in between nearly translucent. "Of course he will."

"But he was almost dead. He was shot three times. How do you know?"

"Because in this universe, we possess the single most important thing for healing."

I blink hard, racking my brain. "What is that?"

She pats my hand. "The care of a community."

# CHAPTER 35

"Well, what can I say? I'm a hero. You can make me waffles every morning to thank me," I say to Mack, and I splash my legs in the water.

I'm sitting on a grassy patch before the shore. Before us is a large stretch of what we would call a pond in our old universe. But now, it's basically a house. We have a regular house too, one that sits on the land where we can sleep inside or watch TV. Really, it's not so different from anywhere else. It's just a little wetter, that's all.

Mack swims up to me and grabs onto my feet, pulling himself in between my legs as he treads water and I sit on the shore.

We've been assigned this spot, and I have to say it suits us well, although we're just settling in.

The fish people of this universe welcomed us with open arms. They rallied together, and with their help, Mack healed from all his wounds. We both healed, really. Gone are the days of isolation and fear.

No more loneliness either. Because we're all connected through the waterways in this universe. Even though not everyone is in the water all the time.

People are varied here. Some look just like the kinds that roam the old universe, regular people—all skin no scales. And some have full-on mermaid fins, flippers, and everything. And others are on a spectrum from everywhere in between. It's not the uniformity that's important, it's the unique pattern that each individual brings.

The world is built to accommodate both water and land. Butterflies are *everywhere* here in a whole rainbow of colors. It's like nothing I've ever seen before.

And the air is so dense with oxygen from all the thick foliage that I never have to fight for a breath again. Of course, I've grown some gills too, and those have been pretty fucking cool. In fact, my scales have made their way all the way to my clavicle, but it seems as though they petered out after that, which means I still have all my hair. I guess that's what my transition looks like so far. But who knows what the future holds? People are fluid here, and they change between scales and skin and scales and skin whenever it suits them.

Other than that, there's plenty that's the same. People still go to work. Fall in love. Have kids.

I know, I was suspicious too. I asked the nurse who took care of us at the hospital. She was really helpful in giving me the rundown on this universe.

"So, is this like a utopia or something?" I asked, my brown knitted together, skeptical. "Because I don't trust that one bit."

(I'm sure my old therapist would still have a lot to say about that, actually).

But she replied in earnest. "Utopia. No. We aren't perfect here, although we do work hard to make a good go of it, don't we? Accept everyone. Take all you little orphan portal hoppers in. Patch up your wounds and bring you into the fold. But no, we aren't a utopia."

I looked up at her from my little hospital bed. "Then what do you call this place?"

But she just smiled and handed me a glass of water. "I think we call it home."

And she's right. That's what it is now. It's home.

And so now, here we are, all settled in on our little plot of land. And water, actually.

Although, there are still a couple of things I miss in the old universe. Really, just one thing.

"You are my hero," Mack says to me. "And I have so many ways in which I want to thank you."

I giggle a little and kick water at him, but he holds on tightly to my hips, rubbing his face and his special little appendage against my now-scaled abdomen.

"I love the way you feel," he says against me, his words muffled. "This dark green suits you well."

"You know, now that you're better . . ." I say, letting my fingertips glide down his neck and shoulders. "I think maybe we have a little business to attend to that we never did on land."

He looks up at me, a glimmer in his eyes. "Oh yeah? And what might that be?"

I know I must look like an absolutely horny freak, but the spell is broken when a group of butterflies flutter over, carrying a package with their little butterfly legs. Yes, this is an actual thing that happens in this crazy universe. I almost couldn't believe it myself. Courier butterflies.

They drop a small package right next to me.

"What's this?" I pick it up. It's a plastic bag . . . and inside is . . ."My phone!"

I clamp my hand over my mouth. "Mack, I had my phone on me when we went through the portal."

I dig into the bag and pull out a little note. It's from the nurse at the hospital.

*Everyone's always losing track of these things when they portal hop. I sent it to a technician, and it's all up and running. You'll send me a thank-you gift later. Cheers!*

I take out the phone, push the side button, and it illuminates in the palm of my hand.

"Do you think it can communicate with our old universe?" Mack asks. He pulls up on the shore to sit beside me, peeping over my shoulder.

"Only one way to find out."

But before I can even type anything, my screen is inundated with messages.

*Kate: WHAT IS THIS ENORMOUS DEPOSIT IN MY BANK ACCOUNT WITH A NOTE THAT SAYS "WETTER IS BETTER"? I KNOW YOU HAVE SOMETHING TO DO WITH THIS JULES DON'T EVEN FUCKING PLAY WITH ME*

From our current universe, Mack ended up depositing a chunk of money into Kate's account. The technology is more advanced here; we're less bound by the laws of what's impossible back in the old universe.

But the majority of the money went to George. And even though I don't see him anymore, I still think about him every day.

Mack's family hasn't realized he's even gone yet. Except for his sister Delaney, who emailed him after several failed attempts to see him at his apartment. Mack has responded, but he's acknowledged that the ground is still tentative. Either way, he's far enough away from everyone that he has some time to sit with his feelings. Maybe one day, he can reach out again. Maybe one day, he can try. The technology in this universe allows us to make contact. For that, I'm grateful.

And because I haven't responded to Kate yet, more texts appear.

*Kate: YOU CRAZY BITCH*

*Kate: You almost killed Jason? He barely made it after you stabbed him! Are you SERIOUS RIGHT NOW? He almost died. Well, I have to say, he had it coming. I fucking hate that guy. You're all over the news! At first they were calling you a crazy bitch, but then some detective discovered the cameras in your apartment . . . which, by the way, did you know Jason had your apartment bugged? Like, are you kidding me? Anyway, everyone's talking about you. And they can't decide if you're a hero or a total psychopath, and I'd say people are pretty damn divided. Most of the women are saying you're star-crossed lovers with the weird fish creature you took into the water with you. A lot of them think Mack is pretty hot. But anyway, where did you go? You're not really in the water, are you?*

The time stamp records several more days had passed before she sent one more text.

*Kate: Wherever you are . . . I miss you. I hope you get this.*

I smile thinking about her. I miss her too. Then I tap away at the keyboard.

*Jules: I love you, Kate. I'm okay, but I'm pretty fucking far away now. Have you and the guys ever considered taking a trip? Maybe one that requires a little portal hopping?*

Typing bubbles appear, and immediately, my heart soars. Then her message appears.

*Kate: Baby, you have my attention. I know a thing about a portal or two but I have to take a nap first. Just tell me where and when, and I'll meet you there. Should I bring a swimsuit?*

"You think Kate could find a portal?" Mack asks.

His fingers are now playing against my thighs. We're both naked, except for the cover of our scales. Even my nipples are covered with scales now, but luckily, they still feel the same. I know because I drummed my fingers along them just to test it out.

I set the phone down. "I think Kate knows more than we ever could."

He leisurely trails his fingers up my thigh all the way to the Y-shaped intersection of my body.

A little shiver runs up my spine.

"About that conversation we were having before . . ." he murmurs.

In his lap, his cock is already hardening. My eyes are on it, my pussy fluttering at the thought. We've never been this free before to do what we wanted. And the freedom is beyond sexy.

I reach over and put my hand on his hardening erection, running my fingertips along the length. It's so big I can barely get my fist around it.

"Can I admit something to you?"

He's leaning back on his hands, head falling back. He hisses a little at my touch but swallows hard and nods. "Always."

"You're really big."

He chuckles and puts his hand over mine so that he's covering my hand, which is now pumping the length of his hardened cock. "Let's just say not everything changed in my transformation."

I watch, mesmerized by the sight of our hands working his cock together, but I shake my head. "No, but you're really big. I'm afraid I won't be able to . . ." I cant my head. "You know."

His eyes glimmer. "What?"

Then I lean toward his ear and whisper, "Fit you inside me."

He groans and wraps his arms around me, pulling us into the water so we're falling beneath the surface. Above us, the aquatic green and gold and pink plants and flowers float all around. Everything is clearer under the water, and the molecules of oxygen and hydrogen connect us in every infinite possible location.

Mack pulls me against him, and we kiss. My hair is floating around us like a halo, my arms floating up as well, as his mouth travels down from my lips to my neck to my clavicle. Then he floats behind me, his hand trailing around my stomach until he's at my back. He pushes at my core with his cock, rubbing it up and down the slick entry.

My eyes roll back, and I reach up behind me to run my hand down the length of his neck. He pushes with one thrust and penetrates me with the head, an immediate shock of pleasure running through my system.

"How does that feel?" he murmurs into my ear.

He pushes a little bit deeper, and I respond by backing into him, meeting him where he's at. "So . . . fucking . . . good."

Once he's seated to the hilt, he snaps his hips into me, his hand making its way down my belly and to my clitoris, circling in dizzy, easy strokes.

"I guess in this universe . . ." he says, snapping his hips again and again, "I fit just fine."

"Yes, god, it's so big." I moan. But I can take him. I can take every last bit of him. And I'm not afraid.

His love is not too big for me.

I can take it all.

Soon, we're furiously fucking, the water swirling around us like a tornado, and we're caught up in the center. I'm pushing against him as he pulls against me, his palm grabbing my breast to hold me even closer to him while his hand works my clitoris.

The feelings swell and evaporate and then swell and catch the tide again until, suddenly, they're washing up on me from every point of my body.

"Keep doing that, just like that," I instruct. "But just a little harder. With your cock. And your hand too . . ."

He nuzzles at my neck, kissing my ear, following my lead.

And as the orgasm finally crashes through me, pulling my body straight and then rocking it to its core, he comes as well. His hips snap in an erratic and frantic rhythm, his breath in my ear. Until the only thing left in any universe anywhere in this entire galaxy is just the two of us.

When it's done, when my climax has finally receded to the shore, I turn around and pull him toward me.

He leans in and kisses me one more time.

And just as he's done before, he leaves me completely breathless.

LE FIN

# About Cat Wynn

Cat Wynn still has her Livejournal from 2001, although she hasn't had the guts to look at it since 2016 which leaves her with a painfully cringey but mercifully hazy memory. She received a typo filled email from Livejournal last year congratulating her on their 21st anniversary together, making Livejournal her longest and most embarassing (but possibly most intimate and honest?) relationship ever. When she studied abroad in college, she devoted her entire Livejournal to a photo archive of every guy she hooked up with. This was a *completely public* journal with *zero censorship* which in 2023 is the most horrifying thing she could ever imagine publishing. But back then she only had six readers, so...you could say she's lived a lucky life.

Now she's a romance writer and co-host on the Tall, Dark & Fictional podcast, and sometimes she writes pop culture critiques even though she clearly has no business critiquing anyone or anything, all things considered.

If you want to read more writing from Cat, you can visit her website catwynnauthor.com or subscribe to her newsletter catwynnauthor.su bstack.com.

# Also by Cat Wynn

### Holiday Games

After the worst year ever, August Pointe can't wait to spend Friendsmas with her besties at her uncle's mountain house. She could really use the comfort of a few familiar faces. But when a blizzard hits, August ends up stuck at the house with a mutual acquaintance she's never met instead. But Jack Harris is a hot, TikTok famous chef. And something about his easy going nature and excellent drink making skills are thawing out August's icy exterior. Plus, he's brought a kitten with him! August is reluctant to get involved, but some Christmas presents are too tempting to keep wrapped up. And her friends think she deserves a little holiday cheer. Still, August isn't sure if it's worth playing bedroom games with a stranger or if she'll just end up doubly heart broken by New Years.

### Hotel Games

Hair stylist Olivia Couper can't wait to celebrate Friendsmas with her besties in a secluded mountain house. So, when Olivia asks Henry, her best friend's grumpy surgeon brother, to carpool, she swears it's a matter

of convenience and *not* a bid for Henry's attention.

Sure, they've been hooking up for years, but they always followed one

unspoken rule: *Never talk about the hook ups.*

Unfortunately, a blizzard hits while Olivia and Henry are on the road,

stranding them in the last hotel room available. And suddenly, Henry

wants to break all the rules.

Olivia's left with a choice: confront her real feelings for Henry or flee to

the mountain house with all her walls intact. It's a game she isn't sure

she's ready to play and a hotel stay she isn't soon to forget.

### Jingle Bell Games

Lara Blunt is a grouch, but she's a grouch who works at the merriest

little Christmas shop in town, The Jingle Bell. Lara can't wait for her

Christmas Eve shift to end so she can sulk at home by herself with a bottle

of rum. Her manager (and the owner's son!) Leo Nicoli, on the other

hand, is full of holiday cheer, and he's had his eyes on Lara since the day

she stomped into his store. Unfortunately for Leo, Lara's been immune

to his charms, and now he's running out of time to win her over.

But when Leo and Lara get locked into a broom closet together right

before closing time, all holiday bets are off. Maybe Leo can finally get

the Christmas gift he's been hoping for—Lara's affection. And maybe

Lara can finally begin to feel a little Christmas spirit, courtesy of the most

festive guy in town. Either way, it's guaranteed to be a Christmas Eve

neither will ever forget

### Airplane Games

Parker Donne wants to plant his feet on the ground, get married and start a family. Unfortunately his niche industry job as a high-end traveling mechanic keeps him wealthy but airborne. He's constantly flying across the globe tending to his rich clients' one-of-a-kind vehicles.

So when Parker finds he's not the only passenger on a private jet back to the states, he knows better than to engage in dead-end flirting. But the chatty woman with the raven hair and blue eyes has stolen his attention — and also his wallet — just for her own amusement. Elliot Sheer is the opposite of what Parker is looking for. She's flighty, temperamental, and uninterested in settling down. And Parker can't even figure out where she lives. She floats from gig to gig as a destination wedding photographer. Tempting but trouble.

Parker won't ever see her again anyway. Except, that he does at the Schiphol Business Lounge and then again at O'Hare Terminal 5. And one more time at Midway baggage claim. And now that he's found her on Instagram he can't pretend he hasn't been seeking her out on purpose too. An International game of cat and mouse. With each crackling encounter it's more clear she won't give him the commitment he wants. But Parker can't stop himself from chasing her through the sky, even when he knows he'll end up crashing to the ground all alone.

### Going Down

Colin Rush is an overworked hotshot at a Big Four consulting firm. His neighbor Emma Smith is a cutesy but reserved first grade teacher who's never so much as glanced in his direction. Needless to say, Colin's positive that Emma's not his type, and, in turn, Emma thinks Colin is an intimidating player, and probably a jerk. Frankly, they avoid each other at all costs.

But they do have one thing in common: they both hate Valentine's Day.

So, when a rainy-day power outage traps Emma and Colin inside their building's elevator, they inadvertently become each others' defacto (and begrudging) Valentines. Now they have no choice but to sit in each other's presence...and maybe even find out what else they have in common, too. Will close quarters allow Cupid to work some holiday magic between them? Or will the elevator be the only thing going down on February 14th?

### Partner Track

Perdie Stone needs just three things in life: Her forever best friend, Lucille. Their adorable rescue pug, Bananas. And last but not least, a coveted partnership at her Charleston law firm.
A partnership she more than deserves when she goes head-to-head with hotshot Ivy League attorney Carter Leplan on a big case and comes out on top. She didn't think anything would feel better than beating the annoyingly gorgeous lawyer at his own game, but that's before a freak storm leaves them both stranded.

Together.

In the last hotel room.

With only one bed.

It's a one-night stand Perdie isn't soon to forget...especially after Carter turns up at her firm and slides right into the job that should have been hers. And right back into her life—a life she thought she had all figured out.

www.ingramcontent.com/pod-product-compliance
Lightning Source LLC
Chambersburg PA
CBHW070451300726
48975CB00007B/2118